A
Matter
Of
Time

Book 4 of The Thistle & Hive Series

Jennae Vale

Acknowledgments

Thank you to my editor, Deb Williams - The Pedantic Punctuator, for all your help and for making the editing process a fun learning experience.

A big thank you also goes to Sheri McGathy, Covers by Sheri, for the beautiful cover design for A Matter Of Time.

Thanks to my family and friends for your support and encouragement throughout this process.

Other Books by Jennae Vale

The Thistle & Hive Series

BOOK ONE - A BRIDGE THROUGH TIME

BOOK TWO - A THISTLE BEYOND TIME

BOOK THREE – SEPARATED BY TIME

Coming in 2016

HER TRUSTED HIGHLANDER
BOOK 1 OF THE MACKALLS OF DUNNET HEAD

Chapter 1

RICHARD LANDED WITH A THUD on the hard ground of an unfamiliar place. "Where the hell am I this time?" he asked of no one in particular. Noting the smell of the ocean and the sight of a large orange bridge spanning a bay to his right, he assumed he was somewhere other than Scotland. "Or, should I ask, *when* am I?" He was just about to pick himself up when the sound of a lovely, sweet and concerned female voice broke through his self-absorbed thoughts.

"Are you hurt?" she questioned.

Richard looked up to find a dark haired beauty with vibrant blue eyes staring down at him. She was by far the loveliest woman he had ever laid eyes upon.

"You took quite a tumble from the looks of it," she said.

"And you are?" Richard stood and dusted himself off.

"Angelina Lawson," she replied, holding out her hand.

Richard wasn't quite sure what to do with her proffered hand, so he did nothing more than hold it gently in his own. "What year is it?" he asked, wanting to confirm his suspicions.

"Seriously! You don't know what year this is? You must have hit your head hard when you fell." She examined him carefully, walking around behind him and then back again. "Do you know where you are?"

The concerned expression on her face was both touching and enchanting. Richard realized he was going to have to remember this definitely wasn't his time and therefore he would need to behave differently. "I'm afraid I don't. Am I in England, perhaps?" Too late he realized he shouldn't have asked, but he really had no way of knowing what England of the future might look like.

"I'm going to call 911," Angelina announced, taking one of those cell phones he'd seen on his last trip to the future from her pocket. "I think you need some medical help."

"No!" Richard almost yelled. "Please, I'm fine. Just a bit shaken up. That's all."

"Are you sure? I don't like the fact you're so fuzzy on a few important details." Angelina tipped her head and was eyeing him with a slightly furrowed brow, which he found irresistible. "You're clothes are unusual. Are you involved in medieval martial arts?" she asked.

Richard saw his opportunity and grabbed it. "Yes. Yes. Medieval martial arts." He had no idea what that was, but if it caused her to view him with less suspicion, he would agree to it.

"Well, that's one thing you know. The guys were here earlier today practicing, you must have been here with them. Although I don't remember seeing you." She was smiling at him now. "Do you know Nick?"

"Nick?" Richard was trying hard to avoid her questioning his presence here. "Yes! I do know Nick." *Whoever he is.*

"Oh, good. I'll just give him a call. I'm sure he'd be happy to help you get back home."

"If only he could," Richard muttered.

"Excuse me? I didn't catch that," Angelina responded.

"Nothing." If he knew what was good for him, he'd just be quiet or he might find himself in one of those jail cells he enjoyed on his last visit to twenty-first century Glendaloch. "Edna," he said aloud. He grimaced when he realized he'd done it again.

"Who's Edna? Is that you wife?" Angelina asked, her focus on the cell phone she held.

"I'm not married," Richard said. "Edna is an old friend."

"There it is," Angelina announced poking at the buttons on the phone. "I'll have Nick on the phone in just a sec."

Richard had no response to that announcement, so he took the time to examine Angelina Lawson from head to toe. She was dressed in extremely tight black breeches and a matching jacket, which showed off her enticing figure. The women of his own time didn't wear clothes anything like this. She wore unusual shoes on her feet, with tiny white bits of fabric peeking up from the top. Her ankles and lower legs were shapely and the fact that they were bare would be considered scandalous in his time. Her hair was long and loose and black, hanging nearly to her waist and her skin held a beautiful golden tone. Angelina's eyes, an icy blue, were set off by thick, long eyelashes. She had full, rose colored lips and Richard found his thoughts wandered to thoughts of kissing them.

"Nick? This is Angelina," she paused and Richard assumed she was listening to the man on the other end of the line. "Hi. I need your help with something." Another pause. "Yeah. I came across one of your guys here by the Marina. It looks like he fell somehow and hit his head. He doesn't know the year or where he is, but he does know you." Again she listened. "What's your name?" she asked Richard.

"Sir Richard Jefford," he replied and hoped he hadn't said the wrong thing, because she raised an eyebrow as though skeptical of his claim.

"He says his name is, Sir Richard Jefford." Angelina didn't have to wait long for a response. "Okay. We'll wait right here for you." Angelina slipped the phone back into her pocket. "That's a relief. He says he knows you and he's on his way here right now."

Richard shifted nervously wondering how someone he didn't know had accepted his presence so easily. *Who could this be and how could he possibly know me?*

"Let's go sit over there." Angelina pointed towards a bench positioned near the water's edge.

"Of course," Richard said. He placed her hand in the crook of his elbow and escorted her.

"You're quite the gentleman, aren't you?" Angelina asked, seemingly flustered by his gesture.

"Always," Richard said. That wasn't necessarily true in the past, but he was a new man now and he intended to be nothing if not proper, from this point forward.

They sat on the bench and Angelina seemed uncomfortable sitting too close, making sure to put some space between them. She turned to face him, daintily tucking one leg underneath her and resting her arm across the back of the bench. Richard was completely entranced. He smiled warmly, but could think of nothing to say.

"Do you remember anything at all?" Angelina asked.

"Yes. I do." Richard responded as he gazed out at the water. Wherever he was, it was exceedingly beautiful. There were many sails visible on the water, along with other, much larger vessels. They moved effortlessly, even without sails.

"Do you remember how you fell?" Angelina questioned.

"Yes." Richard needed to tread carefully here. He wasn't sure what he could tell her that might keep him from being locked up. If he'd answered no to her question it would give the young woman cause for concern and answering yes, while it was the truth, might cause him even more trouble in the long run, but he thought perhaps the honest response was the best.

Angelina sat gazing at him with those beautiful eyes. "Well, are you going to tell me?"

Time to change the subject. "What are those boats over there?" He pointed to one of the larger vessels as it cruised through the water, leaving large swells in its wake.

"That's the ferry arriving from Sausalito," Angelina explained, turning her focus to the water.

"Ah. I see." He didn't see at all. He'd never seen a ferry before and he couldn't believe how it moved so swiftly and effortlessly through the water. He remembered many things from his time in Glendaloch, but he had not seen any boats while he was there, so this was all new to him. "And what of that bridge?" His focus was still on distracting Angelina from asking too many questions about him, but from the expression on her face, the things he was asking her were obviously giving her pause.

"The Golden Gate?" she questioned, as she glanced towards the towering structure.

"The Golden Gate - of course. It's all coming back to me now." Maybe that acknowledgement would satisfy her desire for answers.

Richard and Angelina lapsed into a companionable silence, which Richard was grateful for as it allowed him time to contemplate what had happened and why he'd found himself abruptly shifted into the future.

"I hope Nick gets here soon. He lives right around the corner, so it shouldn't take him too long," Angelina said, glancing around. "Oh, there he is. Nick! Over here!"

Richard was disappointed that this Nick fellow had arrived so swiftly. He'd have liked a bit more time alone with Angelina. Not that he wanted to answer any more of her questions - just to gaze upon her lovely face would have been enough. He turned in the direction Angelina was calling and almost fell off the bench. The man approaching them was an old friend of his.

Sir Nicholas Mackall was striding purposefully towards them dressed in modern day clothing. How on earth had *he* gotten here? Richard stood up and stared in astonishment at his long-time friend and confidante.

"Richard? Is that ye?" Nick was approaching with both arms spread wide. He pulled Richard into a hug and held on to him for dear life. "Saints be praised, it's so good to see ye. How on earth did ye get here?"

"It's a long story, but I imagine much the same way you did. I can't believe I'm seeing you." Richard was trying not to appear completely astonished at the sight of his friend in the modern world, but knew he was failing miserably.

Angelina was standing off to one side, appearing baffled by this turn of events. Sir Nicholas turned to her with a warm smile. "Angelina, this is my long lost friend, Richard Jefford."

"I wouldn't say I was the one who was long lost, Nicholas." Richard smiled broadly and clapped his friend on the back.

"Wait. I'm confused," Angelina said. "I thought he was one of your medieval martial arts guys, but it sounds like you haven't seen each other in quite a long time."

"It has been quite a few years. Can ye imagine it?" Nick said to Angelina, his expression stunned. "Let's head back to my place and I'll explain it all to ye." He met Sir Richard's curious gaze. "Angelina has been kind enough to let me stay in her family's home here in San Francisco as no one was residing there."

There it was! He was in San Francisco. Now, he just needed to find out exactly where that was and how he could get back to England.

"My niece is out of town on an extended holiday and I thought Nick might like a place to stay in the city." Angelina smiled brightly at Nick, who put an arm around her shoulder as they walked.

Disappointment and a touch of jealousy washed over Richard as he watched Nick and Angelina walking together. He mentally shook himself, determined he wouldn't allow jealousy to overtake him. He had turned over a new leaf and left that green-eyed monster behind and he was not about to head down that same path again. "How long have you two known each other?" he asked.

"A few years, isn't it?" Nick answered, glancing at Angelina for confirmation. "We are the very best of friends." He smiled warmly at Angelina and pressed a quick peck on her cheek.

"He's the only man I know who can take no for an answer," Angelina teased.

"Well, it wasnae easy at first, but I understand." Nick turned his attention to Richard. "Angelina isnae interested in romantic entanglements, ye see."

They were approaching a broad street with many 'automobiles', similar to the ones he'd seen in Glendaloch. They stopped and waited for the traffic to come to a halt, before crossing and then heading down a side street. Richard was relieved to hear that Angelina was not Nick's woman, but disappointed to learn she wasn't interested in romance. "Angelina, if I might ask, why are you not interested in finding love?" Richard knew it was pushy, but found he just had to know the answer to that question.

"As silly as it sounds, I don't need the headache of having a man around. I like my life just the way it is. I enjoy the company of men, but not so much that I want to give up my independence. Does that make sense?" she asked.

"I suppose it does," Richard agreed, thinking it made absolutely no sense at all. Catching Nick's eye, Richard's friend shrugged his shoulders as if to say that he didn't understand it either. Richard thought it was probably just as well. He had one goal at the moment and that was to get back home to his family so he could start the process of finding a wife. A woman who would fit in at his castle, who would take charge of running his household. He had no time for a dalliance in this time and place.

Turning another corner, they came to a vibrantly colorful building and Nick led the way up the stairs to an ornate entryway. Richard had never seen such a colorful home. All of the little bits and pieces of wood were painted in different colors.

"Isn't it pretty?" Angelina asked, obviously observing his interest. "I love all the gingerbread on the house. It's a beautiful old Victorian."

"Yes, it's lovely," Richard said. *Gingerbread! I don't see any gingerbread and what is Victorian? What on earth is she talking about?*

Nick must have seen his confusion. "The gingerbread, as 'tis called, is all the wooden trim ye see around the doors and windows. Not what we're used to, but pleasing to the eye, wouldn't ye agree?"

Richard merely nodded in agreement as Nick opened the door for Angelina to pass through. He extended his arm for Richard to go next and then closed the door after they were all inside. Richard experienced a moment of awe as he surveyed the architecture and furnishings of this home. The places he'd seen in Glendaloch had been very nice, but they paled in comparison to what lay before him.

"Nick, I'm concerned that Richard has hit his head. He didn't know what year it was or where he was and I don't know if that's changed." Angelina placed a dainty hand on Richard's arm as she spoke. Richard tried with everything he had not to appear affected by her touch, but deep down inside he was experiencing the most unbelievable level of pleasure. This woman had charmed him, something that had seemed an impossibility when he'd met other women in the past.

"I'm sure 'tis only a concussion. I'll make sure that he's okay, don't ye worry about it, but if ye'd like to stay here tonight, ye can keep an eye on him as well," Nick suggested in a cajoling tone.

"No, I really need to get home and besides, you two must have a lot of catching up to do, I'm sure," Angelina headed towards the door. "Do you want me to put something together for your dinner before I leave?" she asked.

"Nae, love. I'll take care of it. I'll order a pizza. 'Tis my favorite as ye well ken." Nick winked at Angelina in a familiar way that set Richard's teeth on edge. He had to remind himself once again that jealousy was no longer a part of his life.

"I'm surprised you're not sick of it yet," she laughed. "Richard, it was a pleasure to meet you. I'm sure I'll be seeing you again some time."

"I hope so, m'lady." Richard bowed in her direction and was pleased to see Angelina seemed impressed by the gesture.

"Ye'll see him, Angelina. I've an idea to enlist Richard in the tournament at the Renaissance Faire. He's an expert at the medieval martial arts, arenae ye, Richard?"

"I am and I'd be delighted to help in any way I can," Richard said, watching for Angelina's reaction. Why he cared what she thought was beyond him. He had to set his mind on getting back home, not on wooing this beauty.

"Okay. I'll leave you two for now. Have a good night and I'll see you for the next practice," Angelina said.

Richard watched as Nick walked her to the door, tamping down a surge of jealousy as his friend kissed her cheek and closed the door after her.

* * *

Angelina walked to her car, thinking about Richard all the while. He was that take-your-breath-away kind of handsome that she was attracted to and she loved his English accent. Funny how they just happened to be at the Marina at the exact same time. If she hadn't found him and he hadn't needed her help, he might not have reconnected with Nick. Such an odd coincidence. It really was a small world, she told herself. As Angelina approached her car, she had the feeling that someone was watching her. She turned her head in every direction, but found herself completely alone on the street. Her intuition told her to hurry. Quickly unlocking the car door, she hopped in and slammed the door, hitting the lock button as she did. She'd been suffering that same unnerving sensation a lot lately and she didn't like it one bit. It felt as if someone was following her, but there was never anyone there when she checked. It was probably just her overactive imagination at work. She started the car and headed home with thoughts of Sir Richard Jefford dancing through her brain.

Chapter 2

"Tell me what happened," Nick said. "How did ye get here?" He sat opposite Richard in a large, overstuffed chair and waited for Richard's answer.

For his part, Richard sat, legs spread wide, elbows on his knees and head in hands. Lifting his head, he sighed heavily. "It's almost too unbelievable for words, but if you're here in this time with me, then you understand that time travel can actually happen."

"I know all too well what ye speak of," Nick responded.

"I was a moment away from being burned to death by a witch named Brielle, when I was washed over by a wave of water that I'm sure was meant to put out the balls of fire heading towards me. And then in the blink of an eye, I was drawn into a thick fog and when it cleared…" Richard didn't finish his sentence, instead he shook his head in amazement at his predicament.

"Where did the water come from?" Nick asked.

"A witch named Maggie MacKinnon sent it and then yet another witch, Edna Campbell, or so I believe, drew me into the fog. Do you know them?" Richard was wondering if maybe one of them had sent Nick to San Francisco.

"I'm afraid not," Nick answered. "Do ye think one of them may have been behind my trip to the future?"

"Perhaps, but then you haven't told me how you got here. I haven't seen you in years. Not since…" Richard paused.

"…not since I got angry with ye fer yer constant need to ruin the MacKenzies. I'm sorry I left ye, Richard, I'd simply had enough and could see no future in tormenting a clan I had no argument with," Nick apologized.

"You were right to leave me. I needed to stop the foolishness and go home to my own life, with my own people. Unfortunately, even losing your friendship didn't keep me from making an ass of myself, over and over again. It wasn't until just recently that I realized the error of my ways. I was heading to the MacKenzie holdings at Breaghacraig to beg their forgiveness and to tell them I would never bother them again. That's when I met Maggie MacKinnon and in standing with her to defeat an evil witch, one who's actions were directly related to my need for vengeance, I was saved by both she and her aunt, Edna Campbell. I'm not sure why she's sent me here, but I do know that I want more than anything to get back to my home."

"So do I," Nick agreed. "Mayhap we can find a way back together." He stood and went to the bar where he poured them both a generous tot of whiskey. He handed one to Richard and raising his own glass said, "To going home."

"To going home," Richard responded, admiring the amber liquid swirling in his glass. "This couldn't come at a better time." He took a sip. "Mmm, this is quite good."

"Whiskey is one thing that hasn't changed much over time." Nick took a big gulp of his drink and put the glass down. "Shall we order that pizza?"

"What, pray tell, is pizza? I'm assuming it's food, but not something I've ever eaten." Richard took another sip of his whiskey as he watched Nick pick up one of those cell phones. "You have one of those as well?"

"Yes. It's really verra useful. If ye find yerself here longer than ye expect, ye may need to have one." Nick punched at the phone with his large fingers and then held it to his ear. "This is Nick Mackall, I'd like to order my usual." Richard watched his friend and marveled at how he had managed to adapt to this place and time. "Aye. I'll need two. Thank you." Nick tapped the phone again and then put it down. "They'll be here in no time. I think ye'll enjoy this." He laughed as he crossed the room to the window where he closed the blinds and then turned on the lights. "I take it yer familiar with some of the things yer seeing, as ye dinnae appear overly surprised by them."

"I spent some time in twenty first century Glendaloch, so, yes, I've seen cell phones, automobiles, electric lights and some other things." Richard relaxed back into the chair. This wasn't going to be so bad now that he knew he had an ally here to help him.

"When I first arrived here, I was always standing around with me mouth agape. 'Tis a wonder they didnae lock me up fer being tetched in the head." Nick laughed. "I had not a soul to speak with about what had happened and so I had to make my way, sleeping on park benches and relying on the kindness of people I'd meet, for food and drink. Then one day, I was at the Marina, that's where ye landed by the way, and I saw a group practicing with swords and dirks. I couldnae believe me eyes. Oh, and they were verra bad at it, too. I thought I could make meself useful by showing them a thing or two. They were grateful and offered to pay me to teach them. I'm nae fool, so I said I would and that's how I became their instructor. At first, I lived with some of my students, switching between apartments often, never really having a place to call my own."

Richard took advantage of Nick's pause to ask the question that he'd been burning to ask. "How did ye meet Angelina?"

She was at the Marina with one of the men in the group. She wanted to learn medieval martial arts - that's what they call practicing for battle, only they never really battle. It's all for show. Angelina was such a sweet, lovely woman and I wanted to get to know her better, so I thought it would be fun, and to my advantage, to teach her."

"And was it?" Richard asked. He casually sipped his drink, to hide his interest.

"Aye. She learned quickly and before long she was quite good. I learned a thing or two meself." Richard cocked a questioning eyebrow at Nick, who continued. "Angelina was definitely not interested in me. She made that clear right from the start, but a several months later, when she found I was sleeping anywhere I could find a bed, she insisted that I stay here. She is the kindest and most generous woman I've ever had the pleasure to know."

"I understand what you speak of based on my own experience with her earlier." Richard was intrigued by Angelina and more so by his current circumstance. "Nick, I can't help but wonder if there was some reason I found myself transported to this place and time. Based on my knowledge of her, Edna can be a bit of a meddler, and I'm beginning to think she's sent me here for a reason. Could it possibly have been to find you and bring you back with me?"

"I cannae answer that, but if she did then she has my most sincere gratitude." Nick was obviously still amazed at the fact that his good friend was sitting here, having a drink with him. "I never thought I'd see anyone from my own time ever again." And then he laughed a deep, throaty laugh of disbelief.

"And I'm grateful that if I had to travel to the future again, this time I was reunited with someone I've missed having around over the years." Richard raised his glass again in a silent toast and Nick did the same. They finished their drinks and reminisced about their years of drinking, fighting and carousing. They had a lot to share and so the conversation continued without pause until the doorbell rang.

"Our pizza is here," Nick said, getting up to answer the door with an impish glint in his eyes. "Thank ye, young lad. He paid the delivery boy, closing the door after him and took the pizzas to the counter in the kitchen. "Come, we'll eat here," Nick said, pointing to two stools.

Richard rose and joined Nick as he took out two plates and some napkins. He opened the boxes and Richard got his first look at pizza. It both looked and smelled delicious. Nick took a slice and put it on his plate and Richard followed suit. He watched Nick to see how he would eat this strange food and was pleased to see he merely picked it up in his hands and took a big bite. Again, Richard did the same, amazed at the flavors he was tasting. He took another bite and then another. Pausing long enough to speak, Richard said, "I can see why you say this is your favorite."

"Aye. Valerie, the owner of the shop, knows me well. I order from her two or three times a week. Sometimes even more. Angelina is always telling me it's not good to eat the same food all the time, but I respectfully disagree with her."

"And they bring the food right to your door." Richard shook his head in disbelief.

"'Tis truly an amazing time," Nick said. "There are so many things I'll have to show ye."

"Again, I must say how grateful I am to have found you here. I have no doubt that you'll pave the way for me in this world. Tell me about this medieval martial arts that you are a part of." Richard found himself curious about his friend's activities in this modern world and wanted to know more.

"Being that we're five hundred years in the future, everything from our time is called medieval. There has been a recent interest in the way we do or, should I say, *did* battle and groups have cropped up around the world who are interested in learning our ways of engaging in combat. They go all out, even dressing as we do in our own time and they have competitions and a thing called the Renaissance Faire, where people come together to pretend they are in the middle ages. 'Tis another name they use for our time. There is an annual faire here in San Francisco and our group is going to go up against another local group in mock battle. Even though it is *mock* battle, I would still like my group to win, as they are the better men in my eyes."

"Have you armed them all?"

"They provide their own weapons, but they are just for show. They cannae hurt themselves or others with them. Angelina has outfitted them all with clothing representative of our time. She is a talented seamstress and creates costumes for others who attend the faire, both men and women. Eyeing Richard's clothing meaningfully, Nick chuckled. "Of course, neither you nor I will be needing a costume, because we're already kitted out with true medieval clothing. I'm happy yer here. Ye can help me with the training of me men."

"Of course. It will be a pleasure to be of service." Richard eyed the last piece of pizza and Nick nodded to him to take it. He set it on his plate, but before taking a bite he said, "Nick, you never answered my question about how you got here."

"Yer right. I didnae." Nick stood and took his plate to the sink, where he rinsed it before putting it in the dishwasher. "I had been out hunting with me brothers, Duncan and Rory. We had a stag in our sights, ye ken, and we each went in a separate direction to better our chances with our bows. As I moved further away from them, I became aware that we had strayed rather close to a stone bridge which was enshrouded in fog. I thought it strange that the fog appeared only in one spot and me curiosity got the better of me as I headed towards it. I'd completely forgotten about the stag and me brothers. I was mesmerized by the fog and couldnae resist the urge to walk into it. As I did, the ground moved beneath me feet and colors exploded all around me. I scarcely had time to be afeared, before I landed in the bushes at the Marina Green, where I was greeted by a very concerned elderly couple. I thought I must have fallen and hit me head. I searched for me brothers, but never found them."

"You must have been shocked," Richard said.

"Aye. I wandered around for hours, trying to get it straight in me head and then I thought it best to head back to the bushes. I thought if I did, the fog would come again and take me back home, but it never did." Nick picked up Richard's empty plate, rinsed it and put it in the dishwasher. "I had to adapt and I did."

"How long has it been?"

"Two years. Me brothers must have searched all over for me. I cannae imagine what they went through when they couldnae find me." Nick shook his head in disbelief.

"You've never seen the fog again?" Richard asked, feeling a bit uneasy. If Nick had been here two whole years, his prospects for getting back home didn't seem good.

"Nae. I've looked and while there is plenty of fog to be had here in San Francisco, I've nae seen the likes of *that* fog since." Nick refilled both his glass and Richard's. "Now that yer here, I have hope again. We'll find our way back, I've nae doubt."

Richard wished that he was feeling Nick's optimism about their chances. The thought of never being able to return home weighed heavily on his mind.

"Richard, dinnae look so hopeless. I have a good feeling about this." Nick sipped his drink and gave Richard a reassuring smile. "In the meantime, I'll be yer guide to this time and we'll enjoy ourselves as we once did."

Richard offered Nick a half-hearted smile as he considered the prospect of living in this time and place. The only good things would be having Nick's friendship again and the possibility of getting to know Angelina Lawson.

Chapter 3

THE LITTLE COTTAGE BY THE sea, just south of San Francisco, was Angelina's safe haven and as she sat in her car on the gravel drive, admiring her small slice of heaven, she reflected on what it was about this place that grounded her and made her so happy. She loved everything about it - the ocean itself, the sound of the waves crashing onto the beach, the fresh scent of the water and the sounds of the many sea birds lining the narrow strip of beachfront. There was a certain peace to be found here and she never took it for granted. It was home to her and had been for quite some time now. When Jenna and Dylan had gone off on their extended journey to Scotland, they had asked her to move into the family home in the city, but Angelina had never wanted to live there. She'd had many opportunities in the past, but that wasn't the life she wanted. She enjoyed San Francisco well enough on the few occasions that she stayed at the house, however, she wasn't the party girl she had once been and she preferred to spend her nights alone here at the little cottage rather than at the much larger house in the city.

Getting out of the car, Angelina inhaled deeply, enjoying the salty air, when a shiver of apprehension ran up her spine. She spun around and searched the growing darkness, but she saw nothing to make her suspicious. Again, she had the impression someone was watching her, just as she had when she left Nick and Richard earlier. She closed the car door and hurried towards the cottage, where she fumbled with her keys, nerves getting the better of her. The sound of footsteps crunching in the gravel caused her to jump and spin on the spot.

"Angelina," said an elderly woman as she approached.

"Mrs. Whitcomb!" Angelina held a hand to her swiftly beating heart, trying to calm herself.

"I'm sorry. Did I frighten you, dear?" Mrs. Whitcomb, Angelina's friend and neighbor sounded quite concerned.

"I'm just a little jumpy, I guess," Angelina said by way of explanation. "How are you doing, Mrs. Whitcomb?"

"Angelina, I've asked you before to call me Estella," Mrs. Whitcomb admonished. "I'm fine, the husband and I are settling into our new home very nicely."

"Oh, good," Angelina responded as she unlocked her front door. "Please come in, Estella." She reached for the light switch and a soft, warm glow lit the room. Estella followed along behind her. "Would you care to have a seat? I'm going to get a fire started, it's cold in here." It was November and chilly in Northern California, but Angelina preferred her fireplace to the gas heater for keeping her little cottage warm.

Estella took a seat in the cozy living room. "I was wondering if I might borrow a couple of eggs. I'm making a cake for Harry and I realized after I'd already gotten started that I was all out. It's a long drive to the grocery store and I don't see as well at night as I once did."

Angelina's soft gaze landed on Estella. "Of course, you can. I'll get them for you." She marveled at how lively and young Estella seemed, despite her age of nearly eighty years. She retrieved two eggs from the refrigerator and handed them to Estella.

"We're thinking of getting some chickens," Estella said. She searched Angelina's face, perhaps waiting for a protest.

"That sounds like a great idea. Where would you put the coop?" Angelina had thought about having chickens herself, but she knew someone needed to be there on a daily basis to care for them. She wasn't sure she could commit to such an arrangement just yet.

"Out in back by the vegetable garden. There's plenty of room for a coop and a run."

"I'd be happy to help you take care of them when I'm here," Angelina offered. "And maybe in exchange for some eggs, I could help pay for their feed.

"That would be wonderful. Fresh eggs are the best and I know we'd have more than enough to share with you." Estella smiled warmly and stood to go. "Harry wants to build the coop himself, but I'm not sure he's up to the challenge."

"Maybe my friend Nick could help him. I'll ask him and if he agrees, I'll let you know so Harry can buy the lumber." She walked Estella to the door, where they stood for a moment.

"Any help would be a blessing. Thank you so much. I believe we struck gold when we got you for a neighbor." Estella headed out the door and turned to wave goodbye. "I'll bring you a slice of cake tomorrow."

"Thank you, Estella. Be careful walking in the dark," Angelina stood in the doorway and watched as Estella carefully navigated her way across the gravel drive to the path that led to the house next door. "Good night!" Angelina called. Closing the door, she suffered the same uneasy sensation she'd had before Estella arrived. She double checked the locks and made sure all the windows around the house were closed and secured as well. Peeking through the front windows, she realized there was no way she was going to see anything at all out there. The fog had rolled in and the moon was no longer visible, leaving the surrounding area pitch black. She closed the blinds and went to the kitchen to make herself a quick dinner from the contents of the freezer. As she waited for the microwave to beep, she sent a text to Nick. *I'm home. Sorry for the delay texting. My new neighbor stopped by and we were talking.*

The microwave signaled that her food was done and as she removed it, the phone vibrated, letting her know that Nick had answered. *I'm happy you're home safely. Richard and I are catching up on lost time. Will we see you tomorrow?*

I'm not sure. I have some things to do, but if I finish early enough I'll stop by. Angelina loved Nick like a brother. She'd never had one, but she imagined if she had, he would have been just like Nick. At first, he'd come on to her, trying to convince her he was the one for her, but after a brief period of suffering Angelina's gentle rejections, Nick had seen reason in her arguments about not wanting to get involved and they had become the best of friends. She found it amusing that wherever they went, women jealously eyed her, as if she were their competition in the contest for Nick's heart. He loved all the attention and deservedly so. He was a tall, broad shouldered Scotsman, with an adorable accent. Handsome was an understatement in his case. He possessed smoldering good looks, all the way from his mop of wavy brown hair, to his aquiline nose and very masculine chin. His eyes were a tawny gold, with flecks of green and brown and his lips were perfectly formed and a prize many women coveted.

Angelina's phone buzzed again. *Good enough, then. I hope to see you tomorrow. Good night.*

Good night, she texted back. She wished she could shake the uneasy feeling that had followed her since leaving the city. Angelina poured herself a glass of wine and settled into the overstuffed sofa that faced the fireplace. Reaching into the gap between the arm of the sofa and the cushion she rested on, she found her dirk and placed it within easy reach, just in case she needed it.

* * *

A shadowy figure stood watch, hidden amidst the shrubbery surrounding Angelina Lawson's home. Satisfied that he had gone unnoticed, he silently headed back the way he'd come. As he reached his car, which he'd parked in a darkened area around the corner, the man made a phone call.

"Well," asked a voice at the other end. "How'd it go?"

"Fine. She never even noticed me. When the time is right, this should be easy." The man started his car and holding the cell phone to his ear, he began to drive off.

"As long as we can get at her when that big highlander isn't around, I'd agree."

"And if we can't?" The man merged his car onto the freeway, heading back towards the city.

"You'll have to get rid of him."

* * *

"Explain to me what you're doing with that," Richard said, pointing to the cell phone.

"It's called 'texting'. I'm sending and receiving messages from Angelina. With this phone, I not only can keep in touch with everyone I know, but I can access any information I might need. The answer to any question ye could think of, is right here in this phone." Nick handed the phone to Richard so he could examined it more closely.

"I find that hard to believe." Richard was turning the phone every which way. "How can something so small contain the answers to every question? It seems impossible."

"Here, I'll show ye." Nick took the phone back and said, "Ye'll enjoy this, Richard." He pressed the button on the front of the phone and said, "Medieval martial arts." A woman's voice came from the phone and responded, "This is what I found on the web for medieval martial arts."

"Who is that?" Richard was astounded. The shocked expression on his face must have been amusing to Nick, because he burst into laughter.

"Here, see what she found for me." Nick handed the phone back to Richard who nodded seriously as he examined the phone.

"Will she answer any question?" he asked.

"Most of them. What will the weather be like tomorrow?" Nick asked as he retrieved the phone from Richard once again.

"The weather in San Francisco will be sunny, but cool, with temperatures in the high fifties."

Richard couldn't believe that the phone could talk. "What magic is this?"

"Nae magic. Modern technology," Nick said.

"Modern what?" Richard was becoming more and more baffled with each passing moment.

"I'll tell ye more about it tomorrow, Richard. Let me show ye to yer room." Nick threw an arm over Richard's shoulder, "I'm happy to see ye once again, my friend."

"As am I," Richard responded. He wondered how he was going to survive in this world he found himself in. There was much to learn and he'd better get used to it, because going back didn't seem as if it were a possibility at this moment in time.

Chapter 4

RICHARD WOKE TO THE SOUND of clattering and banging coming from the other room. He stretched and yawned and for a brief moment forgot where he was. He sat up and much to his dismay, found he was still in San Francisco. Not a thing had changed during the night, although he'd hoped it would. Throwing the covers off, Richard stood to his full height and took a good look at his surroundings. The bedroom he'd spent the night in was beautifully furnished in a fashion he was unfamiliar with. There was a large, comfortable bed, covered with many different fabric types, end tables with electric lamps, and a dresser for clothing. He explored the one door he hadn't opened last night and found it was a small room, filled with clothes and shoes. He walked inside and stared in disbelief at the huge amount of clothing the room contained.

"Richard," Nick called from the doorway.

"Here," Richard answered as he peeked out from the closet. "Who do all these clothes belong to?"

"The young man who had been living here. The one who went off to Scotland. I believe his name was Dylan," Nick said thoughtfully. "If anything in there fits you, feel free to use it. It appears Dylan was about the same size as the two of us, so I've made use of this closet myself."

"Hmmm…" Richard wondered if this Dylan was the same one as Maggie MacKinnon's man. "Do you know anything about this Dylan?"

"Nae. He was gone when I arrived. Although I believe Angelina has a photo of him on her phone. Why do ye ask?" Nick was leaning against the doorjamb, dressed and ready for the day in modern garb similar to what he'd worn yesterday.

"I think I may know him. He was with me just before I was sent to this time."

"'Tis possible, I suppose," Nick said. "Why don't ye get cleaned up… and put some clothes on for pity's sake. My eyes are painin' me."

Richard was not at all embarrassed. He walked around in the nude in front of his men all the time and they did the same. "Perhaps that's because you've never seen such a fine figure of a man before."

"On the contrary, I have. Every time I look at meself in the mirror." Nick laughed heartily at his own joke. "Are ye hungry? I'll be making some breakfast if ye'd care to join me."

"I would. Let me get dressed and I'll be right there."

Nick left the room and Richard rummaged through the clothes in the closet. He didn't want to create a stir walking around in his own garb. Angelina had been intrigued by it, but obviously people of this time did not dress in that manner. He found a pair of blue pants similar to the ones Nick wore, and a white shirt. He tried them on and despite the fact that they were snugger than he was comfortable with, he was pleased that they seemed to fit. When he'd travelled to the future in Glendaloch, he had continued to wear his own clothing and no one seemed the least bothered by it, but he somehow knew it would be different here. Next he looked for shoes. He wasn't sure he'd be successful, but upon trying on a pair of fine leather boots, he was happy to note that they fit quite comfortably. He took a quick look at himself in the mirrored doors, admiring himself, pleased with what he saw.

Entering the kitchen, Nick whistled at him and nodded his approval. "No one would ever know you weren't from this time. You'll fit right in."

"Is Angelina joining us today?" Richard asked, trying to keep his question casual.

"Mayhap later. She's things to do. Yer taken with her, arenae ye?" Nick teased.

"She's a beautiful woman," Richard responded. "I'd be a fool not to be." He sat at the counter while Nick prepared their breakfast. "It smells delicious. I had no idea you could cook." he said, changing the subject.

"Of course, I can. Ye've been in camp with me, ye should ken that." Nick continued stirring the eggs in the pan. "We've a practice to attend to this morning. I'll introduce ye to me men and ye can take over some of their training." Placing plates on the counter, Nick spooned the eggs onto them. He placed a few pieces of bacon and some buttered toast onto each plate. "Voila," Nick announced with a flourish.

Richard dug right in. "Delicious," he said.

"And ye doubted me abilities! Would ye care fer some coffee?" Nick reached for some cups and filled them without waiting for an answer. "Cream and sugar?"

"I remember that I enjoyed coffee. Yes, to the cream and sugar." Richard stirred the coffee with the spoon Nick handed him and then took a sip. "Mmmm. I'm curious. What is the point of training these men for battle, when there won't be one?"

"I ken yer meaning, Richard, and I wondered the same. 'Tis the discipline involved in perfecting a skill. The men and women who participate, gain confidence they put to use in their daily lives; they learn respect for their opponent and 'tis an excellent form of exercise, something that is also prized in this time. So, ye can see while they may have no cause to use their swords or dirks in real battle, the artistry of wielding the sword benefits them in other ways." Nick picked up his empty plate and took it to the sink. "Are ye done?"

"Yes." Richard handed him his empty plate and holding up his cup, pointed to the coffee pot indicating he'd like a refill. "Are there many women who participate? I know Angelina does, but I didn't think it would be something most women would enjoy."

"Women and children participate as well. In this time, women can do anything a man can do, if they wish." Nick poured another cup for himself and one for Richard. "I teach many at my school, but other than Angelina, none of them will participate in the tournament."

Richard nodded his understanding and sipped his coffee.

"I noticed when ye arrived ye didnae have yer sword with ye." Nick tidied up the counters as he spoke.

"I must have lost it during the time travelling. I admit I feel a bit naked without it." His hand went to the spot his sword would normally hang, reflexively searching for the hilt.

"I know a man who can make ye a beauty. He's a true artist. He'll make it according to yer specifications, of course. We can go see him this morning if ye'd like." Nick turned to the sink and rinsed the dishes. "I'll show ye the brilliant work he did on mine." He dried his hands and then left the room, returning shortly with a beautiful, gleaming sword, which he handed to Richard. The heft of it in his hand felt well balanced, the hilt comfortable to hold. At the very top was a Celtic knot, flawlessly executed and polished to a radiant glow.

"I'd like to meet this man," Richard said, continuing his examination of Nick's sword in admiration of the artistry his eyes beheld.

"And so ye shall!" Nick finished cleaning up and grabbed his jacket. "Ye'll need a jacket. There are more in the hall closet."

Richard opened the door Nick had indicated and found several to choose from. The one that called to him was of a soft black leather. He removed it from the closet and put it on, pleased that it fit him so well.

"Ye'll be fighting the women off with that one," Nick observed. "Come, let's go see Quinn."

"Quinn?"

"The sword maker. He lives nearby. We can walk, so there's no need to wait for Angelina to take us. Can ye believe she willnae allow me to drive the car that's in the garage."

"*Can* you drive one of those *cars*?" Richard asked.

"How difficult can it be? I've watched Angelina drive many times and I believe I could do it. Unfortunately, she says I must pass a driving test to get a license," he harrumphed. "It requires that I prove my identity, and I have nae way to accomplish that, so I walk most places. If Angelina isnae around and I need to travel further, then I take the bus or a cab."

"I can't believe how well you've adapted, my friend," Richard said. "I can only hope that I will do the same."

"I have nae doubt ye will." Nick winked, opening the door and stepping out into the blinding sunshine. He reached into his pocket and pulled out a pair of sunglasses which he donned. "How do I look?"

"Are you seriously going to wear those?" Richard should have known better. Nick had always been a bit of a peacock when it came to his looks.

"Aye. I see others wearing them. The glasses give them an air of mystery and I like being mysterious. Is it working?"

Richard laughed out loud. "I've missed ye, Nick."

* * *

Two well-defined footprints in the damp soil had Angelina rushing indoors and wondering if the feeling of being watched that she'd experienced last night was for good reason. They were large footprints, obviously belonging to a man, probably wearing work boots of some sort and the owner had been facing her house, looking directly towards her living room windows. She shuddered to think that someone may have actually been standing outside watching her. What could their motivation be? She'd have to be more observant, especially since the only other people nearby were Estella and her husband. She had chosen this spot because it was isolated and she enjoyed the peace and quiet it afforded her, but she hadn't stopped to think that it might also put her in harm's way.

There was a knock at the door and Angelina jumped in surprise. "Who's there?" she called.

"It's Estella," came the answer. "I brought you some of the cake I made last night."

Angelina released the breath she had been holding and went to the door, opening it to her sweet neighbor. "Estella, you really shouldn't have. Won't your husband be disappointed you're giving away his cake?"

"There's plenty left for him. He's not supposed to eat a lot of sweets, so I'm merely removing temptation. If I left this there, he'd eat it all before the day was done."

"Come, sit down. Can I get you some coffee? And maybe you'll have some cake with me." Angelina put the coffee on and got some mugs, plates, silverware & napkins, which she set on the table.

"We'll have a little tea party, or should I say, coffee party," Estella said, laughing.

"You're in a good mood," Angelina observed. "What's going on?"

"I was talking with my daughter this morning and she and her family will be joining us for Thanksgiving dinner. I'm so excited to see them all."

"That's wonderful," Angelina said. "What about your sons, will they be coming too?"

"Mmmhmmm… And my grandsons and great grandchildren, too. It will be the first time in ages that we've all been together for the holiday." She smiled warmly at Angelina, who was slicing some cake and putting it on their plates. "Angelina, I was wondering if you'd like to join us. You can bring your handsome friend, Nick." Estella had a mischievous twinkle in her eye.

"Estella," Angelina teased, "you're a married woman and I think you've got a crush on Nick."

"I'm married, but I can still enjoy a good looking man, even at my age." She rolled her eyes saucily and then burst into a fit of giggles.

"Thank you so much for the invitation, Estella. I'm not sure Nick will want to go though. He has a friend in town and he'll probably want to spend the day with him, but I'll ask." Angelina retrieved the coffee pot and poured some for them both. She headed to the refrigerator for the creamer, before grabbing the sugar bowl and heading back to the table.

"Well, his friend is welcome to join us as well. The more the merrier I always say. It makes it more festive, wouldn't you agree?"

"Of course," Angelina said. "You'll have to let me make the pies."

"That would be a blessing. I'm not good with pies," Estella agreed.

"Well, I make a mean pumpkin and my apple is pretty good, too. I'll have to come up with a third, considering how many people you'll have." Angelina sipped her coffee and thought about the many Thanksgivings she'd spent alone, or with other single friends. The more the merrier never came into play for her. She was looking forward to this and she couldn't wait to share it with Nick and Richard. "You know, Estella, Nick's friend is British. He has a lovely accent and he's pretty handsome. Richard will make some nice eye candy for you."

The two women laughed as they enjoyed the cake and each other's company. Angelina found that with Estella's presence, she could almost completely dismiss the footprints outside her little cottage from her mind for a short while; almost, but not quite.

Chapter 5

SPARKS WERE FLYING EVERYWHERE AS Nick and Richard entered the little backyard that housed Quinn O'Connell's sword-making workshop.

"Nick!" The man at the anvil wiped his brow and removed the heavy gloves protecting his hands. "I wasn't expecting you so early."

"Sorry for the surprise visit, but I've got practice later and this seemed the perfect time to stop in with my friend here." Nick motioned to Richard to join him. "This is Richard Jefford. He's in need of a sword."

"Nice to meet you," Quinn held his hand out for Richard to shake.

Richard shook the proffered hand in his own firm grip. "And you as well. I've left my sword back home and I'll need one if I'm to help Nick with his students."

"Of course." Quinn continued to wipe his hands and his brow. "Did you have something in mind, or would you like to see what I've been working on."

"I'd love to see what you've been working on. I'm not used to being without a sword, so the sooner I can have one, the better."

"The blade is finished and now I'm working on the hilt. I can make that part to your specifications and probably have it ready for you in a few days." Quinn shrugged his shoulders and stretched his neck from side to side, obviously relieving some aching muscles.

"This one's been coming to me easily. It happens that way sometimes. I have an idea in my head and it just flows out of me." He smiled at Richard, who had been examining the blade on the table in front of him.

"You do beautiful work," Richard observed.

"Thanks. Here, let me show you what I had in mind for the finishing touches." He pulled a piece of paper from under the table and laid it out for Richard to see. The beautifully detailed drawing showed an incredible sword, one Richard would be proud to own. The blade was etched with scrollwork, the hilt, which consisted of the guard, the grip and the pommel was spectacular. The steel guard was shaped somewhat like an owl's head, with wings spanning either side. The grip was covered in black leather from top to bottom, with bands of etched steel breaking up the leather in two spots so it would match the sheath. The pommel, set atop it all, was a filigree ball of fine strands of steel. Richard was very pleased with the design and could hardly wait to hold the finished product in his hand. Nick had assured him that he wouldn't need a sword here in modern day San Francisco, but Richard wasn't quite so confident.

"That will be more than adequate," Richard said. "In fact, it will be the finest sword I've ever owned."

"Good. I'll get back to work then, if there's nothing else you need." Quinn flipped the protective goggles he was wearing atop his head down so that they covered his eyes and began banging away at the piece of metal in front of him.

"Shall we?" Nick asked.

"Yes," Richard answered, pleased with Quinn's swift return to work. It wouldn't be long before he held the finished sword in his hands.

* * *

The traffic getting from Angelina's home to Nick's place, was relatively light. It was rare that she could make her way across the city without sitting at every stoplight for what seemed like hours. She'd been gliding right along and had made it through just about every intersection without even stopping. She was excited to get to Nick's today, which was unusual in itself. While she enjoyed Nick's company, there really wasn't anything out of the ordinary happening. She'd go to his place to pick him up, and they'd head off to practice. Afterwards, she'd drive him home and maybe they'd have dinner together. It was pretty routine. But today was different, she was experiencing a sense of heightened anticipation and knew that if she really wanted to consider it more closely, she could've identified the feeling as having a lot to do with seeing Nick's friend Richard again. There was something about him that piqued her curiosity. He was so unmistakably masculine. His deep, rumbling voice and ever-so-dark eyes penetrated her soul, so much so, she hadn't been able to get him out of her mind since yesterday. She'd have to be on her guard. Angelina didn't like to show her hand too early with a guy. Of course, she didn't plan on him being more than an enjoyable distraction, but she suspected Richard was someone who could distract her for a good long time, at least until he moved out of Nick's place - or until Angelina decided to move on. She wasn't one to let a man entrench himself too deeply into her life. She preferred to keep it all lighthearted, on the surface. Men were not to be trusted, she'd learned that from her mother's mistakes and she had vowed she would never allow the same thing to happen to her. So far, she'd been as good as her word. Men had come and gone in her life and it never bothered her to let them go. Richard would be no different. That is, of course, if he actually was interested. He certainly seemed as if he was, but she'd know for certain soon enough. Angelina pulled her car into the parking space in front of Nick's. It was her lucky day - no traffic and the best possible parking space. She wondered if her luck would hold out with Richard.

* * *

"Richard, can you get the door?" Nick called from his bedroom.

Richard headed to the front of the house and opened the door to find a vision of loveliness standing on the doorstep, smiling at him.

"Hi," Angelina said. She cocked her head to the side and studied him with a rather odd expression on her face.

"Please, come in," Richard said, moving out of the way for her to pass. "Is everything alright?" She was still gazing at him with that same expression.

"Fine," she responded, straightening her head and licking her lips.

He found himself dumbfounded by her presence and unable to think of a single thing to say to her. He closed the door and followed her into the living room, where she turned and looked him over from head to toe.

"I see you found Dylan's closet," she announced.

"Yes, Nick said it would be acceptable for me to borrow some clothing for now. I hope you don't mind." Richard was uncomfortable under her watchful eye.

"No, of course not, Dylan wouldn't mind. He's very generous that way. Besides, I know Nick has made use of some of those clothes as well. And they fit you very nicely." She was staring at him again, as if she was expecting some reaction from him.

"Is something wrong?" Richard asked.

"No. Why would you think that?"

"I don't know. You're looking at me with such intensity, I was wondering if perhaps I was not wearing the clothes properly." Richard glanced down at his shirt and noted that it *was* buttoned properly. Everything to his eye appeared to be fine.

"I'm sorry. I didn't mean to make you uncomfortable. You just look quite handsome, that's all." She turned and walked away from him, heading into the kitchen. He was glad she did, because her departure meant she wouldn't notice the smug, self-satisfied smile which appeared on his lips. He followed after her, in hopes that he was not misreading her.

"Did Nick make any coffee? I usually need a little pick-me-up around this time of day." Angelina walked over to the coffee pot, apparently pleased to find that there was enough remaining for her to have a cup.

Richard watched her every move in fascination. She poured her coffee and he noted her delicate hands as they held the pot. Those hands were connected to equally beautiful arms. His gaze travelled up to her shoulders and then down to the cleavage exposed by the low cut shirt she wore.

"Now who's examining who?" Angelina asked, placing the coffee pot back on the counter. She turned her full attention on Richard, who couldn't help but notice the smoldering eyes gazing without shame directly into his own.

"Are you flirting with me?" Richard asked.

Angelina shrugged her shoulders, a soft, sensual smile lighting her lips. "Where's Nick?" She hadn't taken her eyes off of him.

"Right here, love." Nick interrupted Richard, just as he was about to touch his fingers to those lovely lips.

Damn poor timing, Richard thought and let his hand drop back to his side.

"What are you to up to?" Nick questioned, obviously noting the sexual tension in the air. He glanced from Angelina to Richard and back again, his eyes narrowed suspiciously.

"Not a thing," Angelina answered. "Are you ready to go?" She took a sip of her coffee and waited for his answer.

"Almost. Richard you're going to need to change for practice," Nick said.

"Of course," Richard answered, noting that Nick had changed into clothing more appropriate for the sixteenth century. "I'll be back shortly." He offered Angelina an amused smile before he headed back to his room to change.

* * *

"Just what are ye up to, ye wee vixen?" Nick asked once Richard was out of hearing range.

"What do you mean? I'm just having some fun," Angelina retorted, as she dumped the rest of her coffee down the drain. Changing the subject, she said, "Nick, I thought I showed you how to make a good cup of coffee. That was terrible." She wrinkled her nose at him and shook her head. "Apparently you're going to need another lesson."

"I can never make it the way ye do. I've tried, but I'm nae an expert like ye are." Nick took the cup from her hand and placed it in the dishwasher. "Now, back to my original question. Dinnae think I didnae notice ye trying to change the subject."

"What? You know me. I've never met a man I didn't want to flirt with. Richard is quite handsome, I'd be a fool to miss out on the opportunity to get to know him better." Angelina smiled coyly at Nick.

"I see. Ye may want to be careful with this one. He's a man of strong feelings, Richard is. I've known him a long time and he's only once been in love - and it's taken him years to get over that one. I know you dinnae want to pursue anything serious, and go ahead if ye like, but be careful not to destroy him in the process," Nick warned.

"You've become quite the softy," Angelina teased.

"I am nae a softy, as ye call it." Nick looked appropriately indignant and Angelina couldn't help but laugh. She absolutely adored Nick. Their sibling-like banter always brought a smile to her face.

"I'm sorry, Nickie. You know I love you," Angelina stood on tiptoe to kiss Nick's cheek and he quickly turned his head so that she ended up giving him a peck on the lips. "You…"

Angelina's response was interrupted by Richard returning to the kitchen. He was dressed once again in the medieval garb he'd been wearing when she first spied him at the Marina. *Perfection,* she thought, smiling warmly in his direction. The scowl on his face only added to that bad boy quality she so liked about him. Without uttering a word, he turned and headed for the door. Angelina realized too late that he had probably witnessed her kiss Nick and he didn't appear very happy about it. Giving Nick a 'why-did-you-do-that' look, she grabbed her purse and they both practically ran to keep up with Richard.

* * *

Angelina waited patiently as the two men folded their large frames into her tiny little car. Richard looked particularly uncomfortable in the back seat. "Are you okay back there?" she asked apologetically.

Richard grimaced as he tried to find a comfortable spot for his legs and when he couldn't, he simply gave up trying and appeared to resign himself to the fact that this was as good as it was going to get.

"Don't worry. We don't have far to go," Angelina reassured him.

They drove to practice in an uncomfortable silence. Angelina hoped she hadn't done something which would ruin her chances with Richard. She'd have to talk to him about it later, when Nick wasn't around. He had no way to know that her relationship with Nick was purely platonic. She could understand how he might get the wrong idea about them.

Arriving at their destination, Angelina got out of the car and stifled her laughter as first Nick, and then Richard, pulled themselves awkwardly out of the vehicle. It was astounding how those two men could make her little car resemble the clown car at the circus. Nick saw the humor in it and couldn't control his laughter. Richard, on the other hand, seemed none too amused. He glared at both Nick and Angelina before storming past them.

"We're going this way, Richard," Nick called out, pointing to his left and the area that had been designated as their practice field.

A dozen young men stood waiting for them, smiling happily as they approached.

"We were wondering where you guys were," said Zeke Barret, a tall, blond haired man with an easy smile.

"We're here now," Nick said. "This is a friend of mine. Sir Richard Jefford. He's from England and he's an expert in medieval martial arts. He's agreed to help with your training."

The group of men all turned to Richard and offered a friendly greeting. Richard bowed slightly in their direction, but remained stubbornly silent. Angelina was beginning to worry about this silence. She didn't know him very well, and hoped she hadn't hurt his feelings too badly.

Nick divided the group into two, directing one group to work with Richard and the other to follow him. As the group walked away, Richard called out. "A sword, Nickie, if you please."

Nick quickly turned back toward Richard. "What did ye call me?"

The smirk on Richard's face said it all. He had waited for his opportunity and when it arrived, he took full advantage of it. "I believe you heard me, Nickie. I need a sword."

"You can borrow mine, Sir Richard," one of the men in Richard's group said.

"Thank you and please, call me Richard." He turned his back on Nick and continued, "I will be working with you one at a time and the rest of you will look on and learn." Richard made quick work of his students. Each and every one of them found themselves flat on their back with a sword at their throat in a matter of seconds. "So, I can see we have much work to do if you wish to excel as swordsmen." Richard stood surrounded by his group of students, who listened carefully to his speech. He explained where each one of them had gone wrong and made suggestions to correct their faults. He handed the sword back to the young man who had lent it to him. "What's your name?" he asked.

"Wade Granville, sir," he responded.

"Wade, pair up with Zeke and the rest of you find a partner. You will parry with each other and I will show you your weaknesses and strengths. Then you will switch partners and we'll do the same thing all over again. Your opponent will not always be the same man, and so it is good to learn how to spar with as many different opponents as possible.

* * *

From across the field Malcolm Granger and his team of combatants observed the newcomer working with Mackall's men. Malcolm wondered who he was and where he'd come from. He was obviously an expert with a sword and could prove to be stiff competition for his men. He preferred to view him as just one more person standing in the way of his goal. He'd need to find out all he could about this man just as he had with Nick, but he felt sure that no matter what it took, he'd win in the end. "Let's go," he called to the men surrounding him.

Chapter 6

STRIDING PURPOSEFULLY ACROSS THE FIELD, followed by a group of men seemingly armed for battle, Malcolm Granger made his way towards Nick and Richard. Halting, arms folded across his chest, Malcolm observed Angelina holding her own against a much larger opponent. She was magnificent with a sword and watching her lithe body as she spun away from her opponent made Malcolm's body react in a way that he couldn't afford at this point. He had much more important things on his mind. If she was still around when he had achieved his goal, then he'd think about making her his. For now, he had to set his plan in motion and wait for the right time to make it happen.

Malcolm was a member of the Royal Academy of Medieval Martial Arts. He enjoyed reminding Nick of this as often as possible. He knew it rankled the other man and that's exactly why he did it. "Your lads are coming along nicely," Malcolm called to Nick, who looked up briefly to acknowledge him. "I see you've hired a new instructor, perhaps you'll introduce us."

Nick nodded to Richard, "Sir Richard Jefford, meet Malcolm Granger, our opponent in the upcoming meet."

Richard stopped what he was doing and walked over to Malcolm, sizing him up as he approached. "I'm please to meet you," he said as he shook Malcolm's hand.

"And you," Malcolm replied. "*Sir* Richard Jefford. Is that name just for show?" he chuckled.

Richard furrowed his brow and stood to his full height. "For show?"

"Yeah. You aren't really a knight, are you? So, obviously it's a name you've made up to fit with the medieval theme." Despite his lighthearted response, Malcolm's smile never reached his eyes.

Richard did not oblige him with an answer, merely turning back to his students to continue his lesson.

"I believe I've insulted *Sir* Richard," Malcolm laughed as Nick approached. "He's quite sensitive, it would seem."

"Ye certainly have a way of ingratiating yerself on everyone ye meet, Malcolm, but that is one I wouldnae suggest you rile." Nick cast his gaze in Richard's direction.

"Really! Is he that good?" Malcolm was delighted - he was getting all the information he needed without even having to work for it.

"He's better than that good. Ye'd be smart to steer clear of him or apologize and hope he doesnae challenge ye."

"Malcolm," Angelina interrupted her workout to come and greet him. "How are you?"

"Hello, my sweet." Malcolm reached out to take her hand and gently kiss it. "A pleasure to see you."

Angelina smiled warmly at him and his eyes lingered on her until Nick interrupted the moment.

"Are ye here to practice, or to cause trouble, Malcolm? We're just about done, so ye can have the field all to yerself."

"We're here to practice, Nick. Why would you think otherwise?" Malcolm glanced back at his men, who all wore challenging expressions and stood shoulder to shoulder behind him. "We're looking forward to the next tournament. I hope it's not too soon for you."

"Nae. We'll be ready fer ye. The question is whether ye'll be ready fer us." Nick called to his men and they all fell into line behind him, sizing up their competition. "We're done here."

Malcolm and his group brushed past Nick, making eye contact with every man they passed. Malcolm spoke just loudly enough to be overheard, "They'll be lucky if there's even one man left standing when we're done with them."

* * *

"Who was that man?" Richard demanded as they made their way back to the car after practice.

"That was Malcolm Granger," Angelina offered.

Richard had observed the exchange between Malcolm and Angelina from a distance. She was a little too friendly with him for Richard's liking. What kind of woman was she? He had caught her earlier kissing Nick, after openly flirting with him and now this Malcolm Granger. She was as infuriating as she was beautiful. "I know his name. Who *is* he?" he growled.

Angelina stiffened at his response. "I was merely answering your question, there's no need to bark at me like that. I don't know what your problem is, but don't take it out on me."

Richard realized he was falling back into the old habit of being unreasonably jealous. If Angelina wanted Nick *or* Malcolm, so be it. He would simply not vie for her attention. He would not allow his heart to be turned to vengeance once again because he couldn't have what he wanted - and he wanted her. It had become painfully clear to him earlier and now he would have to let that go. "I apologize, Angelina, I had no right to speak to you that way. I let my irritation at Granger get to me. There is no excuse for my behavior."

Angelina appeared to soften. "Apology accepted."

Nick, who was seated in front once again, peered back at Richard with a questioning look. "Malcolm Granger is a very wealthy man who is fascinated by anything medieval. He has one of the largest collections of medieval artifacts in the world. Rumor has it that more than a few of them were collected illegally, but he has more than enough money to prevent anyone from investigating their true origins. He's currently searching for a sword from the time of James IV, apparently with no luck, as it has nae been uncovered in any archeological digs to date. He's obsessed with finding it and will spare no expense to get what he wants."

Richard sat stone faced in the back seat, absorbing all of this information and building up a huge dislike for Malcolm Granger.

"He's also our chief competition in winning the Northern California Medieval Martial Arts Finals Championship. He's trained his men well and several of them are experts in other forms of martial arts," Nick explained. "They've won every year since the competition began."

"They'll not win this time," Richard stated as he stared balefully out of the window. "I'll see to it."

"That's what I like to hear," Nick said. "Now, where are we going for dinner, Angelina?"

"Well, I don't know about you, but I'm going home. You two are on your own." Angelina pulled her car into a parking spot in front of Nick's.

"I hope you're not leaving because of me," Richard said, recovering from his momentary anger. "Please, join us for something to eat. I promise to behave myself."

Angelina gazed back at him and his heart skipped a beat. *Damn it, why does she have to be so beautiful?* He tipped his head to the side and did his best to look as sorry as possible.

"Well, when you look at me like that, how can I refuse?" Angelina pulled the key from the ignition and opened the door to get out. "I'm hungry, let's figure out where we're going. Somewhere close by would be good."

Richard noted that her whole demeanor had changed. He knew it was because of his apology and he was pleased with himself for recognizing his own bad behavior and correcting it. He pulled himself out of the infernal back seat and did his best not to curse as he did so. He was happy they would be walking to their next destination, because he really didn't think he could take another minute in that car.

"Shall we go to the diner around the corner?" Nick offered.

"Sure," Angelina responded. "Although all that greasy fried food you like to eat is going to catch up with you, sooner or later."

Nick laughed. "Later, I hope."

* * *

The three walked off down the street, Angelina, between the two men, as they discussed the day's practice and Malcolm Granger.

"I've known Malcolm for a few years," Angelina said. "He's nothing, if not intense."

"Yes, that would be putting it mildly. I'd say Malcolm and I started as friends, drinking buddies ye might say, but shortly after he realized that I was teaching medieval martial arts, he became confrontational and belligerent. The man doesn't like to lose. Granted he never has, as long as I've known him, but he looks at me as a particular threat to his standing in the community. Now that yer here, Richard, he may become even more ruthless. We'll have to wait and see." Nick opened the door to the diner, ushering his friends inside. They settled in the first empty booth, Nick on one side and Angelina the other. Richard opted to sit next to Angelina and a thrill ran through him at the touch of her leg against his thigh. Nick handed menus to them both. "I dinnae need a menu. I know exactly what I want."

Richard stared at the laminated card in his hand wondering what it was for, until he realized it listed the various foods available in this establishment. He wasn't sure he'd made a wise decision sitting next to Angelina. Having her so close was making it uncomfortable for him, but he couldn't exactly get up and walk away and Nick was entirely taking up the other side of the booth. He would simply have to suffer through the pain and pleasure of her nearness.

"I know what Nick is going to have," Angelina said with a laugh. "What about you, Richard? What would you like?"

Richard cleared his throat to stop himself from saying, *you*. "I'll have whatever Nick is having." He glanced away from her penetrating eyes and took in the *diner*. It was a rather unusual place, but he assumed it operated in much the same way as the eating establishments he had seen in Glendaloch.

"Well, that's not very original. I'm going to have the Ahi Tuna Salad. Nick doesn't eat nearly enough veggies."

"Nonsense, Angelina. I'm having french fries. They're made with potatoes," Nick stated with authority.

A young woman came to their table with paper and pen in hand. "My name is Serena, I'll be your server tonight. What can I get you?" She sounded about as interested in serving them as Richard was in the conversation between Nick and Angelina over what Nick was going to eat. Nick ordered something he called a cheeseburger with fries and Angelina ordered her salad.

When it was Richard's turn to order, he repeated Nick's order and put his menu back in the holder Nick had taken it from. As he leaned across Angelina to do so, he had the overwhelming urge to kiss those pouty lips that tempted him from not more than a few inches away. She licked her lips and he groaned.

"Is everything okay," Angelina asked.

He realized too late, he'd foolishly groaned out loud. *What is wrong with you, Richard?* "Fine," he answered as he sat back on the bench. He saw the knowing grin on Angelina's lips and stifled a chuckle. *She knows exactly what she's doing. Two can play this game.*

The waitress returned with water, silverware and napkins. "Your food will be out shortly," she said in the same disinterested tone.

"Thank you," Angelina responded.

Richard gave up trying to contain himself to his half of the bench and spread his legs so that the one that was closest to Angelina was in contact with hers from hip to thigh. He threw his arm over the back of the booth and challenged her with a smile. "This is quite cozy, isn't it?"

Nick, who had been observing the two of them quite closely, stifled a laugh.

Angelina for her part, didn't appear bothered by it at all. Instead, she adjusted her own leg and in the process rubbed up against Richard's. For the next ten minutes or so, they continued to tease one another until thankfully their food arrived, forcing them to drop their little game of cat and mouse, and eat. Richard having never seen one before, couldn't help but be fascinated with Angelina's *salad* and it must have been obvious to her.

"Would you like to try it," she asked, as she picked up a forkful of the unusual leafy greens and held it out to him.

He hardly had time to reply when he found it at his lips, so he opened his mouth and accepted her offering. The flavors were unlike any he'd ever tasted. "Delicious," he said after swallowing the last bit. "Would you like to try mine?"

"I'll have a french fry," Angelina said and waited for him to feed it to her. "Ketchup, please."

Richard looked to Nick for guidance on that one and watched as Nick picked up a fry and dipped it in the red liquid on his plate. Richard reached across and dipped the fry into the ketchup before returning it to Angelina's mouth. The sensual way she accepted it from his fingers was more than he could bear, as a dribble of ketchup landed on her bottom lip. He quickly focused on his own food and tried to avoid further eye contact with her.

He had to admit that the food was very good. If he had no other choice, he imagined he could live here and learn to fit in the way Nick had. His friend would be there to guide him when needed and perhaps this woman who sat beside him would… what was he thinking? He didn't want to stay here and he was going to do everything he could to find a way back to his own time and place. His family needed him. He'd been away much too often over the past few years and it was time for him to settle down and manage the family holdings. He had no idea how he would make that happen, but perhaps when Edna realized that she'd mistakenly sent him to the future, she'd find a way to get him back where he belonged. Unless it was her intention all along to send him here. Perhaps she wanted to keep him out of his own time and away from the MacKenzies. He was getting agitated just thinking about it and his tense posture, he noted, had Nick and Angelina exchanging concerned glances. Once again he had to get himself under control. He smiled warmly at his old friend and his new one. He would manage, no matter how things worked out. What choice did he have?

* * *

What's up with him? Angelina thought as she watched Richard go from relaxed and enjoying their interplay, to tense and distracted. He was intriguing. She'd never met anyone quite like him before. He was everything she looked for in a man, along with a little something extra. Richard had an old world sensibility to him and she liked it. He also appeared to be completely genuine. He didn't act like he was playing a part, trying to be someone he wasn't in an effort to impress her. She'd seen enough of that in her dating life and she could spot it from a mile away. Angelina could tell within a date or two, just what to expect from a man and most of the time it wasn't much, so she let them go. She enjoyed their company and found herself surrounded by different men all the time, but that was her choice. Contrary to popular belief among the women she knew, she wasn't the type to sleep around. She valued herself too much and that was a gift that only went to those who proved to be worthy of it. Yes, she was a flirt. Everyone knew that about her, but her female acquaintances were jealous of her ability to attract men and so they fabricated stories about her, trying to make her appear ready to jump into bed with every man who came her way.

The truth, Angelina knew, was deeply hidden. No one knew her real reasons for keeping men at a distance and they never would if she had anything to say about it.

Chapter 7

THE SOUND OF A WOMAN'S voice coming from the living room fireplace woke Richard with a start a few hours later. Someone had called his name. He had heard it loud and clear, but aside from himself, the room was empty. Nick had apparently gone off to bed a while ago, and left Richard sleeping on the sofa. He sat up, preparing to head to his own bedroom when the voice called to him again.

"Richard. Can ye hear me?" the voice asked.

"Yes. I can hear you." The voice sounded familiar to his ear.

"'Tis Edna, Edna Campbell. I'm checking to make sure ye are all right."

"Yes. I'm fine, but I would very much like to return to my home." Richard hoped Edna was contacting him to tell him just how to do that. "Thank you, for saving my life. I don't know what happened after you removed me from harm's way. Are Maggie and Dylan well?" He had thought of them often since his arrival in San Francisco. He'd only spent a short time with them, but they were the first people outside of his own family who had seen the real Richard. They had accepted him, despite his flawed past and he had been grateful for that acceptance. He considered them friends and wanted to know they were unharmed.

"They are well. As a matter of fact, they are here with me at the inn, preparing for their wedding day."

"And Brielle?" He had to know that she had been dealt with, and would no longer be a threat to any of them.

"Brielle is dead," Edna answered.

"Then there is no reason for me to remain here. I must return to my family. I have been away far too long." Silence was the only response. He thought Edna had left him and was just about to call out to her, when she spoke.

"Richard, ye must stay in San Francisco for a while longer. Ye ken that there are some valuable lessons to be learned there. Lessons about life and love. Once ye have accomplished what I've sent ye to do, then ye will be able to return home."

"What lessons? What must I learn?" Richard was puzzled as to why Edna would keep him here against his will.

"I cannae tell ye? Ye must find yer own way, Richard. I have faith that ye will do exactly what needs to be done. Now, I must go. I willnae visit ye again, but ye ken when the time is right, the fog will be there for ye."

"I cannot stay here, Edna. I must return home immediately, do you understand. Anything I must learn I can learn there, back in my own home." Anger was bubbling up inside of him and the fact that he had little if any control in the matter was making it worse. "You have no right to force me to stay here, Edna. Do you hear me?"

"Calm yerself, Richard. Yer temper willnae get ye home any sooner. You've come a long way, but as I said, you have things to learn and they can only be learned where ye are now. I have faith in ye Richard. Ye *can* change yer ways and living in San Francisco for a while will lead you in the right direction. Ye'll have to trust me on that one. There is nae use in arguing with me."

Richard realized she was right. What could he possibly do to change his situation? Edna was the only one who could get him back home and he didn't wish to anger her or he may find himself stuck in the future forever. "Edna, one more question." He stared into the fireplace, thinking he might be able to see her, but there was nothing unusual in the hearth. "What of Nick?"

"Occasionally a person wanders into the fog when it is being used to transport someone else to or from the past, ye ken. 'Tis how ye managed to get yerself back to the year 1514 the first time ye found yerself in Glendaloch." Edna laughed heartily. "'Tis also how ye found yerself in Glendaloch in the first place." Clearing her throat, Edna continued. "Yer friend is also one of those people. He wasnae meant to be cast into the future, but he walked into the fog at precisely the wrong moment and now finds himself in the year 2014, which is a good thing for ye. When ye return, he may return with ye, if he so desires."

She lapsed into silence and he knew she was gone. Richard could feel it. The room was different now and once again, he was alone. *This is all so unbelievable,* he thought as he headed down the hall to his room and the warmth of a very comfortable bed.

* * *

"There's been a change of plans," Nick was saying into the cell phone he held to his ear. Richard didn't think he'd ever get used to the idea that people could communicate with each other over vast distances, much the way he had communicated with Edna last night. "Yes, yes. We'll practice indoors today. We'll meet this evening. I'd appreciate it if ye'd call the others." Nick paused while someone at the other end of the call obviously responded to him. "Thank ye and we'll see ye tonight." Nick turned to Richard, looking for all the world like the happiest man on earth. "Good mornin' to ye, how did ye sleep?"

"Well," Richard responded, not understanding how anyone could be in such good spirits so early in the day.

"Coffee?" Nick was pouring himself a cup and he grabbed an empty mug for Richard and began pouring before he received a response. "'Tis raining today. I've asked Zeke to call the others and tell them we'll be practicing at the warehouse tonight."

"I'd ask why you're so happy, but I recall that seems to be a constant state for you," Richard said, sounding out of sorts, even to his own ears. "Edna spoke with me last night."

"Edna? The witch? What did she say?" Nick sat across from Richard, giving him his full attention.

"She told me I cannot go home yet. There are some things I must learn, or some such nonsense. She also explained your presence here in San Francisco." Richard proceeded to tell Nick what he had learned during Edna's visitation. "And she said you can return with me when I go back, should you wish."

"I wish!" Nick almost shouted in his delight. "If we can find out what ye need to learn, perhaps we can speed up the process."

"I don't believe it will be that easy. After I went to bed last night, I thought a lot about it and I'm sure the lessons have something to do with my jealousy and anger."

"How will ye do it?"

"I don't know what she expects of me. I imagine we'll have to wait and see what presents itself." Richard frowned. "I don't like not knowing what will happen, but I am prepared to show Edna that I am a changed man."

"Perhaps 'tis not Edna that ye must convince," Nick said. "Nonetheless, I will be here to help ye. No matter what, ye can count on me!"

"I know that I can, my friend." Once again, Richard was overwhelmed with how lucky he was to have a friend like Nick. They'd picked up right where they'd left off when last he saw him.

"Ye ken that if I hadn't walked into that fog, I would've come in search of ye. Yer like one of me brothers, with one exception. I chose to have ye in me life and 'tis happy I am to have ye here now."

What could he possibly say to that? Richard smiled warmly at his friend, knowing that they would each give their life for the other if it were ever necessary.

* * *

Dampness permeated everything in the warehouse. The roof was leaking and puddles formed on the floor in several places. Angelina grabbed towels and buckets and began soaking up the water and strategically placing the buckets under the leaks. The door opened and a group of bedraggled students entered, shaking the rain out of their hair and off their jackets.

"Hey, Angelina," Zeke called. "It's really coming down out there."

"Way to state the obvious," his friend Kyle said, rolling his eyes.

"Glad you could make it," Angelina said, placing the last bucket under a leak before she walked towards them. "I was wondering if any of you would show up tonight."

"Everyone's coming, as far as I know. We all know it's important to get in as much practice as we can before the tournament." Zeke removed his jacket and hung it on a peg by the door. "Malcolm's guys are tough. I'm not sure we'll be able to beat them."

"Positive thinking. You must have faith in yourselves. Nick would hate to hear you talk like that." Angelina's face registered her disapproval, and seeing the reaction of the men at the door, she softened. "I believe you can do it. Sometimes people who are too cocky for their own good fail to see beyond their own high opinion of themselves." That seemed to help. They appeared relieved that she wasn't actually angry with them.

"Where are Nick and Richard?" Kyle asked.

"They'll be here. Probably just stuck in typical rainy day traffic. They were grabbing a cab the last time I spoke with them. Help me mop up the floor so no one slips and falls while you're practicing." She handed out mops to a few of the guys, while the others used the towels she'd already laid out. They got the water situation taken care of and then they pulled out the mats, which they placed in the middle of the room to form a large square for their practice space.

The door flew open and Nick and Richard, looking like two very handsome drowned rats, blew into the room. Richard said nothing. Angelina imagined he was trying to create a strong, silent mystique. Nick, on the other hand, began ordering the others to get their gear on and start sparring.

"Angelina," he kissed her cheek. "Was it bad in here?" He perused the large space and seemed pleased that everything was in order.

"Not too bad. We got it all mopped up before you got here. That roof's going to need to be repaired though. It may need to be replaced completely." She pointed to all the buckets lined up on the floor.

Nick looked up and nodded. "We might not have been much worse off practicing outside," he laughed.

Glancing around, she saw that Richard had quickly gotten to work with the guys. She heard him make it clear he would be sparring individually with each of them once again, and she guessed it was to see if they'd retained any knowledge from the last time he'd had them on their backs. Apparently, they hadn't learned much. He seemed very patient with them as he explained where they'd gone wrong and then gave them an opportunity to try again. When they were successful, he was complimentary as he explained the finer points of swordplay and how they got it right, which went a long way towards making them want to try harder to please him. She couldn't help but stare at Richard as he worked. Aside from Nick, he was the most masculine man she'd ever met. He exuded *man* in every way. She was drawn to him, but something told her that he wasn't someone to be trifled with. He was the kind of guy who played for keeps and she wasn't interested in forever. She was only interested in right now. Best not to get involved with him at all, really. Still as she watched, something inside her chest longed to be near him. She imagined she was under a spell where he was concerned and she didn't understand it.

* * *

Richard cast a quick glance in Angelina's direction. He hadn't stopped to speak with her, which he knew was rude, but a conversation with her would take him off his game and he needed to be alert if he was going to whip these men into shape for their competition. Even still, just being in the same room with her was a distraction. She was even lovelier dressed in her practice gear. How could that be? He was used to seeing the women of his time in gowns. To see a woman in breeches was unusual to say the least, but he found it strangely attractive. The curve of her hips and her shapely bottom were outlined for his eyes to explore. Before his conversation with Edna, Richard's plans had included Angelina, but since he would be going back home, and soon he hoped, he had no intention of getting involved with a woman from this time, no matter how much his heart was drawn to her.

"I see ye peeking at her," Nick said, and he slapped Richard on the back. "And I see her sneaking glances in yer direction."

Richard didn't answer, instead getting between Wade and Jayson as they were about to make contact. He corrected their stances and posture, gave them some words of encouragement and then returned his attention to Nick. "I do not understand what you are getting at."

"Yer interested… and so is she. I'd wager every cent I don't have on it." Nick chuckled as he grabbed Kyle by the back of his shirt and steered him out of harm's way. "Excuse me for a moment," he said to Richard and then proceeded to stand with Kyle, having him mimic every move he made as he advanced on his opponent. "That's it! Ye've got it, now go do exactly as I've shown ye."

Richard watched with interest as Angelina engaged Zeke with her sword. As unusual as it was for a woman to engage in swordplay, she was exquisite in her movements and astonishingly better than a lot of men that he knew. She parried back and forth with Zeke, spinning and jabbing, eventually knocking his sword from his hand and a split second later, she had her own sword at his throat. Zeke stood, arms in the air, in surrender. Richard couldn't help himself, "That was perfect, Angelina. Zeke, you could learn much from what just happened. Did you see how fluid her movements were? How she followed your every move? How you were so caught up in what she was doing, that you froze and allowed her to best you?" He turned his attention back to Angelina. "Where did you learn to fight like that?"

"I've been at this for a few years now. I started out with Malcolm's group, but when Nick came along, his methods were more to my liking. It just comes naturally to me. It's like I know what my opponent is going to do before they do. Do you know what I mean?" She wrinkled her nose in the most fetching way.

Richard fought to get his thoughts back on their conversation, as his attention slipped to her pert little nose and her full, sensual lips. "I do know what you mean. I feel that way myself. I would venture to say that I am so totally engrossed in what I am doing that everything else fades into the background, making it easier for me to read my opponent."

"Yes. It's the Zen of swordplay," she teased. Richard didn't understand her reference and it must have shown on his face. "You know, being in the moment."

"That's a good way to put it," Richard said. "I believe Zeke is waiting for you." He turned and walked away before she could read him, the way she had read Zeke. What she would see was a man who desperately wanted her, despite knowing he couldn't have her. He intended to stick to his decision.

"We're making good progress with them," Nick said as he approached. "With your help I believe we have a chance against Malcolm's crew."

"I don't care for him," Richard stated, distaste showing on his face at the mention of Malcolm's name.

"He's a strange one," Nick conceded. "As I've said, we were friends at first, and then rivals. I'm nae sure what changed, but now he tries to act like a man who would be my friend again, while at the same time sending me signals that he wants to show me who the better warrior is."

"You would be, of course." Richard kept his gaze on their students as he spoke with Nick. "He must know that."

Nick ignored the compliment. "The men he surrounds himself with are excellent in all forms of the martial arts. Sometimes, I think he believes this to be a real battle and that worries me. For this group, it's a fun activity. Something they participate in to let off steam after long hours at their day jobs. Not a one of them has that killer instinct that is crucial to being a true warrior. That's not to say we can't train them to do all the right things, but if it came right down to it, they'd be hard pressed to actually hurt someone. Malcolm's men are the exact opposite and that gives me pause. I don't want anyone here getting hurt."

"And they won't. We'll see to it. How long do we have before the competition?" Richard asked as he sized up the group.

"About two weeks." Nick's face revealed his concern.

"Don't worry. The two of us and Angelina are prepared. Zeke is coming along nicely as are Wade, Kyle, and Jayson. The others will get there by the time of the competition," Richard stated with confidence.

Nick nodded. "As a precaution though, from this point forward I think we should practice every day."

Chapter 8

MALCOLM GRANGER SAT IN DARKNESS behind the large mahogany desk in his office, which was perched at the very top of a skyscraper he not only owned, but occasionally called home. The floor to ceiling windows offered sweeping views of the city and the Bay and on a night like this, it was breathtakingly beautiful. The lights twinkled and reflected in the rain as it came down, pitter-pattering on the windows with every gust of wind. The east side of the bay was bathed in a soft light and the moon peeked out from behind dark clouds. Soon enough, it too would be experiencing this deluge, but for now it was being spared. Lightning flashed across the sky in streaks, sending brilliant light into the darkness around him. Malcolm felt its power coursing through his body with every display of its majesty.

A knock at the door drew his attention, "Yes, come in."

"Mr. Granger," Ellie Foster, Malcolm's administrative assistant, entered the room, apparently not the least put off by the darkness. "I'm going home, unless you need me for something else."

"Good night," Malcolm said. He was feeling magnanimous. "I won't need you tomorrow, so enjoy a day off."

"Thank you, Mr. Granger. I'll see you on Monday then," Ellie said.

"Leave the door open, I'm expecting someone." He didn't explain and Ellie knew him well enough to leave it be. "Yes, sir."

Malcolm stretched back into his chair. He was expecting Joel Prewitt, the head of acquisitions for his collection of medieval artifacts. He hoped Joel had the news he'd been waiting for. His search for the sword had been fruitless to this point, but Joel had been searching the length and breadth of Scotland to locate it, or at the very least to find any evidence of its existence. Malcolm stood and went to his liquor cabinet. He opened it and light flooded the room as he reached for the crystal decanter filled with his favorite scotch. He poured himself a generous portion and walked to the window where the lightning display continued to light up the night like Fourth of July fireworks. His doorbell chimed and Malcolm returned to his desk, pressing the button that would unlock the door allowing Joel to enter. Moments later, he heard the distinct sound of footsteps making their way down the hall to his office door.

"Malcolm," Joel called as he tapped lightly on the door.

"I'm here," Malcolm answered. "Come in and hit the light switch on your way through."

Joel obliged him and turned on the overhead lights. He carried a briefcase, which Malcolm hoped contained information about the artifact he sought. "It's raining cats and dogs out there," Joel stated, shucking off his raincoat.

"I'm not interested in the weather," Malcolm said. "What have you got for me?"

Joel seemed nervous as he placed the briefcase on a nearby table and opened it. He pulled out a folder and walked to Malcolm's desk. "May I?" he asked pointing to a chair.

"Of course." Malcolm was losing patience, Joel seemed to be stalling for time and he didn't like it. "Spit it out. I'm not paying you to waste my time."

"Sorry," Joel sputtered. "I didn't find anything helpful I'm afraid. As I told you, I traveled throughout the highlands and visited many of my contacts. Not a one of them had anything for me. Usually they have at least some small thing, but this time they came up empty."

Malcolm's jaw flexed as he struggled to control his anger. "Damn it!" He pounded his fist on the desk, making Joel jump. "Joel, you're going to have to do better than that!" He stood and paced towards the windows. "Did you retrieve the information I request-ed?"

At this question, Joel seemed to relax. "Yes, sir. I went to see the present day Mackall clan and inquired about one Sir Nicholas

Mackall." He opened the folder and placed its contents on the desk. "These are some genealogical records dating back to the early sixteenth century. According to the family members I met with, Sir Nicholas Mackall disappeared while out on a hunting expedition. There is a gap in the records at the point of his disappearance, and family records show nothing more about him. It's unclear whether he was ever located again, or whether the records were somehow lost or destroyed."

Another curse erupted from Malcolm's mouth. "Was there any record of a Nicholas Mackall in recent times?"

"There is a Nicholas Mackall living in Edinburgh at this time. He is a descendant of Rory Mackall, who would have been one of Sir Nicholas Mackall's brothers." Joel waited while Malcolm digested this information. "They are quite an interesting family, my research shows that there were several brothers and two sisters."

"I don't care about that," Malcolm interrupted, pacing back and forth across the room. "Is this Nicholas Mackall still in Edinburgh?"

"He is. They gave him a call while I was there and we spoke briefly. I can say with certainty that he is there."

"All right. I have another name I'd like you to research for me." Malcolm paused, waiting as Joel took out a pen and his notebook. "Sir Richard Jefford."

Joel scrawled the name into his notebook. "Am I looking in present day records, or genealogical records?"

"Both. You'll be looking in English records and go as far back as you went for Mackall. This is a priority, do you understand?"

"I do. I'll get on it right away." Joel gathered his things, leaving the folder for Sir Malcolm. "I'm sorry about the artifact, sir. I've got some colleagues doing research for me and I hope to have more information soon." He backed towards the door as he spoke, seeming for all the world as if he couldn't get out of there fast enough.

"Let's hope you do," was Malcolm's curt reply.

"Good night, sir." Joel left the room and Malcolm growled as he listened to the sound of his employee's feet beating their way swiftly towards the door.

So, he hadn't received the news he'd been hoping for. He had absolutely no concrete evidence that Sir Nicholas Mackall, from sixteenth century Scotland, was the same Nick Mackall he knew today. Perhaps it had merely been the ramblings of a drunkard, but Nick had been very forthcoming with the information that he was a time traveller from medieval Scotland when they'd first met. Malcolm had been skeptical at first, but the more he thought about it, the more he believed it to be a real possibility. And, if it were true, he needed Nick to help him get back to that time period, so he could retrieve his artifact *before* it became an artifact. That part might be tricky and was exactly why he had his man following Angelina Lawson. Nick would likely not want to go back to his medieval life. After all, who in their right mind would want to leave present day San Francisco with all its wonders, for a backwards existence in medieval times? However, from Malcolm's investigations, he'd discovered Nick had a soft spot for Angelina and if Nick wasn't willing to help Malcolm, then Angelina was fair game to be used as a pawn in his bargaining. For now, Malcolm would wait for more information from Joel, but the thought of being able to travel back in time to retrieve a priceless treasure was intoxicating and a prospect he simply wouldn't let go easily. He had Gabe Adamson following Angelina, so that he could track her activities. If the time came when he needed to use her as an end to his means, then he'd know exactly when it was best to strike.

* * *

"Come on, you two," Angelina called from the doorway of the warehouse. "I'll give you a ride home."

Richard groaned inwardly. He didn't think he would survive another ride in that hellish vehicle, but being close to the woman who was causing him such turmoil might just make it worth a short time with his knees wrapped around his ears.

"Don't look so excited, Richard." Angelina had a teasing lilt to her voice. "My car isn't quite big enough for the two of you, so I stopped by the house earlier and collected Dylan's truck. It's much roomier."

Richard's gaze went heavenward as he thanked his lucky stars for this turn of events.

"That was quite stealthy of you, Angelina. I had no idea you were there." Nick turned off the lights and exiting the building behind Richard and Angelina, locked the door. As they approached the truck, he waved Richard into the front passenger seat. "You sit up front, Richard. I'd like to stretch my legs in the back."

Richard nodded and strode quickly to the driver's side to open the door for Angelina, who smiled in surprise at his gesture. "M'lady," he announced, with a flourish of his arm.

"Wow! I'm getting the royal treatment here." She got in the car and Richard closed the door behind her, before getting in on the other side.

"Seatbelt," Angelina said.

Richard glanced back at Nick for guidance. Nick grinned and popped his head between the two seats, snaking his arm around to pull on the seatbelt beside Richard's shoulder, bringing it across his body and inserting it with a click. "Yes. Put that seatbelt on. We don't want to get a ticket now, do we?" He winked at Richard and turning to Angelina said, "He's such a scofflaw, this one." Chuckling he sat back and put his own seatbelt on.

Richard admired his friend's ability to deflect attention from his ignorance of all things twenty first century. Angelina seemed none the wiser. He surreptitiously took in the interior of the truck and was quite impressed with how luxurious it was in comparison to the much smaller vehicle Angelina seemed to prefer.

"Isn't this more comfy," she asked, as she pulled out of the parking lot and headed into the heart of the city. "Looks like it's starting to rain again." She touched something near the steering wheel and another modern miracle began to clear the water from the windshield. Fascinated though he was, Richard kept his thoughts to himself. The large raindrops began to fall with increasing speed until they pelted the truck in a constant splattering rhythm. Angelina was complaining about the fact that people didn't know how to drive in the rain and Nick was agreeing with her. Richard kept silent, having nothing to add to the conversation. Instead, he gazed out the window at the passing sights. It was dark now, but the streetlights lit their surroundings just enough for him to see. The stop and go of the vehicles around them interrupted their progress, but that was fine with Richard. He was enjoying the opportunity to sit beside this woman, who was an enigma to him. She was a rare beauty, delicate and feminine. The smell of her perfume was driving him crazy with the desire to nuzzle her neck with his nose. Self-control was his greatest ally at this moment, the only thing stopping him from giving in to his needs. Despite her dainty demeanor, Angelina had proven she could wield a sword with the best of them, and he didn't doubt she'd take a dim view of him touching her without her permission. In fact, she was better than their entire group, with the exception of himself and Nick of course.

"Angie," Nick said and Richard raised an eyebrow. He'd never heard Nick call her that before and immediately decided he didn't like the sound of it, preferring the use of her proper name.

"Nickie," she retorted. Richard immediately had the impression this was some sort of game they played with each other.

"Why don't you stay at the house tonight? I don't like the idea of you driving in this weather." Nick paused, waiting for her to respond.

"I don't know," she began doubtfully.

"I won't hear otherwise," Nick stated firmly. "Richard will sleep on the sofa, won't you Richard?"

"Of course, it's very comfortable." Richard tried not to sound too eager at the prospect of Angelina staying with them overnight.

"You don't mind?" Angelina was studying him with those beautiful blue eyes.

"No. I agree with Nick, this is not a good night for you to travel alone." Richard swiftly glanced away from her mesmerizing stare, before he found himself forever trapped in those pools of loveliness.

"Okay, then, I'll stay," she agreed.

"This will be fun," Nick said, smiling widely.

"It'll be like a slumber party," Angelina teased.

"A what?" Both men asked the question at once.

"Oh, never mind. I guess they must call it something different where you're from." She glanced at Richard and then quickly back at Nick before refocusing on the wet road ahead.

"Perhaps if ye explain it to us, then we'll ken yer meaning." Nick poked Richard in the shoulder from behind.

"Yes, do explain please," Richard added.

"It's something that girls do when they're younger. They have sleepovers. Their friends all come with their sleeping bags and pajamas to stay the night. Then they watch movies, eat pizza, gossip and do each other's hair and makeup."

Richard saw Nick's ears perk up at the mention of pizza and he had to admit the idea sounded good to him as well. "What are pajamas?" he asked.

"Pajamas? Sleeping attire." She wrinkled her brow as she eyed him speculatively.

"Ah, yes. Sleeping attire. So how will the *three* of us go about having a slumber party? What will we do?" Richard could see he was making Angelina uncomfortable with his questions, but he had to admit that he was enjoying teasing her. He kept his face serious, knowing she'd be confused by his lack of reaction.

"I was just kidding. Of course we're not going to have a slumber party," she muttered. "We're adults." Angelina kept her eyes on the road, even as a deep chuckle erupted from Richard's chest.

"You're having fun at my expense," Angelina said, peeking in his direction. "I'll remember that."

"I apologize. I couldn't help myself." Richard noticed that Nick was extremely silent in the back seat. Very unlike him. He always had something to say, about absolutely everything. Richard snuck a quick look in his direction and discovered Nick was obviously holding back his own laughter.

"I love you, my friend, but I wouldn't bait the fair Angelina too often. She can be brutal. Believe me, I know," Nick said, trying to stifle a snicker.

"You'd do well to listen to your friend." Those beautiful pools of blue were focused on him again, but this time there was a smile behind them. Richard immediately decided her eyes would be the death of him, even as he returned her heated gaze. He found he couldn't tear himself away this time, instead deciding he might just wade right in and stay for a while.

Chapter 9

THEY ORDERED PIZZA, BUT Angelina made sure that this time they ordered a salad and a veggie pizza for her. She went to the bar and got out a bottle of red wine and some glasses. "Nick would you open this, please?"

Nick dutifully uncorked the bottle and handed it to her.

"Wine?" she asked. "It goes better with pizza than whiskey."

Richard walked across to her and took a glass. God he was handsome. She didn't know if she wanted Nick to stay or go. This could be a disaster, if it didn't go well, so having Nick around was probably for the best. She hadn't felt a pull this strong in forever. It was making her fidgety and she did her best to get it under control, but every time he came within a few feet of her, she could feel his energy - warm, masculine and virile. She reminded herself that she'd already decided it was not a good idea to set her sights on him. Her mind was a little fuzzy right now, as to the reason she had made that decision. He looked so good, and she found herself wondering what he'd look like without the shirt. He was strong, that much she knew from watching him at practice. His chest was broad and muscular, which she could see even with the impediment of his shirt. Her breathing was growing ragged and she knew she had to get her mind focused on something else, because this line of thinking was going to get her into trouble and it was looking a lot like trouble's name was Richard Jefford. Maybe if she faced away from him, it would help.

She made herself busy, putting every last item on the bar in order and when that was done she headed for the kitchen, where she ran her wrists under some cold water to cool the heated blood coursing through her veins and pooling between her thighs.

"Pizza's here," Nick called from the front door.

The thoughts in her head were so loud she hadn't even heard the doorbell. She turned the water off and dried her hands before turning to find Richard leaning sexily against the wall, his dark eyes burning holes through her. Was that lust she saw there? *Oh, God!* She breezed past him, blurting out the first thing she could think of to say. "You might want to get in there before Nick eats it all, because if you leave him alone with a pizza long enough…" She nearly tripped over the area rug on her way past him, but he caught her and steadied her against his hard body. She found her hands resting on his chest and they seemed to move without her knowledge, caressing the rock hard muscles beneath. Finding herself in such close proximity had her quivering and pushing herself away quickly, before he could notice. "Thanks, I'm such a klutz sometimes. Nice pecs, by the way."

* * *

He had no idea what a klutz was, but Richard was more than pleased with the way Angelina had responded to his touch. If being a klutz meant that she would hold herself against him again, and brush her soft hands across his chest, then he was all for it. His appetite seemed to have left him, for everything but this woman. He was hungry for Angelina. Yes, he had told himself not to get involved with her, as he was planning to leave soon, but would it be so wrong to take her to his bed, even if it was only for a brief time? A little voice at the back of his mind told him it would. He was becoming a better man and the new Richard would never compromise a lady's virtue in that way.

After waiting for the evidence of his lust to quiet itself, he entered the living room and settled on the sofa. Angelina brought him a slice of pizza and then sat right next to him. A little too close for comfort, but he had nowhere to go without appearing rude.

Nick had put a movie on the television. Thankfully, Richard was familiar with this device from his visit to Glendaloch, so he remained calm and didn't ask any questions that might arouse Angelina's suspicions. Some things she could no doubt chalk up to the language barrier, but other things would definitely set off alarm bells in her head and Richard didn't want that to happen.

Stretching his arm across the back of the sofa, Richard tried to get comfortable. Not an easy task with such a beautiful creature seated to his right, but he did his best to appear unfazed by her presence.

"Nick loves this movie," Angelina explained. "Ladyhawke is his favorite. I think he's watched it at least a dozen times."

"Hmmm," Richard answered vaguely, not paying any attention to the screen. That little chat he'd had with himself earlier was not helping. The physical pull he felt towards Angelina was beyond his ability to control. His hand was enticingly close to her silky black locks. He wanted to run his fingers through them, to feel the softness for himself, but he stayed his hand. Sheer torture would be the best way to describe his current situation. He listened as Nick and Angelina teased each other with an easy banter. Her laughter reminded him of tiny bells, tinkling pleasantly in his ears. He prayed he'd be able to make it through this night without making a fool of himself.

* * *

"I love that movie," Nick said, getting up from his seat. He turned off most of the lights. "I'm exhausted, so it's off to bed for me."

"Good night," Angelina said.

She observed Richard giving Nick a meaningful look as he turned to leave. *I wonder what that's all about.* They both watched Nick leave the room and headed down the hallway.

"I'll bring pillows and a blanket for ye, Richard," Nick called and true to his word, he appeared a few moments later, depositing the items on a nearby chair. Nick left them alone again and Angelina found herself without a thing to say, painfully aware that the sexual tension in the room was increasing by the second. Richard leaned forward and picked up a large book of photos from the coffee table. He began turning the pages and from Angelina's perspective, seemed as though he was trying to ignore her presence. Things were getting awkward between them, but she didn't want to leave him and go to bed. In fact, despite warning herself against pursuing this man, she found herself watching his full, firm lips and wanting to kiss them.

"That's a book of photos I took around the Bay Area." Angelina pointed to the book and Richard muttered something under his breath, which she didn't quite catch. "I'm sorry, I didn't hear you."

He cleared his throat. "I said they are beautiful. You actually created these?" He sounded astonished.

"Well, I wouldn't say *created*. Photography is a hobby of mine and I had collected so many photos over the years that I decided to put them into a book. That's the only copy."

"It is very precious then," he noted.

"Here, let me show you some of my favorites," Angelina said. She leaned closer to him, her breast brushing his arm as she turned the pages until she reached the one she was looking for, a beautiful shot of the Golden Gate Bridge. The sensation of his arm pressing against her shirt was scorching, but she refused to move away. "I'm particularly proud of this one."

Richard's sharp intake of breath, told her he was equally excited by the touch. She moved closer, placing one hand on his thigh, on the pretense of showing him more photos. *Mmmm. This is nice.* She moved her hair back behind her ear and peeked up at him. His intense dark eyes were waiting for her. He bent his head a little closer, until their lips were mere inches apart.

Kiss me, her muddled brain demanded. Fortunately she still had enough presence of mind to avoid saying the words out loud. What would Richard think of her if she did?

She needn't have worried because he placed one finger under her chin to hold her steady and then warm, soft lips tentatively kissed her own. He paused, remaining completely still. One second passed, and then another. She didn't dare move, or even breathe, not wanting to break the magic between them. Again, he dipped his mouth to hers, but this time, he lingered, moving his hand so that he was gently cradling her head. He moved his other hand up to her face and she couldn't remember ever being kissed like this. *Please, don't stop!*

And he didn't. His kisses grew more impassioned as Angelina molded herself against him. She found herself overcome by an overwhelming desire to be with him, and wondered if he felt it, too. He had to, because the connection between them was amazing - how could he not be aware of it?

Abruptly, Richard stopped and of all things, apologized. "I beg your forgiveness. I have overstepped my bounds." He separated himself from her, placing the book back on the coffee table and putting as much distance between them as he could manage. The expression on his face was difficult to read, his passions tightly shut down. Angelina decided he was a gorgeous man, even when he was looking very stern.

"No need to apologize. I'm glad you kissed me," Angelina said, keeping her voice soft and low. She hoped her eyes were communicating her true feelings on the subject, letting him know she didn't want him to stop.

"It was a mistake and I'm quite tired." Richard gazed at her, all emotion absent from his face.

"Okay," Angelina responded doubtfully, confused by his sudden rejection.

"You're sitting on my bed," he pointed out, nodding at the sofa.

"Oh! I'm sorry." She rose, and shivered as she left the warmth of his body behind. "Good night." Angelina fled in embarrassment, questioning what exactly had just happened.

* * *

Richard, you are such an idiot! You've hurt her, you callous fool! He couldn't believe his own lack of control. He'd kissed her and it had been glorious, but it wasn't something he should have done, or could allow himself to do ever again. *She deserves so much better than you!* The overwhelming heat generated in her presence began to cool. Richard stood and collected the pillow and blankets, wrapping himself up on the sofa despite knowing sleep would not come easily this night.

He tossed and turned, angry with himself. But why, for heaven's sake? He was a man, not a saint, and she was an alluringly beautiful woman. Whoever thought to name her Angelina had known exactly what they were about, because she was an angel indeed. He knew he would consider himself blessed to have someone like her in his life, but in his heart, Richard knew that he was anything but blessed. Cursed was more likely. He calmed himself with thoughts of home. Yes. He'd return home and find a wife to love, but when he pictured this wife of his future, all he could see was Angelina. He finally fell asleep thinking of silky black hair and soft azure eyes.

The next morning dawned with the same rainy gloom of the previous day. The sound of the rain was comforting in its familiarity and Richard arose from his makeshift bed, barefoot and bare chested, to head for the kitchen. He thought he'd try his hand at making coffee. How hard could it be? He'd seen Nick make it and Angelina was proficient too. He'd watched them both carefully and he thought he'd be able to recreate the same result. It would be a nice surprise for them when they awoke.

He found the coffee and the pot. He searched through the cabinet for the papers that the coffee would sit in and eventually found them, right where the coffee had been. He followed all the steps in the order he remembered and was quite pleased with himself when coffee began pouring into the pot beneath. The smell of it permeated the room and wafted down the hallway, as was evidenced by both Nick and Angelina opening their doors simultaneously and stumbling groggily down the hall.

"Ye made coffee?" Nick asked.

"Yes. Why do you look so surprised?" Richard questioned with a proud smile.

Nick shrugged and grabbed cups for the three of them, while Angelina made her way to the refrigerator and grabbed the cream. Richard had already set the sugar out on the counter. He cast his gaze in Angelina's direction, hoping she'd been able to sleep after his shameful exhibition last night. First chance he got, he would explain himself. With that thought in mind, Richard felt much better. He smiled warmly at her and she turned her back to him.

"It's still raining," she observed. "The practice space is going to be flooded again."

"Aye. 'Twill be," Nick concurred. He took a sip of the coffee and his facial expression was almost comical, as he made a show of swallowing the bitter brew.

"Is the coffee not good?" Richard asked, wondering where he had gone wrong.

"Nick, don't tease him. It's not nice," Angelina said. "It's fine Richard. A little strong, but for your first attempt, very good." She continued to avoid eye contact with him.

"Thank you," Richard answered. He couldn't believe that while she was obviously upset with him, she still stood up for him, despite the fact that the coffee was almost undrinkable. She really was an angel.

"Why don't you two go and sit down and I'll see what I can whip up for breakfast. Do you have eggs, Nick?" she asked.

Nick shrugged. "Have a look in the fridge. And make another pot of coffee, if you would. While yer at it, would ye *please* show Richard the correct way to do it?"

Richard stared daggers at his friend and Nick chuckled. "Why do ye look at me like that? Ye ken ye need to know how to make proper coffee." He turned his back on them both and went to sit in the large comfortable chair near the fireplace.

Richard followed Angelina into the kitchen, suffering the distinct impression she wished him to be as far away from her as possible. "Angelina, I'd like to speak with you later, if I might."

"You can speak to me now," she responded sharply.

"Alone. I'd explain my actions last night to you."

"No need to explain. I got the message loud and clear." She busied herself searching through the refrigerator and pulling out eggs and breakfast sausage. Her silent disapproval continued as she pulled pans from the cabinets, all the while making quite the clatter as she thumped them down on the counter.

"Angelina, please…"

"Oh, right. I was supposed to teach you how to make coffee." She proceeded to throw away his efforts, starting over again, and Richard watched carefully as she explained the process. When she was done, she cocked her head to one side. "Got it?"

"Yes. I believe so."

"Good. You can join Nick. I don't need any help."

"I'll go, as long as you promise you'll allow me to speak with you later." He wasn't going to budge from the kitchen until she agreed.

Angelina appeared as if she would argue with him, but instead, she relented. "Okay, okay, I'll listen. I promise. Now go." She made a shooing motion with her hands and somewhat relieved, Richard left her and joined Nick by the fire.

* * *

Breathing a sigh of relief, Angelina busied herself with preparing breakfast. Thank goodness he'd left her alone! It had been difficult, but somehow she'd managed to keep her eyes off his chiseled abs and strong, hard chest. She was feeling vulnerable and that was not okay. She hadn't been vulnerable where a man was concerned in forever, so this had to stop - *now*! She was perfectly capable of detaching herself emotionally from a man. Granted, it wasn't usually after one single extremely hot kiss, but he obviously wasn't interested and so she would live with that. She was friends with Nick, but she wasn't sure she could be friends with Richard. They'd have to keep their interactions on a purely professional level. *What on earth does he want to talk to me about?*

If he was going to tell her that after their kiss he found he wasn't attracted to her, she'd be hurt, but she'd deal with it. She didn't believe that was the case though. She had experienced a magnetic attraction to him and was sure he had as well. So what was his problem? Gritting her teeth in frustration, Angelina took her bad mood out on the eggs, whipping them beyond what was necessary and then adding them to the pan where she was sautéing some vegetables. Once everything was ready, she put together a plate for each of them and set them on the breakfast bar.

"Nick, Richard, food's ready." She poured some fresh coffee and when she went to sit down, found that the two shirtless wonders had each taken an end seat and left the center stool for her. She was used to seeing Nick half dressed. He was very comfortable in his own skin and never gave a thought to whether or not she minded. She didn't, of course. Nick had a great body, but Richard's was even better. And now here she was, having to sit next to him. She was the meat in a half-dressed man sandwich. *Great. Just great.* The last thing she wanted was to be subjected to the force field that seemed to emit from Richard every time she got close to him, drawing her in. Just as she expected, her skin started to burn up the minute she sat down. Her appetite immediately disappeared and instead of eating, she shoveled her food around on the plate while the two men ate every crumb on theirs.

"Are ye going to eat that?" Nick asked eyeing her untouched food.

"No. I'm not very hungry this morning." Angelina pushed her plate towards him and he took half and sent the rest down the counter to Richard.

"Where's yer appetite gone to, lass? Did Richard do something he shouldnae have after I went to bed last night? Is that why ye cannae eat?" Nick's eyes twinkled with mischief.

Angelina didn't answer immediately and she could sense Richard's discomfort in the seat next to her. "Of course not, don't be silly. Nothing of any importance happened. I'm just not hungry. Can't a girl skip a meal without you jumping to ridiculous conclusions?"

Nick chuckled in apparent disbelief. "I've a few phone calls to make, so if ye'll excuse me. Richard will help ye with the dishes, willnae ye?"

"Yes, I'd be happy to." Angelina noticed Richard was giving Nick that pained expression again.

"You go sit in the living room, or do whatever it is you do after breakfast. I can do this myself." The last thing she wanted was to be in close quarters with Richard. She'd barely made it through breakfast and she still had to find a way to get out of their little 'talk'.

"Alright, I'll go take a shower then." Richard departed the kitchen, leaving Angelina to clean up the mess. She quickly got everything done and before Richard had finished showering, she gathered her things and slipped out through the door like a thief in the night, or rather like a woman determined to avoid any further discussions.

* * *

"Where's Angelina?" Richard asked, as he exited his room fresh from the shower.

"I dinnae ken where she went off to in such a hurry, but she didnae even say goodbye. We'll see her later today at practice." Nick stood up and walked towards Richard. "Would ye like to tell me what happened between the two of ye? The air in the room between ye was thick."

"Nothing happened." Richard was embarrassed by his behavior the previous night and didn't feel like sharing with Nick.

"Fine, but I know otherwise. I can read it all over yer face, and Angelina's was nae any better. And I heard ye tell her that ye needed to explain yerself." Nick wore that crooked grin that women found disarming, but Richard found just plain annoying. "I ken yer attraction to her and I see that she feels the same. Why can ye nae just enjoy yerself? Live for the here and now, and dinnae worry for tomorrow."

"If only I could, my friend. You've always been able to do that, but as you know, it's not quite as easy for me." Richard walked to the window and gazed down into the street.

"Mayhap that is what yer here to learn." Nick's expression seemed to suggest he thought he had just solved the puzzle, but Richard wasn't so certain.

"Perhaps it is, but I think there must be something more. I only hope it reveals itself to me soon. I'd like to go home."

Chapter 10

As far as practices went, this one had been uneventful, but progress was made among all the men and Richard was certain that by the time the tournament rolled around they would be more than ready. Much to his disappointment, Angelina had not joined them. She'd called Nick and told him she wasn't feeling well and was going to stay home and rest. Richard knew he was the cause of her absence and he felt terrible about it.

Nick called a cab and they headed back to the house, to discover Quinn waiting for them, and he was carrying Richard's new sword. If anything would draw Richard out of the doldrums, it was the arrival of a shiny, sharp new sword. He hefted it in his hand for the first time and tested the weight of it. It was lighter than he'd expected, but very finely constructed. In fact, he decided after a moment or two, he liked the lightness. Tiring during a long battle was never good and the weight of this sword would assist him in that regard. The hilt was exquisitely crafted, with black leather and steel wrappings and the wing-like extensions on the guard were beautiful to gaze upon and equally utilitarian. Overall, Richard was quite pleased with Quinn's efforts.

"Shall we go in?" Nick suggested. "'Tis cold out and I'd enjoy a glass of whiskey. I'm sure you two would like to join me, eh?" He opened the door and Richard and Quinn followed him inside.

"Quinn, you've done a fine job. This sword is well balanced, light and beautiful. It will serve me well in future battles. Thank you." Richard continued admiring his new sword, inspecting the fine scrollwork on the blade and the black stones embedded in the guard. "You are a most talented craftsman."

"I'm happy you're pleased with it. I make so many swords and the new owners almost never truly appreciate the finer details involved. I can see that you are a man who knows his way around a weapon." Quinn accepted the drink Nick was offering him. "Thank you. When is the next tournament?"

"In a little less than two weeks. Will you be joining us?" Nick handed Richard a glass and then waved them both over to the living room to sit down.

"I'll be there. I know you guys don't fight with real swords, but it's still great fun to watch. Who's your competition this year?" Quinn sipped his drink, directing his gaze over the top of the glass at Nick.

"Malcolm Granger and his lads. I cannae lie. He's been a difficult competitor in the past, but with Richard here, I feel confident that we can win this," Nick said.

"Malcolm Granger - I wouldn't put it past him to fight with real swords. He's ruthless when it comes to winning, you should be careful of him." Quinn's face showed his concern. "He's been a customer of mine in the past. He had some swords that had been found on an archeological dig and he wanted me to replicate them for him, making them look like new, of course. He was willing to pay whatever I wanted to ensure they were perfect. I like to work alone, but he stood over my shoulder watching my every move and giving me direction on the *proper* way to make a medieval sword. He paid me well for the work, but there's something about him that I just don't like."

"I ken yer meaning. He can be a bit of a bastard. Let him bring his best and we'll see if he can win."

Richard listened intently and decided he didn't like what he was hearing. "Do you truly believe he'll use real swords?" If that were the case, their group would be at a distinct and dangerous disadvantage.

"Like I said, I wouldn't put it past him," Quinn answered.

"Then we'll bring ours along. We won't reveal them unless it's necessary, of course, but if he does dare to draw his, we'll be prepared." Richard placed the sword back into the finely crafted sheath, which Quinn had made of matching black leather with steel accents.

"Richard, there is one other thing I'd like to show you. Prior to working on the sword you now hold, I designed a matching dagger. I brought it with me, thinking you might like to have both." Quinn drew a sheathed dagger from the inside pocket of his coat. "No pressure, of course. You don't have to take it if you don't need it or want it." He smiled at Richard, as if he already knew what his response would be.

Palming the dagger, a warm smile spread across Richard's face. Unsheathing the blade, he performed the same ritual he had completed with the sword.

"I can see that you're smitten," Quinn chuckled.

Nick stood up to investigate the dagger that had Richard so enthralled and whistled. "More fine work, Quinn."

"What will you take for both pieces?" Richard asked. He wanted both sword and dagger, but wondered how he could possibly pay for them. He had none of the modern currency that would be required, a problem he'd overlooked until now.

"They're already paid for," Quinn answered.

"Impossible. I've given you no payment." Richard was puzzled, looking back and forth between his friend and Quinn.

"I've paid for them out of the school's funds," Nick explained.

"The school's funds? But why?" Richard didn't think he could accept such a generous gift, especially since he knew that the school was Nick's only source of income.

"Yer working with me to get the group ready fer competition. We never discussed what yer pay would be. Besides, what kind of instructor would ye be, without a sword and dagger of yer own?" Nick cocked an eyebrow at Richard and slapped him on the back.

"You are truly a far greater friend than I deserve," Richard said, embarrassed to find himself a little misty eyed. He had plenty of coin from his own time, but that would do neither of them any good here. "I give you my word, I will work my hardest to see everyone at their best for the tournament." Nick had told him there was a prize of $10,000, which would be awarded to the winning team and Richard was determined to do whatever was necessary, to ensure Nick won the prize money. It would go a long way towards repairing the roof at the practice space and replace the many worn items Richard had noticed.. He wouldn't let his friend down.

Nick raised his glass in a toast. "Here's to luck!"

"To skill," Richard corrected.

＊＊＊

The cozy little restaurant was situated in an alleyway in the financial district. Angelina had agreed to meet Malcolm for drinks and dinner after he called her earlier in the day. It was obvious he had a thing for her, but up until this point, she had avoided his requests for dates. Tonight was different. She needed a distraction, something to help her stop thinking about Richard Jefford, and Malcolm Granger fit the bill. He was waiting for her outside the restaurant as she made her way down the alley, which was lit by dozens of tiny fairy lights reflecting off the wet pavement and giving the alley a romantic, golden glow.

"Angelina," Malcolm greeted. "I'm so happy you could make it. You're looking beautiful tonight." He took her hand, and as was his habit, kissed her knuckles.

"Thank you, Malcolm." There was no physical attraction there between Angelina and Malcolm. When he kissed her hand, no delicious tingles set off alarm bells, the way a mere glance from Richard did. Malcolm was safe. Nothing would happen between them, because Angelina wouldn't allow it.

"I wish you had allowed me to send my car for you. I hate to see you out alone at night." Malcolm opened the door and took her elbow, guiding her inside. The restaurant was dimly lit, a place for romantic liaisons. She hated to disappoint Malcolm, but there was no way she was going to find herself without a way home at the end of the night, and if it came right down to it, she'd be sure to tell him she'd rather keep their relationship platonic.

The maître d' rushed over to them. "Mr. Granger, it's good to see you! Your table is ready, right this way." He led them all the way to the back of the restaurant and into a candlelit alcove, a cozy booth for two away from the prying eyes of the other diners. The maître d' stood there for a moment or two, wringing his hands and clutching the menu to his chest.

"I'll call you when we're ready for dinner, in the meantime, please bring the wine I ordered when I booked." Malcolm ignored the maître d's bowing and scraping and turned his attention to Angelina. "Are you comfortable?"

"Yes, thank you," she lied. In fact, Angelina was feeling anything but comfortable under Malcolm's intense scrutiny. "I had no idea this restaurant was here," she said. "It's very nice."

"I like it. A little hideaway, tucked into an area most people wouldn't even find accidentally. Privacy is of the utmost importance to me, Angelina." His eyes probed hers and she squirmed, ill at ease with his fierce attention. "Ah, here's our wine."

The waiter poured them both a glass of the finest cabernet, obviously a bottle pre-approved by Malcolm. He raised his glass. "Shall we make a toast?"

Angelina nodded nervously, convinced this had been a very bad idea. She should never have agreed to meet Malcolm for a dinner date; it was becoming obvious now that he was interested in pursuing a relationship. She reluctantly raised her glass.

"To us," Malcolm said. "And more particularly to you. I'm a lucky man to have garnered an evening alone with the beautiful Angelina Lawson." He didn't appear to notice Angelina's reluctant smile, instead clinking his glass with hers and then sipping his wine. Angelina followed suit, resisting the urge to throw back the entire glass. Malcolm trailed a path across the back of her hand with his fingers, before she swiftly cleared her throat and pulled her hand away, pretending to adjust the napkin in her lap.

"How are things going in the world of medieval artifacts?" Angelina questioned, hoping to take his mind off her.

"Quite well. You know I always get what I want, one way or another," he said, the double meaning obvious in his response. "I've recently been searching for a medieval sword, one that is said to have belonged to King James the Fourth."

"You mean the Sword of State, gifted to the King by Pope Julius II." Angelina was a medieval history buff, so she was confident this might be the sword he was referring to.

Malcolm eyed her with apparent surprise. "No, that sword is already recovered and in Scotland. As much as I might wish to add it to my collection, it would be difficult to obtain the weapon."

"I should think so," Angelina responded bluntly. "That sword belongs to the people of Scotland and is not for sale."

"Precisely why I'm searching for the brother to the Sword of State. It is identical in many ways, but rather than being blessed by the Pope, it is said to have been magically imbued with the ability to grant its owner great power, and the ability to rule the world." He searched her face and Angelina did her best not to look shocked at his obvious desire for even more power than he already held. She knew that Malcolm was one of the wealthiest men in the world. He could buy anything he wanted - or almost anything - but she was quite determined the one thing he couldn't buy was her.

"Did this sword actually exist? Do you have any proof? And if it did exist, why didn't the King use it to his own benefit?" Angelina nervously spun her wine glass between her fingers.

"Some say that while he was aware of its value, the King wasn't quite prepared to use it at that particular point in time, and so he sent it off somewhere for safe keeping. After his death, the sword would have been left to his son James the Fifth, who was a small child. The regent at the time was his mother and then John Stewart, the second Duke of Albany. At some point during these two reigns, the sword disappeared and therein lies my problem. I have many sources who believe that it most certainly did exist, but they don't know why it went missing or who might have taken it. I intend to find out."

"It could all be just a fabrication, a fictional tale passed down for generations. How can you possibly find something that may not have even existed?" Angelina scoffed.

"As I said, I'm convinced it did exist. I've had my people searching historical records and speaking with archeologists and historians. As a matter of fact, just today, my Acquisitions Director sent me a sixteenth century map, showing the possible location of the sword." He smiled brightly at her and appeared as excited as a small boy on Christmas morning. "If only I could travel back in time…"

"Well, we both know that's impossible." Angelina took another sip of her wine.

Malcolm's facial expression was unreadable. "Do we?"

* * *

"Perhaps we should check on her," Richard suggested. He was still feeling guilty about what had happened the night before, and desperately wanted to talk to Angelina to explain himself. Maybe this was part of the lesson that Edna felt he needed to learn. He had never suffered a moment of guilt until recently. His reputation was not a good one, of that he was certain, but he suddenly found himself caring about other people's thoughts and feelings. Why did he care so damn much? On some level, it had been easier when he didn't, but now he couldn't forget the hurt expression on Angelina's face as she hurried from the room. He had to fix that somehow. He wanted to be back in her good graces again.

"I already did," was Nick's reply.

"And…"

"She's out to dinner with Malcolm Granger." Nick glanced at Richard as if he were waiting for an outburst.

Richard remained silent, much to his own surprise. His face, on the other hand, scowled back at Nick. "He's dangerous, you know," he finally said. "I don't trust him."

"Neither do I," Nick agreed. "There's nae we can do, though. I'll continue texting with her and if she needs our help, she'll let us know."

Richard paced back and forth, stopping occasionally to stare moodily out the window.

"I can see 'tis going to be a long night," Nick observed. "Richard, ye'll be wearing a hole in the floor. Come sit." He refilled the whiskey glasses.

Richard stood there for a moment, experiencing a number of revelations. The life he wanted was his for the taking. He could have had it all along. He had a good friend, a family that loved him and the possibility of a very good life. How could he have missed it? His ridiculous jealousy had needlessly clouded everything in his life. If only he had seen it sooner. Perhaps he could have saved himself this second trip to the future. Richard turned to see Nick observing him carefully.

"Have ye got it all figured out?" he asked, with a knowing expression.

"I think I have," he nodded. "I think I have."

Chapter 11

THE HOUSE WAS IN DARKNESS, but fortunately, Angelina had her own key. She fumbled with the lock, but eventually got it open. "Hello, it's just me!" Angelina called out, just before she found herself engulfed by two strong arms.

"Thank God you're alright," Richard said, as he crushed her to him.

"Richard, I can't breathe!" Angelina gasped. He loosened his grip slightly, but continued to hold her, his warm breath caressing the top of her head. Once again, she was reminded of the power this man had over her. She wanted to sink right into him, but then she remembered he wasn't interested in her in that way. She struggled to get away from his hold and finally freed herself. "Wow, I just had the craziest night ever."

"Did he hurt you?' Richard asked, his eyes fierce with worry.

"No, of course not. Besides, I can take care of myself if I have to. Don't go getting all medieval on me," she said.

Richard eyed her curiously. "What do you mean by that?"

"Nothing. You're just being unnecessarily protective." She removed her coat and set her purse down on the floor as she breezed by Richard on her way to the living room. She sat, not on the sofa, but in the oversized chair by the fire. She wasn't going to give him the opportunity to sit next to her again. She had learned her lesson the hard way on that score. Besides, she was still feeling the effects of that hug he'd given her as she'd come inside. Once her body stopped quivering, she might be able to carry on a normal conversation, but before she could settle herself, damned if he didn't stride over to kneel in front of her!

"Angelina, I beg your forgiveness for my behavior last night. I should never have kissed you."

He appeared to be very sincere and Angelina swallowed uncomfortably before she responded. "I'm willing to accept some of the blame for what happened. I've thought about it and I was sending you signals that I wanted something to happen between us. It's my own fault that you kissed me. And I kissed you back. I thought it was a pretty amazing kiss, but apparently you thought otherwise, so—"

"No! Of course I didn't think otherwise," he interrupted. "It was an amazing kiss." He reached for her hands and she didn't pull them away.

"So why did you get all weird on me?" She tipped her head and softened as she gazed at the first man in her life who had apologized for something she would be willing to do again at a moment's notice.

"I don't want to take advantage of you, Angelina. I'll be leaving soon and I can't take you with me." He sounded so sad, that she almost forgot to be angry.

"Wait a minute. What makes you think that I'd want to go anywhere with you?" The annoyance in her voice had Richard sitting back on his heels. "I don't do commitment, Richard. I'm my own woman and I don't need a man to make my life complete. I'm not interested in being a possession - something to be tossed aside at some man's whim. I'm an independent woman and that's the way I like it."

Richard was smiling warmly at her, despite her rant. "I believe that is what I enjoy the most about you, Angelina. You are a precious flower that cannot be picked, because you are strongest when your feet are firmly rooted in the ground."

She wasn't sure how to respond to that. "I'd like for us to be friends. Can we do that?" She asked him, but she was really asking herself. Could she just be friends with this man, who had such a strong physical presence that her knees grew weak just at the sight of him? It would be hard, but she could do it… she hoped.

"That would make me very happy. I don't think I could stand it if you stayed angry with me." He touched her cheek and the now-familiar heat flashed through her body, settling in the one place she was hoping it would avoid.

"Let's get one thing straight," she said in a raspy whisper. "Friends don't touch each other like that."

He pulled his hand away as if it were on fire. "I'm sorry. I didn't intend to overstep my bounds yet again."

"It's okay. We'll figure this out as we go."

"Are you going to stay here tonight? It seems too late for you to drive home all alone."

Angelina realized with a shock that Richard's concerned face was becoming very precious to her. "I think I will, but only if you let me take the sofa."

"I couldn't possibly. You are a lady to be respected and that means you shall have the bedroom and I shall have the sofa."

"You're doing it again… getting all medieval on me. If you don't take the bedroom, I won't stay. That's final."

Richard must have known that she meant it, because he rolled his eyes and looked up at the ceiling as if seeking divine intervention. "If you insist."

"Okay. You can go to bed now, I'm here and I'm safe. No need for you to worry about me anymore."

* * *

No need to worry about her anymore! What was she thinking? She had no idea how dangerous Malcolm Granger might be. Richard didn't have firsthand knowledge of the man, but he knew plenty of others just like him - men who would do whatever was necessary to get what they wanted. He himself had been one of those men, so he understood how bad this situation could become. If Angelina was what Malcolm had decided he wanted, Richard was going to do his best to ensure that he didn't get her. He relaxed back onto the bed, still feeling guilty that Angelina was sleeping on the sofa. *She's a stubborn one.* He smiled, thinking of her in that light. Yes, she was stubborn, strong willed and the most beguiling woman he had ever met - and she was perfect for him. What a mess this all was. Why couldn't he have met her in his own time? It would be hard to leave her, but it had to be done. Damn it, he didn't even know when that would be. He might be here for a while, which would be sheer torture for him. Seeing her every day, hearing that sweet, sultry voice, smelling the scent of her perfume. He wasn't sure how he'd be able to do it. He wouldn't compromise her virtue by breaking their pact of friendship, no matter how much he wanted to.

No. This would be a test of his willpower over his more primal instincts. Again, he wondered if this was one of those lessons Edna had told him he needed to learn. If so, it was going to be the hardest one of them all.

* * *

Sleep did not come easily for Richard, nor did it last long when it did. He finally stumbled out of bed at the first sign of the morning's light, yearning to see the woman who slept just beyond his bedroom door. The woman who was now going to be his *friend*. He had never been friends with a woman before, preferring bedding them, to getting to know them. He silently crept down the hall and into the living room. Angelina slept soundly on the sofa and he took the moment of opportunity to drink in her beauty. Her silken black locks were strewn across her pillow, perfectly framing her face. He fought the desperate urge to to run his fingers through them. His gaze lowered to her mouth, where her lips had formed the sweetest little pout. He wanted to kiss them. Her long eyelashes brushed the tops of her cheeks, giving her an angelic appearance. How appropriate. He might have stood there all day, watching every slight movement and listening to every soft sigh, but if she awoke and caught him, she'd surely be angry. Tearing himself away, he decided it would be better to give coffee making another try.

Remembering his lessons, Richard made a passable job of brewing the bitter black liquid. He poured a cup for himself and added cream and sugar. *Very good*. He smiled broadly at his victory in the kitchen. He was just about to take a seat at the breakfast bar when he heard a sleepy Angelina calling to him.

"Richard? Is that you making coffee?" She stretched, and he groaned inwardly at the sight of her languorous movements.

"Yes," he answered. "Would you care for a cup?"

"That would be wonderful." Angelina sat up and pulled the blanket up under her chin. "Brrr… it's cold in here." She grabbed the remote and pushed a button to ignite the gas fireplace. "That should help." She smiled at him through sleepy eyes and Richard's heart almost burst with an emotion that was quite unfamiliar to him.

Handing her a cup, he sat opposite her, watching as she took her first sip. Her lips curved upwards in a brilliant smile. "You did it. This is really good," she praised, lifting the cup to her lips again.

"Do you think so? I did everything you taught me," Richard responded, pleased with her approval.

Angelina nodded shyly.

The unfamiliar feeling that had overtaken him was making it hard for Richard to focus on anything but Angelina. He gave himself a mental shake and smiled warmly at her. "How are you feeling this morning, m'lady?"

She cocked an eyebrow at him. He assumed the 'm'lady' was responsible. "I'm fine, I slept really well. How about you?"

"I also slept well," Richard lied.

"I have to go back to Pacifica this morning and I'll probably meet up with you guys later at the warehouse."

Richard was so wrapped up in the fantasy of Angelina that was playing out in his head that he didn't hear her speak and he was startled when she raised her voice.

"Hello. Earth to Richard!"

"Oh, I'm sorry. What were you saying?" He quickly tore his gaze away from her and focused on the cup in his hand.

"I'm going home and I'll be back later for practice."

He didn't feel comfortable letting her go home alone. Something in his gut was warning him that he needed to keep her close. "Angelina, I would love to see your home. Would you take me with you?" He tried his best not to look too eager.

"Sure. If you really want to go, I'd be happy to take you with me. Can you hand me my clothes from the chair?"

Richard hadn't realized until this moment that Angelina had kept the blanket pulled up to her chin to protect her modesty, because she'd taken her clothes off to sleep. He was particularly grateful he *hadn't* known, or sitting here speaking with her would have been doubly difficult. He rose and got her dress and shoes from the chair, depositing them on top of the blanket. He stood there, coffee in hand gazing down at her loveliness.

"Ahem. If you don't mind leaving for a few minutes, I need to get dressed."

"Oh, of course," Richard felt like an idiot. He was certainly making a fool of himself this morning, but thankfully Angelina didn't seem to care. "I'll leave you then." He backed out of the room and down the hall to his bedroom.

* * *

Could that man get any hotter? She hoped she wasn't making a mistake taking him home with her. What harm could come from letting him see where she lived? She could introduce him to Estella and they could go for lunch at the little seaside restaurant down the road. Nothing romantic, just two friends spending the day together. It would be fine. She quickly donned the pretty black dress and strappy heels she'd worn the night before.

Nick emerged from his room and headed straight into the kitchen.

"Good morning to you, too," she teased.

"Is it now? I'm surprised to see you here this early, and so dressed up," Nick teased right back.

"I slept here and you know it." Being as observant as he was, there wasn't much Nick didn't know, and Angelina was certain he would have heard her late arrival.

"And where did Richard sleep?" he asked, obviously working hard not to chuckle.

"In his room," she responded indignantly.

"I see. And you? Did you sleep in there as well?"

Angelina frowned at him in response. "We're going to my house for the day. We'll be back for practice."

Nick looked surprised and Angelina enjoyed the little victory. "Why aren't you inviting me to go along?" he demanded.

"You can come if you like," Angelina made the offer automatically, but she hoped he wouldn't agree to it.

"I have some things to attend to," Nick replied. "You two go and have fun. Oh and Angelina, be gentle with him."

She was about to ask him what he meant by that remark, when Richard returned to the room, "We're going…"

"Yes. I know. You're going to Angelina's house," Nick said. "Try and be back at the warehouse by six, if you can."

Angelina headed for the door and Richard fell into step behind her. She glanced back at Nick, as she opened the front door, and caught him as he winked and waved.

"We're taking Jenna's car," she said to Richard. "Every now and again I have to take it, or the truck, so the batteries don't die." She led him into the garage where the truck and two cars were parked. Angelina pointed to a silver car and Richard opened the driver's side door for her to get in. She started the car and he settled into the passenger side. "Seat belt," she reminded him, when he didn't put it on right away.

"Right." He clicked the buckle into the holder.

Angelina backed the car out of the garage and headed off towards Pacifica. It was a beautiful day, sunny and crisp, and the drive down the coast wouldn't take long. She enjoyed the panorama of the sun glistening on the water as she quietly observed Richard from the corner of her eye. He seemed enthralled by everything they passed, and acted like a man who was experiencing everything for the first time, which seemed strange. There was a great deal she wanted to know about Richard, and Angelina hoped that today she'd get her answers.

Chapter 12

As Angelina pulled onto the gravel drive beside the house, she couldn't help thinking this might not have been the best idea she'd ever had. Having Richard seated next to her for the entire drive had been torture. In fact, she'd be glad to get out of the car and take a deep breath. It would be the first one since they'd gotten into the car.

"This is it," Angelina said, as she stepped onto the driveway.

Richard emerged from the passenger side with a look of wonder upon his handsome face. He turned a full circle, and stopped again once he was facing her. He nodded his apparent approval. "You live here alone," he stated.

"I do. Let's go inside." She led the way to her front door, aware that Richard was scanning the area as if he were searching for something. "Is everything okay?" she asked.

"Yes. I always like to get the lay of the land when I'm somewhere I've never been before." He smiled that sweet, sexy smile of his and Angelina had to force herself to turn away and concentrate on unlocking the door. As they entered the house, Richard once again seemed as if he was searching for something, or someone.

"What exactly are you looking for?" Angelina asked, her curiosity piqued.

"As I said, I like to familiarize myself with my surroundings."

Angelina dropped her purse on the kitchen counter and turned to find Richard standing so close she nearly bumped his chest with her nose. She stepped back and found herself up against the counter.

"I'm sorry. I'm crowding you," Richard said, moving away. Not nearly far enough though, in Angelina's estimation. She could still feel waves of heat emanating from his body.

"Why don't you have a seat? Can I get you something to drink? Water? A soda?" She was nervous and hoped it didn't come across in her voice.

"Water, thank you." Richard exuded confidence as he wandered through her living room, examining her little knickknacks, photos and mementos. "Your home is much like you," he observed. "I like it."

"Here's your water." Angelina handed him the glass and said, "Why don't you sit for a minute while I get changed. Then we can go for a walk along the cliff if you'd like." She tried to be as nonchalant as possible, but she was suffering a distinctly inherent reaction to his close proximity. Her small cottage had always been plenty large enough for her, but Richard somehow made it feel tiny. As she closed the door to her bedroom she was having second thoughts about the idea to bring him home with her. What was she going to do with him all day? She knew what she'd *like* to do, but that wasn't happening. They made a pact to be friends, so she'd stick to that arrangement, no matter how difficult it might be. She grimaced at the prospect. Without conscious thought, she pulled on her sexiest jeans and a t-shirt. Taking a deep breath she walked out of the bedroom and directly into the heated gaze of Richard Jefford.

* * *

Richard looked up when Angelina entered and sucked in a breath at the dazzling beauty who stood before him. She wore the simplest of clothes, but on her, they were breathtaking. He couldn't seem to stop staring. He was definitely going to have a hard time keeping his hands off her. "You look lovely, Angelina," he managed to choke out.

"Thank you," she said, and grabbed a jacket from beside the door. Richard watched, mesmerized, as she wrapped a scarf around her neck and tucked her phone into the back pocket of her jeans. His eyes lingered on her shapely bottom which was now being spoiled by the rectangular outline of the phone. "Shall we?" she asked as she opened the front door.

Richard followed as Angelina exited the house, closing the door behind her. As they were heading down the driveway, an elderly woman approached.

"Estella!" Angelina said, smiling brightly at the woman. "I was hoping we'd see you today. This is my friend Richard. Richard, this is my neighbor and friend Estella."

Estella was beaming at him. "It's a pleasure to meet you, Richard."

"The pleasure is all mine, Estella." Richard took the hand she offered and kissed it. It appeared that Estella was going to swoon, so he grasped her elbow to steady her. She smiled up at him speechlessly.

"This is Nick's friend, the one that I told you about," Angelina said.

"Oh, yes, of course. I hope you'll be joining us for Thanksgiving dinner. I told Angelina to invite both you and Nick." Estella was still gripping his hand and didn't appear to intend on letting it go.

Richard chuckled. "I don't believe she's mentioned it, but I'm sure we'd love to join you."

"I'm sorry, Estella. I meant to tell them about it, but I forgot. We're going for a walk, would you care to join us?" Angelina hoped Estella would, because the older woman would most assuredly keep Richard busy with small talk and endless questions.

"I'm afraid I can't. I'm baking again and I have something in the oven. Would you mind taking Percy along with you?" Estella suggested, sounding hopeful.

Richard didn't know who this Percy was, but he hoped Angelina would refuse. He didn't intend to share her with another man today.

"Sure. We'd love to," Angelina said, much to his dismay. She started walking towards Estella's home and Richard trailed along behind.

As they got closer, Estella called out, "Harry? Harry! Percy's going to go for a walk with Angelina." She turned and spoke to Richard. "I'll be right back with him, wait here."

Richard wasn't certain if she meant Harry, or Percy, or both. He stood with Angelina by his side waiting until a small, fluffy creature came charging out of Estella's house towards them. He instinctively stepped in front of Angelina, to protect her from the strange animal. It began barking and running happy circles around them. "It's a dog," Richard said, surprised.

"Yes, of course - what did you think it was?" Angelina sounded amused by his comment. She stooped down to pet the dog and it wiggled in ecstasy.

"I wasn't quite sure," Richard said. He squatted down so he could get a better look at Percy, who immediately turned his attention to Richard. He held his hand out for Percy to sniff and then petted the little dog. "You're an unusual one, aren't you?" Percy stopped wiggling, tipping his head and sat perfectly still, as if he understood what Richard was saying to him. "And very intelligent as well."

"Do we need a leash, Estella?" Angelina asked.

"No. He's very good off the leash. I'm sure he won't give you a bit of trouble. Will you, Percy?" Estella's adoring gaze settled on her little dog.

"Okay, then, we'll be off. See you in a bit," Angelina said.

* * *

The ocean crashed onto the rocks beneath the path they walked, occasionally sending a splash of surf to the top of the cliff. She was happy to have Percy walking along with them. Richard seemed fascinated by the little dog, and while he was studying Percy, Angelina was safe to ogle Richard all she wanted.

"I've never seen a dog like this before," Richard said. "What breed is he?"

"I don't really know. I think he's a mix of a number of small breeds. He's pretty cute, don't you think?"

"He is," Richard glanced her way and caught her staring at him in open admiration. He smiled warmly. "Angelina, I hope you won't mind my asking, but why is it that you avoid romantic relationships?"

She hadn't been expecting the question and it took her a moment to remember exactly why she had chosen to remain single and uninvolved. "Well," she finally managed, "I haven't had the best of luck with the men I've known, starting with my father."

"What could your father possibly have done, to cause you to turn your back on love?"

"He left." That wasn't the complete truth, but it was all she cared to share. Truthfully, she hadn't given her father much thought over the years. As far as she was concerned, he didn't deserve her attention. Richard remained silent, as if he was waiting for her to explain and she found herself examining that hollow, conflicted feeling she had buried deep in her heart, knowing that her father had not wanted her. "Before my mother met my father, she had been married twice." Angelina screwed up her nose and shook her head. "She wasn't very good at relationships. She had two other daughters - one by each of her husbands. By the time she met my father, she had been divorced for several years and her two daughters were already in high school and college." Angelina kept her gaze focused out over the water as she continued. "My father was a lot younger than my mom. He was apparently looking for a good time, and she filled the bill. After I was born, he hung around for a while, but the responsibility of a wife and a child was too much for him and he left. I never saw or heard from him again."

"I'm so sorry, Angelina," Richard said, his gaze falling on her. She hoped it wasn't pity she could see in his eyes. She neither needed nor wanted that.

"Don't feel sorry for me," she said. "I've gotten along just fine without a father." They walked a bit further before she spoke again. "When I was old enough to start dating, I made some poor choices, just like my mother did. I always seemed to go for the guys who weren't looking for a long term relationship, or if they were, they treated me as if I was a possession." Keeping her gaze lowered, she thought about all the times she had been someone's arm candy. "I think I told you before, I don't want to be any man's possession, something to be tossed aside at their whim." She peeked at him and saw that he was listening very carefully. "After a while, I decided I couldn't trust a man with my heart, so I stopped offering it." She turned and gazed into his handsome face. "This is what I want. I'm the one who calls the shots now, and I prefer it that way." Angelina's heart had hardened over many years of disappointment, and she wasn't about to start softening now that she'd met someone who appeared to be different from all those other men.

Richard stopped walking and when she turned to face him, he took her hands in his. "You are a woman who is meant to be treasured, Angelina, not something to be tossed aside. I know you've been hurt, but don't deny yourself the experience of loving someone and being loved in return." He searched her face, for what, she had no idea. Steadfastly, she reminded herself she was not going to love him, no matter how much she might find herself drawn to him.

The frantic yapping of little Percy drew their attention. A flash of white fur bolted down the path in front of them and then with an anxious yelp, he disappeared.

"Percy! Oh, no!" Angelina exclaimed. They both took off running towards the spot where he'd last been. "Percy!" she called.

Richard peered over the edge of the cliff. "He's down there, he's landed on a ledge," he said. He lay down on his stomach and stretched his arm out over the side but a few tense moments later, he shook his head. "He's too far down, I can't reach him."

Angelina lay down beside Richard, frantic to try and help. She gasped, when she saw the little dog, covered in dirt and whimpering in fear at his predicament. He had landed on a small shelf, which jutted out from the cliff edge. "He's lucky he didn't fall all the way down to the water." Angelina scanned the area around them, hoping to discover a way down to rescue Percy.

Richard stood up and removed his jacket, before he turned back and settled on the edge of the cliff, his feet dangling over the side.

"You can't go down there!" Angelina shouted. "You'll fall. Let me go for help."

"I don't think we have the luxury of time on our side," Richard observed. "Were he to move in the wrong direction, he'd be lost to us and I, for one, do not wish to break that kind of news to Estella." Finding hand and footholds, Richard twisted around and lowered his large frame down the side of the cliff.

Angelina held her breath as she watched him climb down like an expert. Crumbling rock and dirt showered him as he went, but he never faltered in his movements. Finally, after what seemed like hours, he reached Percy. He managed to get his feet wedged on the small shelf and with one hand, scooped Percy up. The little dog showered him with kisses and Richard held him tightly against his chest. He looked up at Angelina and smiled triumphantly. "I've got him," he called.

"I can see that," she replied with an anxious smile. "How are you going to climb back up? You'll need both hands."

He winked at her and quickly stuffed Percy into what had once been a very clean white shirt. Once he was certain that the dog was safe, and there was no chance he'd lose him, he began to climb back up.

Again, Angelina held her breath, praying that he'd make it back to the top without falling. When his head appeared over the edge of the cliff, she heaved a sigh of relief. He carefully placed both palms down on the dirt and hoisted himself onto the pathway. Angelina couldn't help herself, throwing her arms around him and never wanting to let go. The whimpering of little Percy brought her back to the present and she reluctantly let Richard go. He pulled Percy out from his shirt and handed the small dog to her.

"Percy, what were you thinking?" she scolded. Percy's small body started to quiver and a volley of excited barks erupted from his mouth. It was all she could do to hang onto him, as he frantically tried to escape her grasp to chase a small rabbit hopping about in the brush. "So that's what made you run off like that," she observed. "We'll have to tell Estella that he needs to be on a leash for cliff walks, from now on."

They cut their walk short and headed back the way they'd come. As they approached Estella's home, she met them at the door. "Did you have a nice walk?" she asked, mischievously eyeing the two of them before her gaze fell on Richard's dirty clothes and she frowned. "Richard, what happened to your shirt… and why is Percy so dirty?" Estella took Percy from Angelina's arms and bustled inside. "Come in and tell me what happened."

Angelina and Richard exchanged glances as they followed her into the small house. Estella set Percy down and he immediately ran to his water bowl. "Tell me what happened," she repeated, as she looked lovingly at the dog.

Angelina relayed the story, as Estella grew more shocked with every new detail..

"Oh, my," Estella said. She appeared a little unsteady on her feet and Harry swiftly came to her aid, settling her into a nearby chair. "Richard, thank you so much for saving him. He's never done anything like that before."

"It was no trouble at all, Estella. I'm happy he's back here at home with you." Richard placed a comforting hand on Estella's shoulder and she covered it with one of her own.

"And look at your shirt! It's all dirty now. Please, take it off and I'll wash it for you," Estella said, gazing up at him in undisguised admiration.

"Estella! Leave the young man alone," Harry chided.

"Don't worry about it. I'll clean it for him later," Angelina said, hiding a grin at Estella's visible disappointment.

"Well, the least you can do is let me give you some of the chocolate chip cookies I've just baked. Let me get a plate for you." Estella got up and busied herself in the kitchen, returning with a plate overflowing with cookies.

"That's a lot of cookies," Angelina grinned. "Thank you."

Estella's adoring gaze had settled on Richard again. "I hope you'll enjoy them. Are you sure you won't let me wash your shirt?"

Richard seemed to be having a hard time containing his laughter and Angelina could see the twinkle in his eyes. "I'm sure," he chuckled.

"Well, then, enjoy the cookies and if you need anything at all, please come and see me." Estella escorted them to the front door and Angelina saw Harry sit down in his chair, shaking his head at his wife's antics.

"I'll talk to you later, Estella. Remember to keep Percy on a leash when you take him out walking near the cliffs," Angelina reminded her.

"I will."

The door closed behind them and Angelina and Richard both burst into fits of uncontrollable laughter. "Wow! Estella really has a thing for you. Harry's going to have to keep an eye on her," Angelina teased.

"It won't be the first time that a woman of age has shown an interest in me," Richard chuckled.

"So, this is a common problem?" Angelina unlocked her door and Richard followed her inside. Setting the cookies on the table, she said, "I think we should have some lunch before we dive into those cookies. What do you think?"

"Agreed," Richard said. "I could use a clean shirt though. You don't happen to have one around here, do you?" He eyed the room, as if he expected to find a spare man's shirt lying around somewhere.

"Hmmm… actually I have some large t-shirts that I use to sleep in. I think one of them might fit you. Let me go get one, I'll be right back." She smiled sweetly at him, experiencing a newfound admiration for the handsome Englishman. Not only was he undeniably sexy, but he was also brave and selfless, two qualities she didn't run across too often. If ever, in fact.

* * *

Richard waited for her to return to the kitchen, the wonderful aroma of the cookies calling to him until he couldn't resist for a moment longer. They were a curious creation, like nothing he'd ever eaten before and he was anxious to try them. He picked one up, noting that it was still warm. Breaking off a piece, he noticed that the chocolate chips Angelina had mentioned, or at least, he assumed that's what they were, oozed from the cookie as he popped it into his mouth. "Mmmm…" He couldn't believe the amazing flavors exploding in his mouth.

"Here you go," Angelina said, holding out a navy blue item towards him. "I see you couldn't wait to try a cookie," she observed.

"They're delicious. I've never had anything like it before," he said.

Much to his surprise, Angelina touched her finger to his mouth, rubbing it across his lips. "You've got some chocolate on your mouth," she said, before she looked away shyly.

Richard ran his tongue over his lips. "Did I get it?" he asked.

Angelina nodded. "Try that shirt on. If it fits, we'll head down the road to the Fish House Restaurant. They sell great fish and chips. You'll have to see if they're better than what you can get back home in England."

He had no idea what she might be talking about, but he agreed. "Alright, give me a moment to change." He followed Angelina's directions to the bathroom and headed in to change his shirt. While he was at it, he washed his face and hands, drying them on a soft, fluffy towel, before donning the shirt. He pulled it over his head and found it was a little too tight, but nothing that he couldn't deal with. "What do you think?" he asked, upon exiting the bathroom.

Angelina surveyed him silently, with her head cocked to one side.

"I really only need to know what you think of the shirt," he teased, when she hadn't spoken for a full minute. "Does it fit?"

"It fits just fine," she agreed, when she finally managed to draw her eyes away from his chest.

"Good. Let's get these fish and chips you mentioned, so I can come back and eat more of Estella's delicious cookies." Richard chuckled knowingly as he headed for the door.

Chapter 13

"WELL, WHAT NEWS do you have for me?" Malcolm demanded. He needed to know Angelina's every move, if his plan was going to work. He didn't want any screw-ups to ruin everything he'd worked so hard to complete.

"When she left you, she went to Mackall's house." Pierce Holmes was Malcolm's right hand man and the one he trusted above all the others to carry out his orders to the letter and without question. "She spent the night there."

Malcolm was peeved by this piece of news. He had wined and dined Angelina the night before, but to no avail. She remained friendly, but cool and aloof. What on earth did she see in that Scottish oaf? He shook his head resolutely. It didn't matter. He could live without her, but he couldn't live without the sword. "Okay. Where is she today?"

"She left Mackall's around 9:30 a.m. with that other guy," Pierce informed him.

"The Brit?" Malcolm asked.

"Yes, sir. They drove down the coast to her home, went for a walk along the cliff and then went out for lunch at a nearby restaurant. They returned about an hour later and they're still at her house now."

"Hmmm... I don't like the fact that this Jefford guy is getting involved here. While Gabe is watching Angelina, I'd like you to watch Jefford. Hopefully, the two of you won't be tripping over one another. I suppose we should watch Mackall as well, just in case," Malcolm concluded.

"I'll assign Dane to him, unless you have someone else in mind."

"No. He'll do."

"If you don't mind me asking, sir, why don't we just get this over with now? Why are we waiting? We've got a handle on all of them and it would be easy to set the plan in motion." Pierce waited silently on the other end of the line for Malcolm's response.

"Yes, it would be easy to do it now, but I fully intend to beat Mackall at the tournament at the end of November. That arrogant bastard deserves to be put in his place one more time, before I get what I truly want out of him." Malcolm disconnected the phone call and tented his fingers. It was only a matter of waiting a short time longer and then, with any luck at all, he'd be in the early part of the sixteenth century and well on his way to finding the sword that would bring him all the power and glory he wanted.

* * *

"What did you think of the fish and chips?" Angelina asked.

"They were very good," he responded.

"As good as what you would buy back at home?" she asked, showing great interest in his response.

He knew this was a test of his ability to fool her - not that he wanted to, of course, but he needed to out of necessity. She'd think him a crazy fool if she discovered the truth. "They were excellent, but I think not as good as what I'd get at home."

"Oh, boo. I guess next time I'm in England, you'll have to give me the name of your favorite place, so I can try it out for myself."

Angelina walked along beside him and Richard acknowledged to himself that it felt good. It seemed as though she belonged there, by his side. He thought he was capable of doing anything if she was with him, but then he reminded himself he was not staying, and she wasn't looking for love. It was a shame, because she would be so very easy to love.

"Penny for your thoughts," Angelina said, her pure blue eyes gazing up at him.

"I was just thinking what a wonderful day I've had here with you. We had an adventure, some good food and the conversation and company were excellent." Richard was surprised by how completely at ease he was, walking with her. He wanted to hold her hand, but knew she wouldn't like it, so instead he let his arm brush up against hers and enjoyed the sensation that travelled up his arm each time he did so. They reached her front door and she looked up at him with such clear admiration, it astounded him. How could he stop himself? He wanted to kiss her so badly, but he knew he couldn't do that to her. He'd already hurt her feelings the first time he'd kissed her.

She reached up and touched his cheek and he held his breath, afraid that if he moved, the spell would be broken and she'd remove her hand. He needn't have worried though, because her damnable cell phone rang and she pulled it from her pocket.

"It's Nick. Probably wondering where we are," she smiled before she pressed a button on the phone and held it to her ear. "Hi. We'll head your way right now. See you soon." She put the phone back into her pocket. "I guess we'd better get going if we don't want to be late." She seemed a little wistful as she opened the door and went inside. "Let me get my things and we'll go." She hurried around the room, picking up her purse and practice equipment, which was in a duffle bag by the front door. She breezed past him, heading towards the car. "Richard, close the door, please."

He did as she requested and followed her to the car saddened to think their idyllic day was at an end.

* * *

Although she was irritated by Nick's impeccable sense of timing, she was actually grateful he had called when he did. There had been a very real chance she was going to kiss Richard again and Nick's phone call had saved her the embarrassment of Richard telling her for a second time that he couldn't go down that road with her. Yes, she had definitely been spared the consequences of her own foolish actions. But damn it, he was getting more and more difficult to resist!

They drove to the practice space in silence. Angelina was lost in her own thoughts and she assumed from Richard's silence that he was as well. He never even glanced in her direction, instead focusing on the scenery passing by his window. She pulled into a parking spot and they both got out. She ran around to the back of the car to get her equipment out of the trunk and ran straight into Richard. "Oh… I'm sorry," she said, the apology covering much more than just accidentally running into him.

Richard cleared his throat and he seemed as if he was about to say something, but she turned away and hurried into the warehouse, not daring to look back. She was, no doubt, the biggest coward in the world, but right now she needed some breathing room.

"There you are!" Nick's voice boomed across from the far end of the warehouse. He was surrounded by students, working intently with their partners. Tonight's group not only consisted of the men who would participate in the tournament against Malcolm and his crew, but a number of women, teenagers and even small children were going through their paces. Nick was moving around from group to group, but it was obvious that he was in need of some help from Angelina and Richard.

"Sorry we're late," Angelina said. "Who do you need me to work with?"

"Let's have you work with the ladies, if you don't mind," Nick suggested.

She didn't mind in the least, it was a pleasure to work with this group. They loved the class and she felt good about providing them with the skills they needed to take care of themselves.

"Richard," Nick said, "would you please work with the little ones?"

Richard looked puzzled by Nick's request, but he agreed. Angelina watched as Richard approached the group and introduced himself. He had the children sit in a circle and she listened as he asked them to tell him something about themselves.

"Angelina," Nick said, nodding in the direction of the women.

"Sorry." Angelina headed off towards her group and began pairing them off so she could evaluate where they needed help. She noticed that Nick had sent Zeke over to work with the teenagers and they seemed very happy about it.

The evening passed in a blur. She made good progress with her ladies' group and was impressed with their ability to follow her instructions with just one simple explanation. She couldn't help but be mesmerized by Richard as he worked with the children. They ranged in age from about six through to twelve. It was adorable watching him parry with the youngest child. He was sweet with them. A little voice in the back of her head was telling her to take note. *So he's good with dogs and children. Is that supposed to make me fall for him? I can't let that happen, no matter how perfect he seems. He'll only hurt me in the end, just like the others I've made the mistake of giving my heart to.*

Still, she couldn't quite reconcile her warning with the man she saw in front of her. He wasn't anything like any of the men from her past. She'd always been able to walk away from any man, with her independence intact. Richard made her feel things she wasn't sure she wanted to feel. Even though she was perfectly capable of taking care of herself, there were times she was exhausted by it. Times when she wanted to be taken care of, wanted to turn to someone at the end of the day and say, *'Hold me. Love me.'* She hadn't allowed herself to do that up until now and she was frightened of the prospect of trying it. She tore herself away from thoughts of Richard and pulled herself back to the here and now, congratulating the women on their great progress and then heading off to hide in the back office and pull herself together before she drove Richard and Nick home.

* * *

Richard couldn't believe how much he'd enjoyed working with the children. He hadn't had much cause to spend time with the young ones around the castle, so he was surprised by their friendly natures and how hard they'd worked, to gain his approval. He'd never really thought about having children of his own before now, but this experience had him thinking about starting a family, and soon. Richard wasn't sure how that was going to happen, but he fervently hoped it would. He just needed to learn those lessons Edna had spoken of and then he'd be able to go home, the changed man he wanted to be.

"Ye did well with the wee ones," Nick said as he approached. "They seem to love ye."

"Love me?" Richard repeated blankly.

"Aye. I heard them all chattering happily about ye as they pre-pared to leave. Ye've made quite an impression on them." Nick began the cleanup work that was a natural byproduct of their classes. "I believe we'll have them do an exhibition at the tournament. The teenagers and the ladies can participate as well. It will be good publicity for my school and should bring me new students by the New Year."

"Where has Angelina gone off to?" Richard asked. He spun on his heel, searching for her among the departing students.

"She's here somewhere. She cannae leave without us, she's our ride home." Nick continued picking up items that had been left on the floor. "I'll need to send an email to the students informing them of the exhibition times, once I've spoken with the event organizers about adding them to the program."

"You amaze me, Nick. You've adapted so well to your surroundings. Even though I know you're not from this time, it's easy for me to forget when I hear you talking about the school."

"'Twasn't always like this, I can assure ye. I made many mistakes and got many funny looks when I first arrived. I made it a point to quickly learn what would make me blend in." He stopped what he was doing and stood up straight, stretching his back as he rose. "There she is," Nick announced, pointing to Angelina as she exited the office.

"We were wondering where you were." Richard smiled appreciatively as he watched Angelina walk towards them.

"For the record, I wasnae wondering. 'Twas him," Nick nodded his head in Richard's direction.

"I was just cleaning up your desk, Nick. I don't know how you can find anything in there." She gave Nick a disapproving scowl and then immediately smiled, to let him know she was just teasing. "Are you almost done out here? I want to get home as early as I can."

Richard didn't like the thought of her returning home alone. "Why? Why must you go home?" He realized immediately that he sounded like a besotted schoolboy, but it was too late, the words had already left his mouth.

Angelina, for her part, appeared unfazed by the question. "I have things I need to do there. I've been spending so much time with the two of you, I've let some things go and it's time for me to take care of them."

"I see." But he didn't really see at all. He wanted her here, where he could keep an eye on her. For some reason, he couldn't shake the idea that she might be in danger, and he would prefer she was by his side.

"Richard, she'll be fine," Nick stated quietly, so that only Richard would hear. In a louder voice, he spoke to Angelina. "Let's go then. I believe we're done here."

They locked up and walked to the car. "Angelina, how are the three of us supposed to fit in here?" Nick asked, surveying the sporty little car.

"Oops! I forgot I was going to need to get you both back home. If I'd been thinking, I would have brought the truck. Oh, well, we'll have to make do. Nick, you sit in the back this time. I know it's cramped back there, but I'll try not to go over any bumps and I'll get you both home as quickly as I can." She exchanged an impish grin with Richard as Nick tried his best to fold himself into the back seat.

"Richard, move your seat forward," Nick grumbled.

"What?" Richard asked. "How do I do that?"

"There's a button on the side of your seat. If you push it, your seat will move forward," Nick harrumphed impatiently.

Richard had a difficult time locating the button Nick spoke of, and he was surprised when Angelina leaned across his body and reached down beside the seat to operate it for him. Richard felt the seat lurch forward, but he was completely focused on the sensation of Angelina's breasts nestled between his legs and he groaned involuntarily.

"There, is that better, Nick?" Angelina asked.

"Much," Nick answered. "How is it for you, Richard?" Nick laughed, peeking around the seat back to observe his friend's pained look as Angelina slithered back into her own seat.

Richard offered Nick a dirty look, but didn't bother answering. It had been a rhetorical question and Nick obviously knew everything he needed to about the situation. As far as Richard was concerned his friend was enjoying the situation far too much.

As they pulled out of the parking lot, Richard gazed silently out the window, his head filled with thoughts of Angelina.

Chapter 14

THANKSGIVING MORNING ARRIVED IN THE form of a clear, but cool day. The sun was shining brightly and showed promise of warming the air for the afternoon football game that was planned in the field next to Estella's home. Angelina had eluded Richard and Nick over the past few days. She had gone to practice, worked with her students and prepared all the paperwork necessary for the tournament and the exhibitions with little or no interaction with the men. Overall, it had made the time fly by and now here she was, getting ready to celebrate Thanksgiving in the way it was meant to be celebrated - with a real family. Over the years, Angelina had spent many holidays on her own and she'd gotten used to it. Being used to it didn't mean she didn't long for the type of holiday she imagined everyone else in the country celebrating.

Nick and Richard would be joining her soon. Zeke was dropping them off, on his way to his own mother's house, which had left Angelina plenty of time to make the pies for dessert. Between Estella and her daughter, everything else was under control - the turkey, stuffing, gravy and vegetables were all taken care of and Estella had told her they'd made an assortment of quick breads as well. When Angelina had visited earlier, the aroma from the kitchen had permeated the entire house and had her mouth watering. Just as she was getting her own mincemeat pie in the oven, the front door opened and Nick and Richard walked in, both carrying bouquets of flowers.

"Good day to ye, lass," Nick said. "We come bearing flowers for ye and the Lady Estella."

"They're beautiful! Thank you!" Angelina kissed Nick on the cheek and hesitated a moment before doing the same to Richard. "I just put my first pie in the oven and I'm about to get the others prepared. Would you like to help me?"

"If ye dinnae mind, I believe I'll take these flowers over to Estella and see what wondrous food she's cooking," Nick said, heading for the door. "Richard, would ye like to join me?"

"I'll stay and help here," Richard said. He sauntered into the kitchen, bouquet still in hand.

Angelina took the flowers from him, retrieved a vase from under the sink, filled it with water and then set the flowers in a pretty arrangement. She stood back and admired them. "Thank you, they're beautiful."

"Their beauty is a mere shadow of your own." Richard was standing too close for comfort, making the small kitchen seem even tinier in his presence.

"If you want to go visit Estella with Nick, it's okay, I can manage the pies on my own." She realized she was already trying to get rid of him, but was uncertain why she was reacting in this manner. She'd been thinking about him all morning, imagining him walking through the door, tall, dark and handsome. And here he was, and she hadn't been disappointed. He was all of that and more. So why was she so determined to avoid him?

"I'd like to stay," Richard said. His eyes seemed to be burning holes right through her.

"Okay, then. I'm going to put you to work, so I hope you've got some cooking skills."

"I follow directions very well, m'lady. I promise I won't disappoint you." He did a little mock bow and his eyes danced with amusement.

Angelina fastened an apron around his waist and handed him a rolling pin. She instructed him on how to roll out the pie dough and true to his word he did exactly as she showed him and made a perfect round for the pie plate. Next he cut up the apples while she prepared the pumpkin for the pumpkin pie. They worked side-by-side in the kitchen with hardly a word spoken between them, other than the occasional question from Richard on what she needed him to do next and her brief answers. Angelina found it to be a comfortable silence and she gradually began to relax. Having Richard here helping her, gave Angelina a warm, fuzzy feeling she hadn't expected. When the last pie was in the oven, she removed her own apron and untied his.

Richard turned to Angelina with an amused expression on his face.

"What's so funny?" she asked.

In answer, he grazed his thumb across her cheek. Trapped as she was between him and the counter, she couldn't tear her gaze away from his smoldering eyes. She stood perfectly still as he reached behind her for a towel and proceeded to wipe some flour from her face. The air between them was thick with emotion and Angelina found it difficult to take more than a shallow breath. She couldn't get past him without touching him, so she stayed exactly where she was and hoped he would move. He didn't. Clearing her throat, she made small talk, spouting words that sounded inane, even to her own ears.

"Once those pies are done, we'll set them to cool and head on over to Estella's." She fidgeted nervously with her hair and finally, unable to take another moment of awkwardness quickly turned her back to him. That was a mistake, because she could feel his hot breath on her neck. His calloused fingers sent chills down her spine as he moved her hair away from her neck. "Angelina, I know you've been avoiding me these past days, but I don't understand why." His deep voice rumbled through her body as she waited to see what he'd do next. "Why are we fighting this attraction we have for one another? You're all I can think about, all I want. Would it be so wrong, to let down our guards and enjoy each other?"

Angelina couldn't speak. Her body was tingling, from head to toe and her breaths were coming in tiny gasps. She wanted to turn and be held in his arms, to experience his lips engulfing hers in passionate kisses, but how could she? They'd agreed to be friends and now, he was saying all the things she so desperately wanted to hear. Finally managing to inhale a deep breath, she spoke. "Richard, I can't do this right now." She pushed her way past him and practically broke into a run as she headed for her bedroom and closed the door behind her. Leaning against it, she did her best to get a grip on herself, to ensure she wouldn't run out and throw herself at him.

* * *

Richard watched in disappointment as Angelina ran away, shutting the door on him as she went into her bedroom. He stood outside her door, not knowing what to do to make the situation better. "Angelina. I'm sorry," he apologized. "Please, come out. We can talk about this later if you like, but I don't want it to spoil your day. Please…"

"I'll be out in a minute. I'm just getting changed," she said through the door. "I'm not angry with you, I'm just confused. I need time to think."

Resting his head against the door, he closed his eyes in relief. Perhaps she would think about what he was offering, and come to him. Since he had no choice but to wait for her decision, he walked into the living room where everything he saw was so very Angelina. Beautiful photos of the coast and framed photos of people he assumed were members of her family were set here and there on bookshelves, end tables and the fireplace mantel. One in particular caught his attention and picking it up, he recognized Dylan, standing on the beach next to a large, oddly shaped board. Next to that was a photo of a young lady he'd also seen before. She had been with Cormac that day when he'd crossed the bridge from Glendaloch back into his own time. He smiled, realizing it wasn't merely a coincidence that he had ended up here with Angelina. "Edna," he said out loud and then he laughed at the absurdity of it all. Edna was the keeper of the bridge, and as such, she obviously decided who could travel through time and where they would travel. Everything that had happened over these past few months had been carefully orchestrated by her and Richard knew she must have a very important reason for sending him to this particular time and place. He was certain both Angelina and Nick were a part of the plan, but that was all he knew. The rest would reveal itself soon and he decided he could relax and let events unfold for themselves. He still had to learn the lessons Edna had spoken of in order to return home, but he knew she would present him with opportunities to do just that. All he had to do was wait.

The smell of Angelina's perfume announced her presence behind him.

"I was just looking at your photos." Richard wondered if he should mention Dylan. He decided it might be best to keep that information to himself and when he had the chance to speak with Edna again, he'd ask her about it. "Are these all members of your family?"

"Not all of them. This is a photo of my mother," she said, pointing to a woman who looked a lot like herself.

"She's a beautiful woman, as is her daughter." He smiled as he glanced from the photo to Angelina, who still seemed uncomfortable.

"This is my cousin, Jenna." She held up the photo of the young woman he recognized. "And this is Dylan. He's not really related to me, but I still think of him as a cousin." She stared lovingly at the photo. "Both of them went off to Scotland and they haven't even called me to tell me they're okay." She sounded both angry and worried as she spoke about them.

"I'm sure they're fine," he said, trying to reassure her. He knew, of course, that they were both doing well and were happily living their lives in his medieval world. Angelina, on the other hand, must have felt as if she'd been deserted. "If there were something wrong, I'm sure you would have heard by now."

She nodded, but still seemed quite sad. "I guess I thought they were the family members I could count on, and now I see that may not have been the case at all."

Without thinking, he wrapped her in his arms, doing his best to soothe her hurt. He stroked her hair and her back with his large hands and her muscles gradually relaxed. "Come. This is to be a happy day, is it not? The pies smell wonderful, I can hardly wait to try them."

"You'll have to wait a while." She smiled up at him as he held her close. "Estella wouldn't be happy with us if we had the pie before our Thanksgiving dinner."

* * *

The day couldn't have been any better. Estella's family included her two sons and daughter, their adult children and their spouses, along with her great grandchildren. Everyone gathered in the adjacent field to play a game of touch football while they waited for the food to be ready. Nick and Richard listened intently as Estella's son, Sean, explained the finer points of the game and then divided everyone into equal teams. The great grandchildren, ranging in age from about four through to eight were excited to be included and jumped up and down as they waited for the game to begin. Angelina and Nick were on one team, with Sean, his wife, their two sons and their wives. Richard was on the other team with Brian, Estella's other son, along with his wife, their son and daughter and their spouses. Estella's daughter, Bella, and her husband were acting as referees, and the youngest children were divided evenly between the two teams. The game was a lot of fun and the children were all given opportunities to score touchdowns. The smallest girl had taken a shine to Richard, and tailed him wherever he went. Brian threw the ball his way and Richard reached up and plucked it out of the sky, handing it to little Sienna. He lifted her into the air and ran with her across the goal line. She squealed in delight the whole way and when he finally put her down she did her very own version of a touchdown dance. Richard ruffled her hair and laughed at her antics.

"Dinner's ready," Estella called and everyone headed into the house. No one cared who had won the game, it had all been in good fun and it had been an enjoyable way to pass the time before their meal.

* * *

"Thank ye so much for a delicious feast, m'lady Estella." Nick bowed low and kissed the elderly woman's hand. Estella beamed at this, seemingly enamored with Nick's actions.

"Nick, if you keep that up, I don't know how I'll compete with you," Harry chuckled.

"Have no fear, Harry. I would not rob ye of yer own true love." Nick was beginning to slur his words, after a long day of feasting and drinking.

"Thank you for having us, Estella. It was a pleasure meeting all of you - I guess I don't have to tell you what a special woman your mother is," Angelina said, addressing Estella's children.

"We know," Sean assured her, putting his arm around his mother's shoulders and giving her a gentle squeeze. "She's the best. Dad's not so bad either," he teased.

Harry appeared embarrassed by this proclamation, but chimed in, "I'm a very lucky man. I have the best family in the world."

Everyone said their goodbyes, with hugs and kisses all around and then Nick, Richard and Angelina made their way back to her little cottage.

"I need to sleep," Nick announced.

"I'll get you set up in the guest room." Angelina unlocked the front door and led them inside. "Follow me."

Nick dutifully followed her down the hall, Richard right behind him, making sure that Nick made it down the narrow hall without incident. She barely got the covers pulled down before Nick face-planted himself onto the bed, one arm and leg hanging off the side, and passed out. She couldn't help laughing at the comical way he had landed. "Help me get him all the way onto the bed."

Richard turned Nick onto his back with little effort, which solved the problem of the dangling arm and leg. He removed Nick's boots and covered him with the blanket, before they both stood for a moment watching Nick sleep and then exiting the room together. "He'll sleep well," Richard said, closing the door.

"He'll be sorry tomorrow though, I think," Angelina added.

Richard chuckled and followed Angelina back into the living room, where she started a fire in the fireplace. The setting sun had brought quite a chill to the air and the fire would warm the small room nicely. They both sat in silence, staring into the flames, each lost to their own thoughts. The soft glow of the fire was the only light in the room and the mesmerizing popping and crackling of the wood the only sound. As they sat down, Richard drew Angelina's attention to a light outside that seemed to be moving from left to right and back again.

"What's that?" he asked, getting up to look through the window.

"That's odd. I don't know what it is." She joined him at the window. Before she could utter another word, Richard had turned swiftly and darted for the door, opening it and silently heading out into the darkness. *What is he doing?* she wondered. She followed him but as she got to the door, she heard someone curse. Glancing back towards the window, she noticed the light they'd seen suddenly disappear and then she heard the sound of someone running through the brush. She made it outside, just as Richard disappeared from sight. It was a new moon, so there was no ambient light to help her see what was happening. She tried to follow Richard, but only got as far as the edge of her property when he came back, carrying a flashlight.

"Someone was outside your cottage. They dropped this light stick when they ran off. I was unable to catch up with them before they got to their car and drove away." Richard took her by the arm and led her back toward the house. "You shouldn't have followed me out."

"What?" Angelina bristled. "Why not? I've told you before that I can take care of myself!"

"I'm very aware that you can take care of yourself." Richard gave the area one final scan before joining Angelina inside. "I'd like it if you'd allow me to take care of you this time. Call it my male pride, or whatever you'd like, but while I know you are completely capable of besting most men when you have a sword and dagger in hand, what is the harm in allowing me to do what I do best?"

The hurt expression on his face had Angelina thinking carefully about his question. Hadn't she recently been thinking about how nice it would be to have someone who wanted to take care of her and here he was, standing right in front of her, offering her his protection and she'd been angry about it. That was no way to treat him. "I'm sorry, Richard. You're right. I guess after all these years of fending for myself, I have yet to learn how to let someone else do it for me. I'll do my best to allow it."

"I don't want you to stop being who you are, because that's what makes you so beautiful to me. I love your independent nature and the fact that you don't need anyone's help, but every now and again, let me take care of you. Allow me that small joy on occasion."

How could she possibly refuse him? He was the fairytale knight in shining armor that she'd dreamed of as a child, and he'd come to rescue her from herself.

"Do you have any idea who that might have been?" Richard peered through the window into the darkness and then turned back to her for an answer.

"I don't know, but I don't think it's the first time they've been here." Angelina sat on the sofa and Richard settled beside her.

"Do you mean to tell me that this has happened before?"

"Several days ago, I found footprints in the damp dirt near the spot where that light was coming from and I've had the feeling recently that someone is watching me, but I can't imagine who it would be, or why they would bother." Angelina had to admit to herself, that this was becoming more frightening as she added all the little incidents together.

"And you didn't tell Nick or me about it?" Richard sounded as if he couldn't believe his ears.

"No. I thought it was my imagination at first, but now I know it wasn't." She searched his face for any sign of his mood. "You're not mad at me, are you?"

Richard shook his head in apparent disbelief. "Angelina, if anything had happened to you, both Nick and I would be devastated. Please, don't allow this to happen again. At the first sign of anything unusual, I expect you to tell us." The concern on his face touched Angelina's heart. He really did care about her and she knew now that she could definitely count on him to be there for her, no matter the situation.

"I'm sorry," she said, as Richard put his arm around her and pulled her close. She snuggled up against him, the warmth of his body reassuring her that everything was going to be all right.

Chapter 15

ANGELINA SAVORED THE COMFORT OF being wrapped in Richard's arms, the steady beat of his heart against her ear, his manly scent enveloping her senses. The soft sounds of the burning wood, crackling in the fireplace was the only other sound intruding on this special moment and Angelina found herself overwhelmed by the intense desire to have Richard make love to her. They had danced around their attraction to one another from the first day they'd met, but in this moment, Angelina made up her mind she was going to have him. When she wriggled out of his arms, Richard groaned in protest, but she grabbed his hand and drew him along the hallway toward her bedroom.

"Angelina?" Richard posed her name as a question as she drew him into her room. She remained mute, closing the door behind them. Coiling her arms around his neck, she drew his head down, and proceeded to kiss him with every ounce of the passion that had been building up for days. She nipped at his lips with her teeth and he picked up on the cue, answering her, kiss for kiss. His arms were vise-like, holding her firmly against his chest. Their tongues entwined, hungrily tasting one another, learning each other. Angelina lowered her arms from his neck, slipping her hands between them to unbutton Richard's jeans. Unzipping the fly, she found him ready and waiting for her. She wasn't about to let the fact that he was so much taller than her be a hindrance, and she pulled his shirt up and over his head. She had wanted to do that since meeting him and she came to a standstill for a moment, admiring what she had revealed. He was beautiful. Angelina greedily ran her hands over his chest and down to his abs.

Richard, for his part, had managed to do some undressing of his own. Angelina wasn't sure how it had happened, but she was standing there, completely naked. Richard was kissing her neck and nipping at her earlobe. The sensations she was experiencing under his gentle touch were unlike any she'd ever had before. Maybe this is what it was like, when you really cared for the other person. Moans escaped her lips when Richard reached between her thighs and slid his fingers through her warm, wet slit making contact with her sensitive pearl. Angelina's legs trembled as she opened herself up to him, riding his hand as he slid his fingers in and out of her slick sheath. Her breath came in small gasps and the sensations were building with every passing second. Angelina grasped Richard's shoulders when he dropped onto his knees. He gripped her thighs with his hands and used his mouth to lick and nibble at her nub, sending her soaring into ecstasy and she collapsed across his shoulder, calling out his name on a sigh.

* * *

Richard lifted Angelina into his arms and laid her across the bed, trailing kisses from her neck to her breasts. First one, and then the other, was lavished with his attention and he marveled at the way Angelina's body responded to his every touch. This was the woman he wanted, and this was exactly how he wanted her. Seeing how much she enjoyed his caresses made him grow even harder. Every moan brought him to the brink and the way she bit her lip and writhed beneath his touch was more pleasure than he could bear. His body strummed with tension and he couldn't wait a second longer. Dragging his attention away from her breasts, Richard levered himself over the top of Angelina, settling between her thighs. He ached to enter her, but first he teased her entrance with the tip of his manhood, ensuring she was ready for him. She squirmed beneath him, her desire to have him inside of her written plainly in her rapturous expression. He could not deny her and in one pulsating beat, he entered her fully. As he moved inside her, he marveled at the soft, velvety walls holding tightly over his rigid length. The need to spill his seed was overwhelming, but he wished to wait for Angelina to join him in climax. They would reach for the stars together. As highly sensitized as they both were in this moment, their bodies hummed and pulsed together, erupting in a crescendo of ecstasy.

They lay entwined in each other's arms, legs twisted together and panting from exertion. Angelina gently kissed his chest and his heart almost burst with the love he held for her. "Angelina..." he began to speak, but she covered his lips with her finger, stopping him.

"Shhh. Don't say anything. This is perfect without words."

* * *

Held securely in his arms, Angelina didn't want to hear any false declarations of love. Didn't men always say they loved you, after they had sex? Saying it now would mean nothing to her and besides, she had made it clear she wasn't looking for love. Richard had a body as close to physical perfection as she had ever seen and she was certain she wanted to be with him because she was drawn in by sheer animal magnetism, not by love. Now that she had experienced his lovemaking, she was certain she could move on from the heated desire she had been experiencing when she was around him. They would be friends, as they'd agreed, but nothing more. She wouldn't open her heart to him, not when she knew he would no doubt move on, as soon as the next-best-thing came along. Experience had shown this was always the case.

If she examined her emotions more closely, Angelina knew she was the one who sabotaged her relationships - in every single instance. She'd never given any man the opportunity for more than a casual dalliance, because she truly believed, deep down, that no man would stay with her for the long haul. Why should Richard be any different? *Because he is,* her mind quietly whispered.

Angry with herself, Angelina disentangled herself from Richard and stood up.

"Where are you going, love?" Richard propped himself up on his elbows to watch her.

"I'll be right back." She grabbed her robe and headed out toward the kitchen. She needed a few minutes away from him, to gather her thoughts. Lying next to him she'd been overcome with emotions which were clouding her thoughts, so she decided a little space was best right now. Pouring herself a glass of water Angelina sat at the kitchen table and gave her traitorous heart a stern lecture. *I can't become attached to him. He told me so himself. He's not staying; he's going to leave soon.*

* * *

Richard intuitively knew Angelina was at odds with herself. They had agreed that they would only be friends. She had insisted that was what she wanted, and yet she was the one who had sent them down this path. She was the one who'd drawn him into her bedroom, she'd clearly wanted to make love with him and now, Richard suspected she was experiencing remorse over the decision. He decided he wouldn't push her. This was something she had to come to terms with on her own and he would wait for her to decide on their way forward, one way or the other. He lay there in the silky, soft sheets, longing to have her beside him, but he wouldn't pressure her.

He lay awake for more than half an hour, before the door opened softly, revealing Angelina's slight figure in a shaft of light from the hallway. "I've brought you some water," she announced, holding out a glass.

He let the cool liquid slide down his throat, realizing he had been parched. How sweet it was, of her to think of him. He placed the glass down and opened his arms to her, holding his breath to see how she would react. Angelina climbed into the bed and lay across his chest and Richard wrapped his arms around her, holding her close to his heart. He gently kissed the top of her head and closed his eyes. Sleeping with her in his arms was everything he wanted at this moment. She had granted him this opportunity, but what would the morning bring?

Chapter 16

THE SUN WAS BARELY VISIBLE through the coastal fog, but as it peeked through the windows, Richard knew morning had indeed arrived and he'd spent the entire night with Angelina in his arms. He lay perfectly still, not wanting to disturb her, as the nights events came flooding back. He'd slept fitfully, spending most of the night reliving their love making and wanting to do it again, but Angelina had put the wall up around herself once again.

He had also listened for anything out of the ordinary that might break the silence of the night, remembering their intruder. The first order of business today was to find out who was following Angelina and why. With that thought in mind, he carefully got up from the bed without disturbing her. His gaze fell on her face for a long moment and he was quite certain her angelic beauty was unparalleled. Tearing himself away, Richard threw on his jeans and marched across the hall to the room where Nick was sleeping.

"Nick!" He shook his friend who, for all intents and purposes, remained completely unresponsive. "Nick!" He tried again, pulling off the blanket and removing the pillow from beneath Nick's head.

A groan from the bed confirmed he had made progress. "What do ye want of me?" Nick rolled onto his back and covered his eyes with his arm. "'Tis too bloody early for this, Richard."

"Angelina's in danger! I must speak with you now." Richard stood upright, towering over Nick, his eyes blazing with the desire to solve this problem. He nudged Nick with his foot, to prevent him from falling back to sleep.

"Alright, alright! I'm awake. What's this ye say about Angelina being in danger?" Nick sat upright, before grabbing his head. Richard knew he was probably suffering the ill effects of all the drinking he'd done the day before. "Water, please?" he managed to croak out.

"I'll get the water; you get up and meet me in the kitchen. Whatever you do, don't go back to sleep," Richard threatened.

Richard went into the kitchen to pour a glass of water and waited impatiently for Nick. He sat at the small kitchen table and tapped his fingers on the tabletop in irritation. Finally, Nick appeared and sank into a chair opposite Richard, who shoved the glass of water in his direction.

"I can see yer angry, Richard, but do not misplace yer anger on me. I'm here now and I'm listening. Tell me what's got a thistle up yer arse." Nick took a long drink of water before placing the glass back down on the table and meeting Richard's glare with one of his own.

Richard proceeded to tell Nick what had happened the night before and how Angelina thought someone had been following her for a while. "Can you think of anyone who might want to follow Angelina?"

Nick appeared to be contemplating what Richard had just told him, and took a minute or two to respond. "No. I cannae think of anyone," he finally admitted. He joined Richard in rhythmically tapping the table with his fingers.

"We must find out who and why. We cannot allow any harm to come to her."

"Calm yerself. We'll keep her safe. One of us must be with her at all times, until we know exactly what is going on." Nick got up and refilled his glass before he began rummaging through the cabinets, obviously in search of something.

Angelina's voice came from the doorway, startling Richard. "Aspirin are in the cabinet next to the sink. Just above the glasses." She retrieved the coffee pot from the counter and eyed the two men. "Coffee?"

* * *

Angelina had caught the tail end of their conversation and she wasn't happy.

She began preparing the coffee and from the corner of her eye, saw that Nick had found what he needed for his hangover. "I can take care of myself, you know," she announced, irritated that these men were planning to handle this situation as if she were a helpless female. "I heard what you were saying and it's not necessary for anyone to stay with me. You've seen me fight."

"Yes, we have, but that doesn't mean that you'll never come upon an opponent who could overwhelm you and do you harm. And it may not be a single attacker, whomever is after you might send more than one man to do the job." Richard seemed to be visibly gauging her reaction before he continued. "It could happen to any of us, Angelina, not only you. I'm not suggesting that because you're a woman, you need our protection. All I'm saying is there is strength in numbers. We are stronger together than we are apart."

She had to admit he made sense, but it went against everything she believed in to need a man's help with anything. She silently continued working on breakfast, giving herself time to ponder what he'd just said.

The difficulty was, she wasn't certain she *wanted* to have Richard around all the time. While she had been happy only moments before about being wrapped protectively in Richard's arms all night and the earth shattering love making that she'd experienced, she wasn't sure what to do about Richard in the long term. One minute he was the one holding back and then it seemed it was Angelina who was back-pedaling. This back and forth volley of emotions was driving her crazy.

They both needed to make up their minds about what they wanted and put an end to their mutual suffering. A casual fling might work for her, but she had the feeling that wasn't what Richard wanted. It would be all or nothing for him and she wasn't sure she could do that. She never had before and even though what she felt for him was different to anything she'd felt for anyone in her past, she was afraid to make herself vulnerable to any man, even Richard. And the prospect of having Richard babysitting her while this stalker was following her - well, she certainly didn't like that idea. She needed time and space to figure things out.

She could see Nick and Richard exchanging glances and mouthing words to each other. The sight of two grown men behaving like little girls talking behind someone's back made her want to laugh. She giggled quietly and set plates of food down in front of them.

"Oh, I dinnae believe I could eat a thing," Nick said, rubbing his stomach and eyeing the food uncertainly.

"You'll feel better if you eat," Angelina encouraged him, but Nick didn't look convinced.

She sat down and put some eggs and toast on her own plate. She poured a cup of coffee for herself, before pouring some for the two men and then quietly went about eating her breakfast.

Nick, who had said he couldn't eat a thing, made a miraculous recovery, wolfing down everything on his plate and heading back for seconds. Angelina smiled softly to herself - she knew him so well. Richard ate at a more sedate pace and she eyed him discreetly when she was certain he wasn't looking in her direction. He was the one she wanted to know more about. How was it that these two had become friends? Nick was lighthearted and always talking, while Richard was the exact opposite, serious and quiet. He was mysterious and she found she liked that character trait. Angelina wanted to know more, especially after last night and hoped that by asking questions, she'd be able to make up her own mind better. "How did you two meet?"

Nick and Richard exchanged concerned glances. "You tell her," Richard said. "You were always a much better story teller than I."

Nick drained his coffee cup and refilled it, before he began. "Well, ye see, Richard and I are verra different in many ways - he's English and I'm Scottish."

"Obviously," Angelina said in an amused tone.

"Richard has a Scottish cousin, who is a close friend of the Mackall Clan. We met at a wedding when we were much younger. How old would ye say we were, Richard?"

Angelina cast her eyes in Richard's direction and once again was met by his searing gaze, the one that warmed her body and made her squirm in her seat.

"We were but lads," Richard answered. "Perhaps fifteen or sixteen."

"Richard was smitten by a lass from the MacKenzie clan."

Angelina noted that Richard appeared uncomfortable at the mention of this girl, and Nick was watching him carefully for his reaction. "Really? Was she pretty?"

"Verra," Nick continued. "We could hardly separate him from her side, but alas, she was in love with another and our Richard never stood a chance."

"I'm sorry, Richard," Angelina said.

"Why? There's no need to be sorry." Richard sat rigidly upright in his chair, seeming as if he'd much prefer to flee, than to continue listening to Nick's story.

"She broke your heart." Angelina could see the truth in his face, even if he was not willing to admit it.

"My heart is fine. Nick, continue telling how *we* met," Richard said, giving Nick a deadly glare.

"Fine then, enough about the lass. When she departed, Richard and I spent time riding out around his cousin's lands and talking about things that fifteen-year-old boys talk about. We became fast friends and spent many years together, before losing touch." Nick again eyed Richard warily, but he seemed relaxed once again.

"So what happened? How'd you lose touch?" Angelina asked.

Richard took up the story from here. "My behavior became difficult for Nick to tolerate. So he went home and that was the last I saw of him until I arrived here."

Angelina was sure that there were some holes in the story, but she'd let it go for now. If Richard wanted to tell her more about it, he would. One thing was certain though - the mention of that girl had caused him to react like a man with something to hide.

Chapter 17

WITH ONLY A FEW MORE days before the tournament, Richard made his rounds from group to group, making sure everyone was prepared. He kept a watchful eye on Angelina, as did Nick. She wasn't happy about it, but had agreed to go along with their wishes until they could figure out who had been following her. They were all aware of the sensation of being watched now. Whoever it was, they were quite stealthy, because so far they'd been unable to catch even a glimpse. Angelina had told Estella that she would be staying in the city until after the competition ended. She hadn't wanted to worry the elderly woman about being followed, but Richard insisted it was best to warn Estella and Harry that someone had been spotted on Angelina's property, so they could protect themselves if need be. He knew Harry was an ex-Marine, and that despite his age, he was very capable of handling an intruder if it came to that. Harry reassured Richard that he had weapons, and he knew how to use them.

Students were coming by the warehouse to collect their medieval costumes and to do some last minute parrying practice, in anticipation of the upcoming exhibitions they would participate in. Those taking part in the tournament had been there almost constantly and had gained the confidence they would need in order to defeat Granger's team. Richard and Nick were quite confident about their chances, but everyone continued to work long hours to achieve their goal. Where it had once been personal for only Nick, the others had all developed a deep sense of pride in their team and their abilities. They understood that Granger believed his team would defeat them easily and they were determined to prove him wrong.

They all took turns working with the children, who were adorable in their medieval costumes. Angelina had worked hard, alongside the team moms, to design authentic costumes for everyone. To keep anxiety levels to a minimum, Nick and Richard tried to keep things lighthearted and fun, encouraging the others to think only of the present and let the future take care of itself. A party atmosphere overtook the warehouse, when a dozen pizzas were delivered, along with salads, drinks and dessert. The children changed out of their costumes and everyone sat around on the floor with paper plates full of food. Laughter and excited chatter filled the large space, echoing off the rafters.

"You should be quite proud of your accomplishments," Richard said, glancing around the room at the happy faces of Nick's students. "Not many would be able to come to a strange place and find a way to fit in so seamlessly."

Nick appeared suitably humble. "You haven't done so badly yourself."

"I've had you to help me. I'm hopeful that once this competition is finished, we will be able to return home."

"You've heard from Edna then?" Nick asked.

"No. It's just a feeling I've had of late. I don't know where it's coming from, but I believe it."

"Are you becoming a soothsayer, Richard?" Nick questioned curiously.

Richard thought about this as he watched Angelina approach them. "I don't believe so, but with Edna, one never knows what to expect."

"Who's Edna?" Angelina asked when she reached them. "You've mentioned her once before."

"Have I?" Richard tried to remember when that might have been.

"Yes. When I found you that day on the Marina. You said her name and I asked you if she was your wife, remember?"

"Ah, yes. Nick and I were just speaking of the competition. How do you feel about it? Do you think everyone's ready," Richard said, trying to divert Angelina's attention.

"Who's Edna?" Angelina repeated stubbornly.

Apparently his diversionary tactics hadn't worked. "She's an old friend from the… from my past." He could see that Angelina was determined to continue and he swallowed heavily.

"From your past in England?" Angelina cocked her head to one side and studied him.

"Yes." Perhaps if he kept his answers simple, she wouldn't persist, but he got the distinct impression that Angelina was deliberately trying to start an argument.

"Do you know her, Nick?" she asked.

"No. I'm afraid not. She's one of Richard's friends, he met her nae too long ago, isn't that right?"

Was Nick trying to make matters worse? Richard glared in his direction and Nick smirked in acknowledgement, clearly enjoying Richard's discomfort.

"If you met her *not so long ago*, then how can she be an old friend?" Angelina demanded.

"Nick is mistaken." Richard was getting quite uncomfortable under Angelina's intense scrutiny. This was not going well. Instead of shutting down her inquiries, he seemed to have merely piqued her interest and, it appeared, an intense streak of jealousy.

"Fine then. If you don't want me to know, then don't tell me." Turning away from them, Angelina stomped off towards Zeke and Wade, leaving Nick and Richard behind.

"Thanks for your help," Richard grumbled.

"Sorry, I wasnae trying to cause trouble, just having some fun. I had nae idea she'd walk away so angry."

Richard knew Nick well enough to know his apology was sincere and he nodded his acceptance. "I don't know what to do, Nick. The woman baffles me. There is an obvious attraction there, yet despite everything, she keeps me at arm's length."

"What are your intentions towards her?" Nick asked.

This gave Richard pause and he realized he hadn't really thought this out. "I want her, Nick. More than I've ever wanted any woman in my life." The truth struck him, the words flowing from his mouth without conscious effort.

"More than Irene?"

"Yes. But, I also want to go back home, and I know I cannot take her with me. I can't even tell her the truth."

"You could try. She may be more open to what you have to say than you think, even if it's far-fetched. I know Angelina - she'd prefer that to lying."

"I agree. She is an honorable woman who's been lied to in the past. I don't want to lie to her. I want to be truthful, but I'm afraid it may be too much for her, and then I'd never see her again."

"When you go back, you'll never see her again anyway. What do you have to lose?" Nick pointed out.

"How do you tell someone you're from the past and you'd like them to return to the sixteenth century with you?" What he needed was some sort of sign. Some divine intervention that would tell him it was all right to approach Angelina with the truth. Somehow, he doubted that was going happen. He hadn't heard from Edna again, although he assumed she must have been keeping track of things somehow. He was frustrated with his situation, but knew he would have to let it go for now.

* * *

What on earth is he trying to hide? Richard remained a complete mystery to Angelina and she was annoyed with herself for even *wanting* to know more about him. After the other night, she had thought she might start peeling back the layers, but he seemed determined to skirt around her questions. Her distrust of men had always been an issue despite the fact that her gut instincts were telling her she might be able to trust *this* man. How could she though, if he was obviously hiding something? Her attraction for him had grown even stronger this past week, knocking down the walls she kept in place to protect herself from hurt and disappointment. Maybe he wasn't any different than all the others who'd tried to win her heart, after all.

Angelina patiently awaited her opportunity, and once Nick and Richard were deeply ensconced in conversation with some of the other members of the team, she had slipped away. Being in constant contact with them - with Richard in particular - was starting to get to her. She was drawn to him like a bee to honey and seemed helpless to stop herself. She definitely needed to have some time to herself and already angry with him for avoiding her questions about the elusive Edna, she was going to slip out while nobody noticed. She seized her chance, hopping into her car for the short drive to a nearby coffee shop. She hoped Richard and Nick might not even notice she was missing. If they did… well, she didn't want to think about that. They'd be furious with her, but she needed some time. With any luck, she'd sneak in to practice again before they even noticed.

As she entered the coffee shop, she noted the lack of patrons. While unusual, it simply meant she could choose a nice spot to sit and enjoy her coffee without interruption. She got a cup of her favorite pumpkin spice coffee and nestled into a corner spot with a view of the door. She was exhausted. They'd been working day and night since Thanksgiving to get ready for the competition and she needed to clear her head and take a deep breath. If she didn't, she wasn't sure how effective she'd be against her own opponent.

As she sat daydreaming, she heard the sound of the coffee shop door opening and closing and then felt the presence of someone standing nearby. Startled back to the present, she nearly jumped out of her seat as she lifted her eyes to see Malcom Granger standing before her.

"This is a surprise, Angelina. I wouldn't expect to see you here all alone." His lips smiled, but the rest of his face remained impassive.

"Malcolm, you scared me," Angelina said.

"That wasn't my intention. May I?" he asked, pointing to the chair opposite her.

"Sure. Please, join me. What are you up to today?" she asked, trying to ignore the unsettled, nervous feeling which had overcome her with Malcolm's arrival.

"The same as you, I would imagine. Getting ready for this weekend." A server brought him a coffee and he barely acknowledged their presence.

Angelina thought the server looked familiar. He didn't work here, or if he did, she hadn't seen him before. She had seen him somewhere though - but she couldn't think where.

"Is everything okay?" Malcolm interrupted her thoughts.

"Yeah, I'm fine, just a bit tired. I needed a little pick me up, so here I am."

Malcolm leaned forward across the table. "Angelina, I wanted to speak with you about something. You're fairly open minded, aren't you?"

It sounded more like a statement than a question and Angelina nodded as she sipped her coffee, which she found she was enjoying less by the minute.

"I have a proposition for you. Hopefully you'll think it a worthwhile endeavor."

"What is it?" She wasn't certain she really wanted to know. After her *date* with him, she had been so freaked out that she had avoided him at every turn.

"I realize our date the other night didn't go well, but you are an intelligent woman and I think I can ask for your help in this matter without worry."

"My curiosity is piqued." She was holding onto her coffee cup for dear life. Malcolm was examining her face, as if he expected to find something there. She wiped at her lips with a napkin.

"I'm sorry. I'm making you uncomfortable. You're beauty has me mesmerized and I'm afraid I'm not very good at disguising my interest in you."

How on earth should she respond to that? She remained mute, and concentrated on staring at the napkin holder.

"Let me get right to the point. Do you believe in time travel?" Malcolm sipped his coffee and patiently waited for her to answer.

Angelina suspected her eyebrows had hit her hairline, she was so stunned by his question. "Time travel? No, I don't think so. Why do you ask?"

"Well, I believe your friends, Richard and Nick, are time travelers from medieval Scotland." He held up a hand to stop her immediate protest. "Before you say anything, I know you must think I've lost my mind, but think about what you know about them, and then think about what you *don't* know."

Angelina's head was spinning. If she didn't know better, it might be possible to believe Nick and Richard were from the past, given their way of speaking, and their reactions to so many things, but since time travel wasn't viable, there had to be another explanation for the questions she had about them. "I think I'd better get back to practice, Malcolm. They'll miss me if I'm gone too long." She began to rise, but Malcolm swiftly grabbed her wrist.

"Please. Just a few more moments of your time."

She sat down warily because he obviously wasn't going to let her leave without creating a scene.

"I'm sure you'll need more time to process what I've just told you, but I'm equally as certain you'll come to agree with my findings. In any case, I need your help to convince them to take me with them back in time."

Angelina was concerned about Malcolm's mental state. He really *believed* this whole time travel thing and unbelievably, he thought he could do it too! "Okay. Let's suppose you're right, and time travel is possible. If Richard and Nick have time travelled to San Francisco, wouldn't they have gone back by now? What's keeping them here?"

"I think it's more *who's* keeping them here. They must know how to get back. There's got to be a portal somewhere in the city, and I need their help to find it."

"Portal?" Angelina repeated blankly.

Malcolm nodded. "Of course. There must be some kind of wormhole that they've travelled through to reach us from their time and consequently, I'm certain they know where it is hidden. I need to find it, Angelina. It's of the utmost importance."

"Why?"

"The Twin Sword, the brother to the Sword of State that I told you about during our dinner date. I must locate the Twin Sword." At her incredulous look, he continued. "Don't you see? The sword has never been found and if I can go back in time to retrieve it before it's lost forever, I will have the find of the century!"

"Malcolm, I think you need some help." She could see he didn't appreciate her pitying look, so she switched to humoring him. "Going back in time could be very dangerous. What if you got stuck there?"

"That's why I need your help, to convince your friends to take me there and bring me back. If anyone can convince them, it's you." He took her hand and gazed pleadingly into her eyes. "Please."

Angelina knew that if she wanted to get out of there safely, she'd have to agree to help him. "Okay. I'll see what I can do."

His face lit with a brilliant smile. "Thank you. You won't regret this. We'll speak again after the tournament."

Angelina rose from her chair with Malcolm still holding her hand. She practically yanked it away, before she quickly exited the coffee shop and headed for her car.

* * *

"Good work," Malcolm said, as Pierce approached him.

"She hasn't spent a moment apart from our two friends, so I knew this would be your only opportunity to speak with her. As soon as I knew she was heading in here, I made the phone call. Do you think she'll do as you ask?" Pierce gazed towards the door where Angelina had just departed.

"She'll tell them, but whether or not they are willing to help is debatable. We'll see. In the meantime, keep following her." Malcolm sipped his coffee, and grimaced because it had grown cold. "Get me another cup before you go."

Pierce did as he was told and Malcolm mulled over his conversation with Angelina. No doubt, she thought he was losing his mind, but he didn't care. He was very used to getting what he wanted and he was quite certain he would this time as well. More than anything, he wanted the Twin Sword, but once he had that, Angelina was next on his list. He didn't like the look in her eye when she looked at him - the one that resembled a frightened rabbit. No, he wanted her respect and adulation, which he knew he would have once he had the sword. Power and money were an irresistible combination to most women, and he was sure Angelina Lawson was no different than any other.

* * *

Richard was beside himself with worry. Angelina had waited until both he and Nick were engrossed in conversation and had obviously slipped away. Her car was gone and she wasn't responding to Nick's frantic phone calls. The other students had all left for the day and he was just about to head out to comb the surrounding area when the door opened and she strolled in as if nothing had happened.

"Where have you been?" His worry was translating into anger and Angelina was not receiving it well.

"I had to get away from you for a little while. I needed to clear my head. Sorry I didn't ask permission first," she snapped.

"Permission would not have been granted! You know you are in danger, that someone is following you - following all of us, and yet you still decided to run off at the first opportunity! Did you think that I wouldn't care? That I wouldn't be concerned for your wellbeing?" His hands were fisted at his sides as he desperately controlled the urge to shake some sense into her. She had to see that it had been wrong to leave the way she had. "What if something had happened to you?" His voice softened, revealing his true concern.

"It would be my own fault then. I can take care of myself."

If she'd stomped her foot at that moment, it wouldn't have been out of character. He'd heard that statement before from Angelina and she was beginning to sound like a petulant child. He was worried about her, couldn't she see that? It meant he *cared*.

After minutes of silence between them, she appeared to come to that realization on her own. "I'm sorry, Richard. It was wrong of me."

He didn't want to be angry with her and he didn't want *her* to be angry with him. He wanted to hold her close and protect her. It was what he knew how to do and if it meant his heart could stop racing in his chest, it was what he hoped she'd allow him to do.

Chapter 18

HAVING MALCOLM TURN UP OUT of nowhere had made Angelina realize she needed to be more careful. Perhaps he had been the one who was following her, or maybe was having her followed. The more she thought about it, the more she suspected she was right. "Richard, please don't be angry with me. I'm okay. Nothing happened and I promise I won't do it again," she tried to soothe him. He was really very sweet for thinking it was necessary to protect her. How could she blame him for that? Of course, once she told him whom she'd seen while she was out, she was sure he'd blow a gasket.

"There you are," Nick called from the office. "Did you nae think we might be worried about ye?"

"Don't you start," she answered. "I've already heard all about it from Richard. I hope you two can forgive me. My independent streak came out and I ran for it. I've already promised Richard I won't do it again." She eyed the two of them warily, before telling them the rest of her story. "I have to tell you something and I hope you won't get all medieval on me, but I went to grab a cup of coffee…"

"And you didnae bring me one?" Nick teased.

Richard threw him a stern look. "Continue, please."

"Well, I sat down to enjoy a moment of alone time and the next thing I knew, Malcolm Granger was standing there. It was as if he knew I was going to be there alone."

"My instincts were right," Richard said. "He *is* the one following you, and his cohorts are probably following Nick and me."

"I don't think he's following me personally, that would be beneath Malcolm. He has a lot of people he pays to do things exactly like that."

"What did he want?" Richard asked, and Angelina could see he was making a concerted effort to sound unbothered by what he'd just heard.

"Well, this is really weird… but he thinks that the two of you are time travelers." She eyed them both, searching their faces for any hint that Malcolm might have been telling the truth, but they both remained stone faced.

"Time travelers!" Nick finally laughed. "That's ridiculous and I hope ye told him so."

"I did, but he really believes it. He wants me to help convince the two of you to take him back in time, so he can get hold of some sword he thinks has been lost to history."

"Did he tell ye what sword?" Nick asked.

"The Twin Sword," Angelina answered and gave them a brief description of what Malcolm had told her about the sword he sought. "He said it has never been recovered and he wants to go back in time to get it, before it's lost forever. So, since he thinks you two are time travelers, he wants you to help him go back and forth."

Neither man said anything. Richard stared at his feet and Nick stared up at the ceiling. She didn't imagine they'd find the answers they were looking for in either place.

"He said he'll talk to me more about it after the competition. Maybe the two of you should have a conversation with him. I don't like being stuck in the middle of this nonsense."

"She's right," Richard said. "Let's intervene after the competition. Keep him away from Angelina."

"Agreed," Nick stated. "In the meantime, Angelina, please dinnae wander off on yer own again. Poor Richard's heart cannae take the strain." He glanced Richard's way and chuckled at the look of outrage on his face. Nick apparently knew exactly how to push Richard's buttons and Angelina was more aware than ever that Richard had strong feelings for her. What she was going to do with that knowledge, was still an unknown.

* * *

"I need to go for a walk, a long walk," Angelina stated. "I'm feeling claustrophobic after being cooped up all day. One of you is going to have to go with me, or I'm going to head off alone." She knew that would get an immediate response and sure enough, it did.

"I'll go," Richard volunteered.

"What a surprise," Nick added, with his usual chuckle. "Keep in touch, so I know yer alright."

"We will. I have my phone." She happily grabbed her coat from the hook by the door. Angelina took long walks almost every day and when she missed a day or two, she got to the stage where she was ready to crawl out of her skin. Donning her coat, she glanced to the door where Richard was already waiting for her. "Let's go."

They closed the door behind them and started down the street. Angelina figured this might be a good time to see what else she could discover about him.

"The tournament is tomorrow. Are you excited?" she asked.

"Excited? No. When meeting another man in combat, whether it's a real battle or a mock one, I prefer to remain as even-tempered as possible. Some like to get themselves all worked up into a frenzy, but I prefer to let the battle guide my responses."

"Real battle? When have you ever engaged in real battle?"

Richard hesitated briefly before answering. "A time or two."

She could see he wasn't going to volunteer the information she was seeking. She'd have to dig for it. "Only a time or two?"

"It was nothing of interest. I wouldn't want to bore you with the details." He took her arm and escorted her across the street.

Why was it that every time he touched her, she could think of nothing but the sensation of having his hands on her? It threw her off her thought processes and she took a moment to regain control. When she did, she continued to pepper him with questions, which he adeptly evaded. She got the impression he was very good at it.

"Isn't it beautiful today? The air is crisp and the sky is so blue - I love the autumn months." They entered Golden Gate Park and they were walking briskly past the riding arena, when Angelina heard a woman shout frantically. Richard took her hand and they rushed toward the source, only to discover a woman who seemed clearly out of her depth with the horse she was attempting to ride.

"May I assist you?" Richard asked the startled woman. Without saying a word, she handed the reins over to Richard. He spoke softly and soothingly to the great beast. "He reminds me of my own horse, Arion. He needs some exercise to work off some of his energy, before you attempt to ride him." He deftly escorted the horse into the riding ring and mounted without any trouble. The horse seemed to be thinking about misbehaving, but when he realized that Richard was no novice, thought better of it. Richard put him into a full gallop and raced around the ring. He put him through his paces and worked him until the horse had quieted considerably. Angelina was enthralled by what he was doing and incredibly impressed by his skill. Coming to the side of the ring, Richard dismounted and held the reins out to the woman, who seemed nervous. "He's quite tired now. I doubt he'll give you any more trouble." He gave her a leg up and once she was settled, he said, "Don't be nervous. He can sense your anxiety. You must be a strong leader for him, as it's what he needs. If you're nervous or frightened, he'll follow suit."

The woman's eyes never left Richard as he spoke. "I understand what you're telling me, but I find it hard not to be afraid."

"Let him run around until he's tired before you ride him. That will help and I would suggest you not go riding on your own again."

"He's always been so good for me in the past. I thought it would be fine to come here to ride today. When he started acting up it scared me." She seemed embarrassed to admit this.

"It's a brisk day and a little wind up his nose had him feeling good. He was merely celebrating his good fortune to be here today. As I said before, don't go riding on your own - accidents can happen even to the most seasoned riders and if there's no one nearby to aid you, you may find yourself in a very bad predicament.

She nodded and turned the horse, walking him around the ring without incident. When she glanced at Richard again, she was beaming. "He's being so good!"

"He will be. Do you mind if we stay and watch you ride?" Richard asked. It was obvious he didn't think it was a good idea to leave the woman alone.

"No. Not at all. I'll feel better knowing you're here. Would you mind helping me with some problems I'm having? With the horse I mean," she giggled.

Richard proceeded to answer her questions about keeping the horse on the bit, sitting the trot and flying lead changes. Angelina watched in wonder as he guided her through each answer until she seemed to swing from timid and hesitant, to completely confident and in control. When they were finished, he helped her down from the horse and Angelina suffered a twinge of jealousy that Richard's hands were not on *her* waist. It was becoming clearer and clearer that Richard was a very special man.

"Now, remember what I've told you and you'll be fine, Noreen," Richard said. He removed the bridle from the horse and handed it to the woman.

"Thank you again. If it wasn't for you, I don't know what would have happened." Noreen leaned into her truck for her purse. She pulled out some cash, which she held out to Richard. "Please take this. You spent a full hour with me and gave me some invaluable advice."

"I couldn't possibly. It was not my intention to be paid for my services." Richard folded his arms across his chest, but Noreen was determined and she tucked the money between his arms. "I'd love another lesson some time, do you have a card?"

Richard appeared thoroughly confused by that question and he looked to Angelina for guidance. "No, he doesn't. He's not a riding instructor."

Noreen seemed surprised. "Well, you certainly should be," she said, directing her answer in Richard's direction. "Here. Take mine." She handed him a business card. "If you have the time, call me and maybe we can schedule a time to get together."

Richard did that funny little bow thing that he always did. "Thank you, m'lady, I will."

Angelina grabbed his hand and yanked him away. "I think she wanted more than riding lessons from you," she muttered.

Richard cocked an eyebrow. "I don't understand."

"Come on. You're not going to tell me that you didn't catch on." Angelina was suddenly feeling very possessive of Richard and snatched the card out of his hand, throwing it in the nearest trash bin. "The nerve of her, coming on to you like that! And right in front of me! What if I had been your girlfriend, or wife, or something?"

"What on earth are you speaking of, Angelina, and why do you seem so angry?" Richard questioned.

Was he teasing her? She couldn't be sure, but there seemed to be a glint in his eye and a slight curl to his lip that could be the beginnings of a smile. "Are you having fun at my expense?" she demanded.

"Why would you think that?" He wrapped an arm around her shoulders and drew her close, tucking her head into his chest.

And there it was again, that sensation she always felt when she was too close to him. Was he aware of what he did to her?

* * *

Richard knew jealousy when he saw it. He'd been a jealous man for most of his adult life, but he liked the way it looked on Angelina. It showed she cared and didn't want to share him with anyone else. He wondered if she was aware of it, or if she would continue to lie to herself about her feelings. Loosening his hold, he waited to see if Angelina would move away and was surprised when she didn't, holding on for a few moments longer. Finally relinquishing her hold on him, her eyelashes fluttered and she peeked up at him with a shy smile on her lips, her hands resting lightly on his abdomen. Richard laughed out loud and swept her up into his arms, twirling her around and around. When was the last time he had felt so light and carefree? He couldn't ever remember a time when he had. Angelina held on tightly, her arms locked around his neck and a wide smile on her face. He couldn't help what he was about to do, any more than he could help breathing. He drew her up closer and lowering his head, his lips met hers in a hot and passionate kiss, which Angelina accepted fully. She moaned and positioned herself so that her legs were wrapped around his waist, allowing him to kiss her more deeply, his tongue testing the crease of her lips, which she parted to give him access. Richard took a few steps forward with her in his arms, staring into her eyes with a look of desire that could not be denied. He backed Angelina into a nearby tree to hold her in place as his mouth ravaged hers. He wanted her desperately, and her answering kisses seemed to be a signal of her willingness. He would have taken her right there, but thought better of it as he restrained himself and gently lowered her to her feet instead. Breathing deeply, he threw his head back and closed his eyes, doing his best to think of anything but Angelina. If he didn't find something else to focus on, he'd never be able to turn around - his erection was such that it was almost bursting from his pants. He thought about God, his home and his mother and finally things began to settle down enough for him to step away from her. She looked so beautiful, her skin slightly flushed and her lips red and swollen - and her breasts heaved delightfully with each breath she took. He mentally shook himself and had to again think of anything else to keep from picking up where he had just left off. Being out in the open would not have been a problem back home, but here, where there were so many people always about, it was quite unseem-ly. He would remain a gentleman, no matter how much he wished he wasn't.

* * *

Damn it! Why did he stop kissing her again? He wasn't running away from her, he wasn't apologizing, but he had a rather pained expression on his face. Angelina was very confused by it all. It was hard to hide and she could certainly *feel* that he wanted her. What should she do? They were constantly playing a game of push and pull. She wanted him, but she didn't *want* to want him. She was sending him conflicting signals and expecting him to read them. She'd never been in a situation like this before, so she did what came naturally and that was to comfort him. Reaching up, she cradled his face in the palm of her hand and he covered it with his own, caressing her. His eyes finally met hers and Angelina knew in that very instant that something had changed. Her carefully guarded heart was revealing itself. She wanted more from Richard. More than she'd ever imagined was possible.

Richard lowered her hand and placed an arm around her shoulders guiding her back onto the pathway. Angelina didn't care where they were going, as long as he continued to hold her close by his side. They headed out of the park and crossed the Great Highway, walking through the sand dunes and onto Ocean Beach, where they settled on a driftwood log and gazed out onto the sparkling sapphire water and crashing waves. They weren't alone by any stretch of the imagination, but they only had eyes for each other.

Richard stared deeply into her eyes, his gaze never faltering. "The beauty of this place, while unusual to me, cannot be denied, but it pales in comparison to the woman I see before me."

Angelina wasn't sure how to respond. His words were the most genuine and honest she had heard from any man she'd ever known. It brought tears to her eyes, which she quickly blinked away.

Richard was very observant though. "Are those tears I see?" He brushed an errant drop from her cheek with his thumb. "I apologize. Perhaps I've overstepped my bounds once again. My goal was not to make you cry, but to let you know you are cherished."

The concerned expression on his face was not the one Angelina wanted to see. She wanted to replace it with the one she'd seen only moments before. "Not sad tears or angry tears. You've touched my heart. I've kept it well sheltered over the years, but it doesn't want to remain shuttered away anymore. No one has ever uttered such sweet and lovely words to me."

Relief flooded Richard's face and Angelina could see it in his brilliant, yet rare smile. She found herself overcome with emotion and rather than cry, she chose to laugh. To laugh at the silliness of her life, prior to this moment. To laugh at all the time she had spent hiding from the world so she couldn't be hurt. To laugh at how good it felt, to be seen through fresh eyes.

At first, it seemed Richard might have thought she lost her mind, but then he joined her and the two of them laughed until their sides ached. "Do you know how long it's been, since I've had the opportunity to laugh like that?" He held her face between his hands. "Thank you, love. I am so very grateful to have met you on this strange journey I find myself on."

A burden had been lifted from both their shoulders it seemed.

Chapter 19

Zeke Barret was holding his own against Gabe Adamson from Malcolm Granger's team. Richard kept a close watch and was happy to note that Zeke was employing many of the techniques he had been taught. Gabe seemed to be tiring, so it was only a matter of time before Zeke would get the better of him. So far, every one of Nick's team had won against their opponents. Zeke was the last one to fight before Richard and Nick would go up against Malcolm Granger and Pierce Holmes. Richard couldn't wait to get this finished. Nick would have the money to repair his warehouse, and Richard could devote his time to returning home. No matter how much he adored Angelina, he couldn't continue to live in this strange modern world. It would be difficult to leave Angelina behind, but Richard couldn't even think about bringing up the subject of time travel with her, let alone trying to convince her to go back with him. She'd scoffed when she'd told him and Nick about Malcolm's desire to travel to the past, and he knew he'd never convince her that time travel was truly possible. His greatest fear however, was what would happen to her after he left. Malcolm Granger had shown a keen interest in her, and Richard hated the idea of leaving her alone to fend for herself against him.

"You're deep in thought," Angelina said when she approached him. She had been the only woman in their group to go up against one of Malcolm's men and she had taken his sword out of his hand in record time.

"I was thinking about how well you did today," he answered.

"Then why the scowl?" She tipped her head to one side, and her beguiling smile melted his heart.

"I'm very proud of you, Angelina. My scowl was not for you, but for our adversary."

"Ah, yes. Malcolm. Then it's a justified scowl after all, but I'd hate to see you adding wrinkles to that pretty face of yours because of him."

Richard cocked an eyebrow in question. Sometimes, he simply had no idea what Angelina was talking about.

"Didn't your mother ever tell you that your face might get stuck like that?"

Richard laughed. "Yes. She did tell me. So I take it you don't like my scowl?"

"I'm very enamored with your face, no matter the expression." She was flirting with him and he enjoyed it. Yesterday had been a revelation to them both. Angelina had let her walls come crashing down, and Richard had learned how to love a woman without the need to possess her. The knowledge that he had come to love Angelina was something he was only just now admitting to himself. No matter what happened in the coming days, he would always have that. He, Richard Jefford, a man known for his jealous rages, had learned how to love a woman without expecting anything in return - but he was pleasantly surprised to know Angelina had feelings for him, too. They hadn't made love again since that night at her house, but they had made plans to explore their relationship further after the tournament was over.

"We have some time before the next round. It looks like Zeke was another winner for us. There's no way Malcolm can take home the prize today, but he'll be doubly difficult to defeat because he's angry."

"I thought you said that it was better to keep your emotions under control in battle."

"I did. That is what works best for me and for most, but an angry bull is an angry bull. One who must be carefully watched, because their fury makes them dangerous. I believe it works against him in the long run, but that does not make the fight any easier to win."

They walked around the Faire hand-in-hand. Richard was like a young lad once again, seeing everything from a much more optimistic perspective. Angelina had done that for him. They found a place to sit and watch the little ones, who were battling stuffed dummies with their wooden swords. Some were being led around on little ponies, the goal being to poke their sword through some strategically placed rings. They would all receive ribbons and prizes for their efforts and Richard enjoyed watching them go through their paces. What would it be like, to have a child of his own? He realized he wanted that more than anything, well almost anything. He wanted Angelina more.

"I think I was born in the wrong time period," Angelina casually observed.

Richard nearly fell off his seat. "I'm sorry, what did you say?"

"I said, I think I was born in the wrong time period. I've always dreamed of living in medieval times." She searched his face, for what, he didn't know, but he schooled his expression so that he didn't look as astonished as he felt. "I love the clothing, the chivalrous knights, and the castles. I know it wasn't all sunshine and lollipops," she added, and Richard tried not to look confused by her choice of words, "but I really think it's where I belong. I mean, *belonged.*" She smiled up at him. "Do you know what I mean?"

"Surprisingly, I do. It's where I belong as well."

"Wouldn't it be amazing? I wish there really was a way to experience it."

There is, my lady fair. Richard had to stop himself from saying the words out loud. She'd never understand that he really was from that time or that she could possibly return there with him. He didn't even know if that was ultimately a part of Edna's plan and the maddening woman had been absent ever since that first night she'd spoken with him.

"I think that's why I love these fairs and the medieval martial arts so much." The wistful expression on her face had Richard thinking about what it would be like, to have her in his world as his wife. They'd live in the family castle, of course, and they'd have children together and build a sweet and beautiful family. He could live a respectable life and finally put his past behind him.

"Richard!" Nick called. "We're up next."

He'd have to put the dream on hold for now. He took Angelina's hand and walked with her back to Nick's side, where he stood with Malcolm and Pierce.

"I hope you're both ready to get your asses kicked," Malcolm said smugly. "Your team might have won the $10,000, but neither of *you* are going to leave here a winner." Both he and Pierce sneered at them as they entered the ring.

Nick chuckled and patted Richard on the back. "I don't believe Mr. Granger or his friend will be verra happy with the outcome of this event."

"Agreed," Richard nodded. He walked to the center of the arena, and Nick followed. The four men saluted one another with their swords and then assumed their fighting stances opposite each other. Since this was the most anticipated match of the day, the area surrounding the arena was jammed with onlookers. Richard could see Angelina and the rest of their team, standing by the gate. He focused on his opponent and deliberately put everything else out of his thoughts. Their carefully choreographed dance began. He and Nick had worked on this together and he felt certain that they would have no problems defeating Malcolm and his man. If they could get one of the men out of the competition, that would leave the other to fight the two of them alone. Richard was confident there was no possibility anyone could beat them. They had been a feared pair in their own time, but of course, no one here was aware of that. Richard believed the crowd had no idea they were in for quite the show.

The rules of the game called for no bloodshed. As Quinn had warned, Malcolm and Pierce *were* using real swords. Richard and Nick had theirs as well, but they were experienced swordsmen who could wield their weapons without harm coming to any one of them. It wasn't until they started parrying back and forth, when both Richard and Nick realized they might be the only ones following the rule to avoid bloodshed. Malcolm and Pierce seemed intent on the exact opposite. Richard quickly exchanged glances with Nick, who nodded and then began to battle in earnest. Richard did the same, engaging Pierce, blocking his every blow. The clang of the metal was dulled only by the sound of the audience, calling out to them in surprise at the ferocity of the exchange. Richard spun to avoid Pierce and nearly knocked the sword from Pierce's hand on his return blow, but much to his astonishment, Pierce held a dagger in his left hand, as did Malcolm. That was not part of the competition rules, but obviously these two were moving far beyond competing for a prize. They were out for blood. In the split second when Richard glanced in Nick's direction, Pierce jabbed at him with his blade, making contact with Richard's arm and slicing it open. The crowd gasped, but Richard remained unfazed. It only served to make him focus more closely on his opponent, whom he was determined was going to go down in defeat with but a few more strokes of his blade. Richard could kill the man, if the desire took him. It would be easy, but that was not what this was supposed to be about. Of course, Malcolm and Pierce had no idea this was merely a game being played by two true medieval warriors against two men who thought they were, but who had no idea what they were truly up against..

"Are ye ready, Richard?" Nick called as they continued to fight.

"I believe I am," Richard answered.

"Alright then, let's finish this."

With a fury that neither Malcolm nor Pierce had been expecting, the two friends went at them, sending them flying backwards to escape the blades slashing towards them. There was only so far they could retreat, and when they were up against the edge of the arena, Nick and Richard simultaneously flipped their opponent's swords up into the air, where they spun for a moment, before landing with a thud in the dirt. The crowd cheered, clapping their hands and stomping their feet. Next came the daggers, which were no match for Richard and Nick's sword skills as they were wrestled away from Malcolm and Pierce and joined the swords on the ground.

Malcolm was visibly furious as he grabbed Pierce by the arm and strode angrily from the arena. Before Richard had a moment to think, Angelina was by his side, examining his arm. "We need to get you over to the EMT. I think you might need stitches."

Deliriously happy, Richard tapped the tip of her nose with his finger and winked to let her know he was okay.

Angelina hovered over him like a mother hen as he sat there, loving every minute of her sweet concern. He wasn't fazed by the stitches in the least. He'd been injured before, much worse if truth be told, and he had the scars to prove it. What he felt even more keenly, was the way Angelina bit her lower lip and held tightly to his hand, squeezing a little harder with each stitch.

"I don't think I've ever had a patient who didn't at least grimace while I was doing this," the EMT stated as he cleaned the wound one final time and then put his equipment away. "Those will dissolve on their own, but try not to get them wet while you're showering."

Richard didn't respond. He was too busy memorizing every inch of Angelina's face.

* * *

The sight of blood oozing through Richard's shirtsleeve had Angelina stifling a scream and cursing Malcolm Granger for what had apparently been a carefully orchestrated attempt to hurt Nick and Richard. The two men had swiftly disappeared into the crowd and it was lucky they did, because otherwise she'd have drawn her own sword and challenged them.

"My sweet Angelina, worry not. It is but a minor wound and your man has done an admirable job of sewing me up. There will hardly be a scar visible when it heals." Richard gently lifted her chin with his finger. "I'm fine," he repeated.

Tears were brimming against her eyelashes and threatening to spill, as Richard pulled her into his embrace, loving the feel of her as she molded herself to him. He softly kissed the top of her head as she sniffled and wiped at her eyes.

"I need a tissue. Will you walk with me to the ladies room?"

"Of course I will. I cannot bear to take my eyes from you, not even for a moment."

The sky was dark now, but the Faire continued, with music and laughter filling the night air. She hadn't seen Nick, but he would definitely be the life of the party, as he had been in years past. "I'll be right out."

Richard released her from his grasp. "I'll be waiting."

Angelina found some paper towels, blotting her tears dry and examining her puffy eyes in the small mirror above the sink. In an effort to erase all signs of her crying, she ran cold water and splashed her face, before drying it and heading back outside.

"Richard—" A hand came out of the darkness to cover her mouth and too late, she noticed Richard sprawled out on the ground in front of her. She struggled to free herself in an effort to go to him, but found that her arms were being held on either side by two large men whose faces she couldn't see in the dark. Another, much larger man picked Richard up and threw him over his shoulder and then she heard an all-too familiar voice.

"There's no use struggling, Angelina," Malcolm Granger whispered in her ear. "This way," he called to his men. As they walked, the sounds of the Faire faded until Angelina knew they were no longer within shouting distance and no one would come looking for them for quite some time. Her heart sank. Where was Malcolm taking them? What did he plan to do with them? Was he so angry because he lost the final battle? She had plenty of questions, but was unable to voice them as Pierce Holmes removed his hand from her mouth and then quickly replaced it with duct tape. Fear and anger bubbled through her chest, but she remembered what Richard told her and settled her mind, removing those two emotions and leaving her head clear to fight this battle when the time came.

Chapter 20

MALCOLM GRANGER HAD RECENTLY PURCHASED an old San Francisco restaurant, one that resembled a medieval castle on the outside and with much renovation, now resembled one on the inside as well. It sat perched on the top of a hill, looking very out of place in modern day San Francisco. The car pulled into a dimly lit underground parking area where the doors were opened and Angelina was ushered out of the car. Richard, who had been slumped in the seat next to her, was dragged from the car and once again thrown over the same man's shoulder for the walk to the very non-medieval elevator that would take them upstairs.

"What do you think of my new castle?" Malcolm asked.

The duct tape over her mouth made it impossible to answer the question, but Angelina hoped the glare she sent in Malcolm's direction would speak volumes about her opinion.

"Oh, I'm sorry, I forgot to remove the tape. Please, don't scream when I take it off. It'll do you absolutely no good." Malcolm ripped the tape from her mouth and Angelina swallowed back the urge to cry out at the pain. "Watch your step getting out of the elevator."

Angelina made her way into what she assumed would be the equivalent of a great hall in most legitimate castles. It was decorated with many of the medieval artifacts that Malcolm was well known for having collected. For future reference, she memorized her surroundings, knowing that it might come in handy when she and Richard made their escape. There was no question in her mind - they *would* be escaping.

"Well? You haven't said anything. Do you like it?" Malcolm stood in front of a large stone fireplace that when lit probably heated the entire floor.

Angelina took the opportunity to glance around the room, noting the position of doors, windows and other possible escape routes. "It looks like you," she said reluctantly.

"It does, doesn't it? I was very happy when this place came on the market and I was able to purchase it for a song. Many months of work have led to it becoming the most authentic medieval castle in the United States. It's almost complete. The only thing it needs is the Twin Sword, and you're going to help me get it. It will then hold a place of honor above the fireplace."

"I don't know how you expect me to help you get something which has never been found." Angelina glanced worriedly in Richard's direction. He hadn't moved yet and it concerned her. "What did you do to Richard?"

"Don't worry, he'll wake up soon. Just a little hit on the head, nothing for you to worry about." Malcolm crossed the room to face Angelina. "I'm afraid I can't let you have the run of the place, for obvious reasons. I have accommodations for you upstairs. You and your friend will stay there, until you agree to help me."

"Help you go back in time? That's absolutely ludicrous, not to mention impossible," Angelina protested.

"Is it now? I'm sure your two friends can tell you all about it, and how truly possible it is. I'll be contacting Nick shortly, to let him know that I have you both. The ransom will be his cooperation in returning to sixteenth century Scotland with me to retrieve the sword and then bring me back again.

"What makes you think Nick is a time traveller?"

"He told me so."

Angelina couldn't hide her astonishment. "I don't believe you."

"It's true. He was quite drunk when he volunteered the information. At first I thought it just the ramblings of a man who was very inebriated, but after I thought about it for a while, I took note of his odd language and behavior, and I started looking into it further. The information that I've gathered leads me to believe what he told me that night was true." Malcolm walked over to a nearby table and poured himself a glass of wine. "My man has been scouring Great Britain, looking to acquire the Twin Sword, with no luck. Once I heard Nick's strange tale, I requested some genealogy investigation and the results confirm your friend, Nick, is definitely from sixteenth century Scotland. And so is this gentleman here." Malcolm gestured toward Richard's prone figure.

Angelina fought against the urge to shake her head in utter disbelief. Malcolm was insane. What he had suggested couldn't possibly be true, but even as she denied it to herself, she realized that both Nick and Richard *had* appeared out of nowhere and neither of them spoke about their backgrounds, except in generalities. Wasn't she, in fact, always telling them not to go getting *all medieval* on her? Angelina simply couldn't wrap her head around it. She was starting to feel as out of touch with reality as Malcolm clearly was.

"Nothing to say on the topic?" Malcolm asked. He chuckled to himself and took a large gulp of wine. "Pierce, take our guests upstairs please. I'm not in the mood for entertaining at the moment, and I must craft a ransom note for our friend, Nick." He turned his back on Angelina and she found herself being marched to a narrow spiral staircase by Pierce and a second burly man, who had been holding her in a secure grip. A third man carried Richard, following along behind. Angelina could see the men's faces clearly now, and recognized them as part of Malcolm's team they'd fought today.

* * *

Richard heard the entire conversation as he pretended to remain unconscious. His head was throbbing, but his thoughts were anything but muddled. As soon as the door closed, he could sense Angelina hovering over him and he opened his eyes warily.

Relief flooded her pretty features. "Oh, thank God! I was wondering why you weren't waking up."

"I've been conscious the whole time. I'm sorry I frightened you, but I felt it best to continue the ruse."

"So you heard everything he said?" Angelina helped Richard up from the floor and gently examined the back of his head. Her fingers came away from his scalp, sticky with blood. "Today's not your day. Let me see if I can find something to clean that up with." Richard watched as she left his side and scanned the room. Elaborately decorated, every last detail, down to the hardware on the doors, screamed medieval. This must be a guest room, as it was outfitted with a large bed covered in furs. At the foot of the bed was an intricately carved bench covered in burgundy velvet. The room looked as if it should be in a museum display. In the far corner was a door and she grabbed the handle, before turning back to him with a worried frown. "I'm hoping this is a bathroom. I'll be right back."

A few moments later, she returned with bandages, a small scissors, and some disinfectant - everything needed to take care of Richard's wound, and she urged him to sit down on the bench at the foot of the bed.

"We must plan our escape," Richard said when Angelina gingerly began washing the blood from the back of his head.

"While I was in the bathroom, I noticed another door. It's locked, but if we can find a way to open it, we might be able to find a way out of here. I've tried to pay attention to the position of every door and window that I've seen, in hopes that the information would come in handy."

"It's smart that you did. It may be the only way we'll escape."

Angelina studied his head closely. "The cut's not too big. It definitely doesn't require any stitches and it seems to have stopped bleeding. How do you feel?"

"Aside from a damned headache, fine." He smiled warmly at her, and could see from the way the frown creasing her forehead disappeared, that it went a long way to making her feel better about their predicament. "I'm sure Nick has noticed we're missing by now. He'll be searching for us, even before that fool sends him the ransom note he mentioned."

"I hope Nick will be okay, I don't want him to get hurt trying to rescue us."

"Nick will be careful. Believe it or not, we've been in somewhat similar circumstances some years ago."

"You were kidnapped?" Angelina said doubtfully.

"Not us. A friend," he explained. "Nick and I came up with a plan to retrieve him, without having to pay the ransom. It was actually quite clever. I'm sure Nick will remember and if possible use the same plan again. It's quite fortuitous that Malcolm has constructed this building into a medieval fortress. Nick will know exactly what to do and in the meantime, we will not stand idly by and wait. We'll do our best to secure our own release."

* * *

Angelina's head was spinning as Richard spoke so matter-of-factly about kidnappings and ransoms, and medieval fortresses. *Was Malcolm right? Were Richard and Nick from another time?* She just had to know the truth. "Richard, is Malcolm telling the truth? Are you and Nick really time travelers?"

There was a long pause before he responded, and Angelina saw the tiny droop in his shoulders that confirmed the answer before he spoke. "I'm afraid we are," he answered.

Her shock must have shown on her face, because Richard spoke in a rush as he tried to explain.

"Please, don't be angry with us. We kept it quiet, for your protection as well as our own. It was best that no one know the truth about us, because frankly, most people wouldn't believe it. You can see the problems we're facing now, after Nick's drunken confession to Granger."

"I'm sorry, but I'm still having a hard time believing any of this could even remotely have a chance of being true."

Richard watched her patiently. "I give you my word, Angelina. It's the truth. I am Sir Richard Jefford and I was sent travelling through time to your modern day San Francisco. I was born in the year 1484.

She searched his face for any sign that he was lying to her, but there was nothing but honesty in his clear gaze. Angelina suddenly had a desperate need to sit down because her legs were weak and her head filled with a strange buzzing sound. She stumbled across to the bed, and flopped down, where she sat staring aimlessly into the distance.

* * *

Richard knelt in front of her. Taking her hands in his and bringing them to his lips, he kissed the palms of both. "This is not the way I would have chosen to tell you my story. There is more to tell, if you care to hear it." He was afraid to tell her the whole of it, but knew honesty would be best and if he lost her because of this, then so be it - it was no more than he deserved.

"Knowing you're really from the sixteenth century is about all I can handle right now. That would make you over five hundred years old!" She exclaimed in disbelief. "Can we save the rest for another time?"

She seemed weary to her bones and more vulnerable than he'd ever seen her. Since he'd known her, Angelina had always been so strong and in control. It took every ounce of his self-restraint not to scoop her up and cradle her in his arms, but he was frightened of how she might react. "May I hold you in my arms while you rest?"

He'd never felt the need to ask before, but his respect for her was deeply felt and if she didn't want him near her, he would not force the issue.

Angelina nodded and lay down on the bed, making enough room for Richard to join her. He wrapped her in his arms and cradled her head on his chest. "Sleep if you can. Tomorrow may require us to be at our best."

"What about Malcolm?"

"Don't worry about him, I don't think he'll be bothering us tonight. It's late and after the beating Nick and I gave him and his friend, he no doubt needs his rest as well. Close your eyes, love." Once again, he kissed the top of her head. As he nuzzled her hair, Richard closed his mind to all thoughts of Malcolm Granger and their predicament and breathed deeply and steadily, knowing that if he was relaxed, it would help Angelina to relax. The smell of her perfume wafted around his nose and when the sound of her breathing grew deeper and rhythmic, he knew Angelina would soon be asleep. He closed his own eyes, knowing the morning would be with them too quickly.

* * *

Nick paced back and forth in front of Angelina's truck. The parking lot of the tournament was empty, with the exception of his team. They had refused to leave him, but he was at a loss as to what he should do next. *Where could they be? Why didn't they tell me they were leaving?* Their disappearance made no sense whatsoever and the fact that the truck was still here only served to increase his unease.

"What do you think happened?" Zeke questioned.

"I have nae idea, but I dinnae believe it to be anything good. Neither of them would up and leave without telling someone. When last I saw them, Richard was having his arm tended to by the EMT. I had to go and accept the award we won and when I came back they were gone. Did any of ye see where they may have gone?"

"Afraid not," Wade answered. Kyle and Jason shook their heads.

"So, no one saw a thing. I suspect our Mr. Granger may have had something to do with this, though I cannae be sure. The bastard hates my guts, and he went out of his way to cheat during the tournament, I wouldnae put anything past him." Nick threw his equipment into the back of the truck. "If it was him, where would he have taken them?"

"I heard Granger just remodeled an old restaurant, one that looks like a medieval castle and he's living in it. Maybe he took them there. But what do you think he wants with them?" Zeke's puzzled expression mirrored everyone else's.

"He told Angelina that he believes I'm a time traveller and he wants to go back in time to recover a special sword for his collection-" Nick stopped abruptly and pressed his thumb and forefinger to his temples. He was so frazzled, he'd spoken without thinking, and now his group were looking at him as though he'd grown a tail and two horns.

The expressions around him ranged from completely puzzled to outright curiosity. "So, are you? A time traveller, I mean?" Wade asked slowly.

Nick wasn't sure how to respond, but he'd already said far too much, and there was no taking it back. He felt the need to be honest with these men. "Aye. I am."

Silence descended on the group as they all digested what Nick had said.

"Well, say something," Nick pleaded. "Dinnae just stand there, looking bewildered."

Kyle was the first to find his voice. "Wow," he said. "So, how'd you end up here?"

The others all nodded their apparent satisfaction with Kyle's initial question and Nick leaned back against the truck and told them everything. When he was done, he was surprised that they were all still there, and hadn't taken off for the hills upon hearing his outrageous story.

"So how do we get them back?" Jayson questioned.

"I didnae think it would be 'we'," Nick admitted with a faint smile.

"We're going to help you, of course. Angelina and Richard are our friends, too," Kyle said.

"I'd be verra grateful for your help. I have an idea, but I think we need to wait for Granger to tell us what he wants, to be certain we're on the right track. I should go home and wait to hear from him, but I dinnae ken how to drive this blasted truck."

"Do you have the keys?" Zeke questioned.

"I'm afraid not." Nick peered in the driver's side window, hoping one of them had accidentally left a door unlocked, but to no avail.

Zeke stepped forward. "Lucky for you, I know how to get inside and I also know how to hot wire the truck."

Nick furrowed his brow at Zeke's response, but had to admit he was impressed when within seconds, the door to the truck was open and Zeke had positioned himself under the steering wheel where he fiddled with some wires. The truck roared to life and Zeke settled into the driver's seat with a wide grin. "Get in."

Nick sat in the passenger seat, while the rest of the group got into the back. "I'll nae ask how you knew what to do with the truck," Nick said wryly.

"You probably don't want to know," Zeke replied.

Once they reached Nick's home, the men piled into the living room. Wade pulled out his cell phone. "I'm going to see if I can find any info on that castle."

"Good idea," Jayson said, making himself comfortable on the sofa. "The more we know, the better it will be for us."

"Here it is," Wade said a few minutes later, as he showed everyone the display on his phone.

"We're not going to be able to see much that way. Nick, do you have a computer we can use?" Zeke asked.

"I dinnae have one, I'm afraid. But I think Angelina left her laptop here earlier today. She didnae want to take it with her to the tournament."

"Where is it?"

Nick went out to the hall table and retrieved the laptop, handing it to Wade. "Do you know her password?" Wade asked.

Nick frowned. "Password?"

"I'll take that as a no. Don't worry, I'll figure it out." Wade strode over to the breakfast bar and opening the computer, went to work.

Nick had no idea what to do next, but he was learning some things about these men that he hadn't known before. They perhaps had less than perfect backgrounds, but he was swiftly learning they were honorable and loyal. He hoped he wouldnae have to use their skills to retrieve his friends, but he would do whatever was necessary.

"Do you have anything to eat?" Jayson asked a few minutes later. "I'm kinda hungry."

"Me, too," Kyle added.

"I usually order takeout, so the refrigerator is nae verra well-stocked, although I think Angelina did bring some food over with her this morning."

"Let me see what I can rustle up." Jayson headed to the refrigerator and started pulling items out. Next, he opened the cabinets and retrieved a few more jars and cans. "You've got plenty here to cook something. "You wanna give me a hand Zeke?"

"Sure." Zeke headed into the kitchen and between the two of them, they found managed to prepare what Jayson called "breakfast for dinner."

"I'm guessing Angelina was planning to make you guys breakfast tomorrow, so that's now become tonight's dinner."

"I've got it!" Wade announced. "I'm in. I'll log onto the internet and we'll have the info we need in no time." Nick came to stand behind Wade and peeked over his shoulder while he retrieved an image of the castle on Angelina's computer. "I'll bet I can get the building plans. When Granger remodeled, he would've had to file for permits with the city."

Nick was beginning to think he might be the luckiest man in San Francisco. He wouldnae be able to do any of this, without this group of men. His team. They were proving to be so much more than that. "I'm grateful to each and every one of ye fer yer help. Zeke, I've been wantin' to speak with ye about becoming a partner in the martial arts school."

Zeke appeared stunned at this announcement.

"I've been thinking about this for a while and even took the liberty of having papers drawn up. I've been holding onto them, waiting for the appropriate time to speak with ye about it. Now, with all that's happening, I'm nae too sure I'll be here after tomorrow. I may be able to return home and so I'd like to have a plan in place that would put ye in charge of the school. First thing tomorrow morning, I'll take the prize check to the bank, it's to be used for all the repair work that needs to be done."

Zeke seemed humbled by Nick's announcement. "You'd really do that for me?" Zeke asked, his voice choked with emotion. "No one's ever given me a chance like this before. I won't let you down." He threw his arms around Nick and crushed him in a hug.

"I'll be counting on the rest of ye as well, to help him as best ye can." Nick gently disentangled himself from Zeke. The warmth he felt for these four men was not easy for him to put into words, but he hoped they knew he respected each of them and valued their friendship.

"Foods up!" Jayson called. They all grabbed a plate and helped themselves to eggs, bacon and hash browns. "I made coffee, too. I thought we might need to stay awake a while longer, so we can make a plan."

"Good thinking," Nick said in acknowledgement. "And good food."

As they ate, Wade found the information he'd been searching for and before long, had the blue prints to the castle on the computer screen.

"Eat, Wade. We'll look at those in a minute." Zeke shoved a plate at Wade. "Get some food and sit down with us."

Nick was reminded of his brothers, Rory and Duncan, who were always ready to help at a moment's notice. These men were not brothers by blood, but they were brothers just the same and he was proud of them. They had won their battles today and they were determined to help him win the freedom of his friends. That was, if in fact, they were with Malcolm. He hadnae stopped to think of any other scenario, but as the thought popped into his head, he quickly dismissed it, knowing intuitively exactly where they were. He just prayed nae harm had come to them.

Chapter 21

A KNOCK AT THE DOOR had Nick leaping to his feet. The sun hadn't even risen yet, and already it had begun. Zeke, who was also awakened by the loud knocking, held his hand up to Nick, signaling that he would get the door. Nick positioned himself to one side, where he wouldn't be seen when Zeke opened the door.

"Give this to Nick Mackall." Dane Smith, one of Malcolm's henchmen, thrust an envelope in Zeke's face. "I'll wait for his answer."

"Then you'll wait out there," Zeke announced, slamming the door in Smith's face.

He handed the envelope to Nick, who tore it open and read the note.

"What's it say?" Zeke asked.

"It's as I expected. He wants me to take him back to the sixteenth century, help him find the Twin Sword and then return him safely to his own time."

"Twin Sword? What's that?" Wade questioned. The others had woken and crowded around Nick as he stared at the note.

"There's a tradition - or perhaps I should say - there *was* a tradition. When a new Catholic monarch was crowned, one who showed deference to the Catholic Church, they received the gift of a sword that had been blessed by the Pope. King James the fourth received just such a sword from Pope Julius the second, along with another that the Pope knew nothing about. This second sword came to be known as the Twin Sword because it was identical to the first in every way but one - 'twas not blessed by the Pope, but infused with dark magick by an unknown sorcerer. It is said that the man or woman who possesses the Twin Sword will unleash unbelievable powers - powers that will allow them to rule the world. King James was verra wary of the power of this second sword. Fearing its dark magick, he chose to lock it away until he found a way to destroy it. He wanted nothing to do with it, as he believed anyone using it would become a slave to its power and to the sorcerer who created it."

"The Pope sent him both swords and didn't know it?" Jayson sounded as if he couldn't believe what he was hearing.

"Nae. Somewhere between Rome and Edinburgh, the Twin Sword appeared in the same box containing the Pope's gift along with an unsigned note from its creator," Nick explained.

"What happened to the Twin Sword, after James decided he didn't want it?" Zeke asked.

"King James hid it away in a rock vault, somewhere on the Campbell Clan's land. Before he could find a way to destroy it, James himself died and his infant son, James the fifth, ascended to the throne. Regents ruled in the bairn's place, until the boy was old enough to rule himself, but by that time, everyone involved in hiding the sword had died and since no one knew where it was, it was soon forgotten. I'm surprised Malcolm even knows of its existence."

"I'm not. He has a reputation for searching out and acquiring very rare treasures," Wade said.

"We cannae let him get his hands on it." Nick began to pace back and forth across the living room. "Open the door," he suddenly announced.

Zeke did as he was directed and Smith, who had been sitting on the stairs, rose to his full height.

"Tell Granger I cannae help him. I dinnae ken how to get back to the past. If I did, do you nae think I would have already gone home?"

"Mr. Granger thought that might be your answer, and he doesn't believe you. He said to tell you that if you won't help him, he'll be forced to kill your friends. You have twenty four hours to make up your mind." With that, Smith turned and headed down the stairs to the street below.

Zeke closed the door and leaned against it with a worried frown.

"We willnae need twenty four hours," Nick stated confidently. "We'll get them out before the deadline. Richard will be working from the inside to secure their escape, and we'll be doing our best from the outside."

* * *

"Good morning," Malcolm Granger greeted Richard and Angelina from the dining table in the great hall. They both remained stubbornly silent and their captor waved towards two empty chairs. "Please, sit down. Have some breakfast. I do hope you slept well last night?" Malcolm placed a forkful of food into his mouth and casually watched them as he chewed.

Richard pulled out a chair for Angelina and then sat in the vacant chair beside her.

"I've sent word to your friend, Nick. He knows of your predicament, but he is choosing not to help you."

Angelina glanced Richard's way and gave him a meaningful look, and then helped herself to some of the food. He did the same.

"You two aren't very talkative. Not morning people?" An unpleasant smirk crossed Granger's lips. "Fortunately, I'm a generous fellow. I've given him twenty four hours to change his mind."

"What happens then?" Richard poured himself some coffee.

"I'm afraid I'll have to follow through with my threat to kill you both. It's nothing personal, of course."

Richard grasped Angelina's hand under the table to reassure her. "What did you ask of him?"

"I told him I need him to take me back to the sixteenth century, retrieve the Twin Sword, and then return us safely back to the twenty first century."

"And if he does this, you promised to let us go?" Richard didn't believe they'd be getting out of this alive, but he wanted to hear confirmation from Malcolm.

"I haven't made a decision about that yet. If Nick continues to refuse his help, however, the matter will be moot." Granger stared at Richard triumphantly.

Richard ignored him, but the mounting tension in Angelina's body was obvious and once again, Richard gripped her hand, hoping to prevent her from taking any action they might regret. She responded by nodding infinitesimally, ensuring that Malcolm didn't notice the movement.

"You know, Angelina, after we had dinner the other night and then our little chat at the coffee shop, I had hoped you'd be more willing to help me. I'm sure by now you've reached the conclusion that everything I told you was true. It's a shame you didn't believe me then, perhaps if you had, you wouldn't be sitting here today." Malcolm barked out a menacing laugh. "You could have shared in the power I will attain, once I get my hands on the sword. You still could." His lascivious leer had Richard bristling with anger, and this time, it was Angelina who was comforting him with a gentle squeeze of his thigh.

"Malcolm, you don't know me very well if you think for even one moment that I would betray Nick or Richard." Angelina's gaze never wavered, and she stared at Malcolm with cool disdain.

"Well, if you change your mind, you can tell the guard at your door. He'll be certain to get the message to me. Just remember, if you assist in this project, you could have everything your heart desires."

Richard was pleased when she didn't engage in argument with Malcolm. It would do no good at this point, but Malcolm had given him an idea - one that might just get them out of this predicament.

Malcolm stood up, placing his napkin on the table. "I have things to see to. When you're finished here, my men will escort you back to your room. Don't even think about trying to overcome them, they have orders to run you through if necessary. You would be smart to remember that and behave accordingly."

"No guns?" Angelina questioned.

"I like to keep things authentically medieval." With that announcement, he left the room.

Angelina glanced Richard's way and he reassured her with a smile. A finger to his lips warned her to remain silent.

* * *

The door to their room was locked behind them and Angelina immediately turned to Richard and whispered, "What's the plan?"

"We'll wait a short while, to give the illusion you've been thinking about Malcolm's proposition, and then you'll ask the guard to send word that you've changed your mind."

"But I haven't! I'm not going to save myself at your expense."

Richard held up a hand. "I know. Hear me out. When the guard leaves, we'll go through the bathroom and break into the adjoining room, leaving this door locked. I had a look on the way upstairs, and

I believe the room next door to this one is vacant. By the time the guard gets back, hopefully we'll have found a way out of this place."

"It could work." Angelina furrowed her brow as she worked through the plan in her head. "It's worth a try."

"I'm sure Nick is on his way by now. If our plan fails, I'm certain he'll have something up his sleeve." Richard placed his hands on her shoulders. "It's going to be alright, Angelina. Trust in me. I'll not let any harm come to you."

"I know you won't, and I won't let any harm come to you." She winked at him and he couldn't help but laugh. It was just like Angelina to be more concerned about him than herself. "Come here," she beckoned. "I need a kiss." Her lips curved in a seductive smile that drew Richard right to her. She wrapped her arms around his neck and gently kissed his lips. Richard wanted her so badly it hurt, but for now, it would have to wait.

"Not the right time or the right place. I know," Angelina laughed, as if she'd read his mind.

"I promise you, as soon as we are out of danger..." He didn't get the opportunity to finish, before Angelina leaned into him, her warm lips capturing his, and pressing her body seductively against him. A growl escaped him as he took what she offered, passionately kissing her, letting himself explore all of the places he'd been longing to touch once again. Her small moans of pleasure drove him on. He tangled his hands in her glorious black locks as he kissed down her throat and felt her warm breath against his ear. He continued kissing down her body, stopping to linger at the vee of her shirt. He nimbly undid the buttons and pressed his lips to her breasts, taking first one and then the other gently into his mouth. He reluctantly pulled away and looked up into her beautiful face. Common sense warred with primal need. He was just about to pick her up and carry her to the bed when a sound outside of their room brought them crashing back to reality. They both stopped, completely still and listened intently. There was the muffled sound of voices, followed by the sound of a chair being scraped across the floor and then silence, which told them a new guard had settled in by their door.

"Richard, we need to get out of here. I want you so much I can hardly stand it."

Her words brought him great joy. This woman, this treasure, wanted *him*. His heart was nearly bursting with happiness.

"I don't know what's going to happen, but I do know I want you by my side from this moment on." He caressed her cheek with his hand and thought how lucky he was to have met her. "Angelina, will you come with me, back to my time and my castle? If you would, I can image no greater gift I could receive. I would spend the rest of my days loving you."

The smile on her lips, those beautifully full, rosy lips, told him everything he needed to know, but when she spoke, she asked the question cautiously. "I think I just heard you say you loved me, or am I wrong?"

"No, you are not wrong. I love you, my dearest Angelina. I would be proud and happy to call you my own. Will you come with me?"

"I will!" She wrapped her arms around his waist and rested her head on his chest as he enfolded her in his arms. Richard finally understood what true love felt like and he was going to experience all it had to offer as he spent the rest of his days with Angelina.

* * *

Nick and his men arrived outside Malcolm's castle, long after the sun had gone down. They made their way silently to the entry of the underground garage, an access point they felt would be their best bet for breaking into Granger's fortress. Wade was assigned the task of disarming the alarm system and video cameras, which they had located from the blueprints they'd accessed the night before. He had it knocked out in short order and they proceeded on to the garage entry. Again, Wade's expertise with electronics came into play as he unlocked the mechanism holding the gate closed. At this point they fanned out, two heading for the back of the castle, two for the front and Nick hurried toward the elevator. He knew it was risky, but he hoped that by now, Malcolm had retired for the night and they would find Richard and Angelina before anyone was any the wiser. After all, he'd done this before, minus the modern technology, of course, and it had always worked.

Luckily for Nick, after spending such a long time in the modern world, he had become familiar with objects like elevators, so when he entered, he knew exactly what to do and was only mildly apprehensive when the doors closed, leaving him enclosed in a small three foot by three foot box. The elevator stopped on the next floor and the doors quietly slid open. Nick peeked out into the darkened hallway. Hugging the walls, he made his way towards the great hall and was surprised to see light coming from under the doorway. *Damn my luck!* He made his way slowly to the room's entrance, listening for sounds that it was still occupied. From this vantage point, he could see very little and just as he was about to move closer, he felt the point of a blade at his back.

"Move into the great hall, Mackall. I've been expecting you." Malcolm Granger's gruff voice sounded in his ear. "Sit, please. I believe we'll be joined by the others shortly."

Nick did as he was told, feverishly thinking about ways to turn the tables on Malcolm. Noises down the hall alerted him to a scuffle taking place nearby and before long, Zeke, Wade, Jayson and Kyle were escorted into the room.

"Pierce, if you'll go and retrieve our guests, we'll be able to get started here."

* * *

Richard held his finger to his mouth, warning Angelina to remain silent. The noises coming from the hallway told them something was happening. Some loud thuds and groans were followed by a chorus of harsh voices.

"Let's get him downstairs and then we'll come back for them," someone said.

"Now's our chance," Angelina whispered. "I think I can pick the lock." She started searching her pockets for something that she could use.

"No need. We don't have any choice; we've got to get out before they come back." Richard kicked out at the door, splintering the wood and knocking it from its hinges. "Come." He grabbed Angelina's hand and ran into the hallway. "This way." They headed in the opposite direction, away from the commotion coming from the direction of the great hall. Running in the darkness was not ideal, but they managed to find their way to a back stairway, which Richard assumed might lead them to the kitchen. From there, he hoped to find a door leading outside. As they reached the bottom of the stairs he stopped short, and Angelina ran into his back. He steadied her and waited at the foot of the stairs, listening intently for the presence of any guards nearby. When he heard nothing, he stepped into the kitchen, Angelina holding tightly to his hand. Again, they headed for a doorway they hoped would lead them away from the great hall and capture, but as they reached it, a heavyset figure appeared. Malcolm's man, Gabe, stood before them, sword and dagger in hand.

"Turn around and walk," he ordered.

Since neither of them were armed, they had little choice but to do as they had been ordered. They entered the great hall, to discover Nick and his men being held at sword point, their own swords and daggers piled on the nearby table.

"Were you hoping for a rematch? Because if you were, I believe we've won this round. I must applaud you for your efforts, though. Fortunately, my alarm and surveillance system are programmed to reactivate if they're ever disarmed by an intruder. So, while you thought you were deactivating my system, you actually set it in motion. The silent alarm went off warning us that you were here and the cameras hidden throughout the castle showed us exactly where you were at every moment. Even knowing about the cameras, you'd be hard pressed to locate them throughout the castle, which makes for some interesting viewing on my part." Malcolm pointedly eyed Angelina and Richard. "I've had my eye on you two since you arrived. When you thought you were alone in your room, well, let's just say I'm quite disappointed in you, Angelina. I never took you for the type of woman who would throw herself at a man."

Richard bristled with fury and made to lunge at Malcolm, but Angelina grabbed his arm to hold him back. "Don't, Richard. His opinions don't matter to me."

"Now that I have you all here, let's discuss the matter at hand." Malcolm strode across to the fireplace and leaned against the stone facade. "I want the Twin Sword, and you are going to help me get it."

"I'm afraid we cannae help ye, Malcolm," Nick said. "I was tellin' the truth - Richard and I are nae here of our own doing. Ye see, a witch sent us and the only way we can get back is with her help."

"Well, then, you'd better start asking for her help and quickly, if you don't wish any harm to come to our Miss Lawson." Malcolm inclined his head and one of his men yanked Angelina away from Richard, who found a sword held at his throat when he tried to aid her. "Don't be stupid, Sir Richard. Your death will not improve the situation."

Richard turned an angry glare on Malcolm, who chuckled in response. "Edna Campbell is not a woman to be trifled with Granger," Richard shouted, hoping that somehow, Edna would hear him and magically produce the fog to transport them back where they belonged.

"And why is that? Because she's a witch? I'm sure I could convince her that it would benefit her greatly to help me with my quest."

He remained in his position by the fireplace. "Bring Angelina here," Malcolm ordered, and Smith took her by the arm and dragged her over to him. "Now, we'll see just how committed you are to keeping me from my sword."

Chapter 22

"RICHARD NEEDS OUR HELP, Maggie!" Edna and Maggie were both standing by the inn's fireplace, staring into the flames and watching as Malcolm Granger threatened the young woman.

"What can we do, Auntie?" Maggie asked, worry etching her features. "We cannae allow him to harm her, or Richard."

"We willnae allow that to happen, dear. We'll work together to free them. I believe 'tis time for Richard to come home." Edna closed her eyes and began muttering an incantation. She reached out and Maggie grasped her hand. As the two began chanting in unison, the scene in the flames became clearer. Startled faces turned to stare at them through the flames they were creating in Malcolm's hearth in San Francisco. Each person was frozen in place, paralyzed by Edna's spell. The flames in the hearth grew in size and ferocity until finally, Edna spoke.

"Richard, can ye hear me?" she asked.

"Yes, Edna, I can hear you," came his answer.

"Do as I say. The others surrounding you are unable to move."

He glanced around, as if to confirm for himself that what she had said was true.

"Listen carefully, Richard; I am here to help ye. I want ye to lay a hand on the shoulder of each person ye wish me to release from the spell and when you do that, they'll regain their ability to move. Ye must leave swiftly and get back to the place where ye first arrived in

San Francisco. The fog will be waiting for ye. I cannae hold these other men for verra much longer, so ye must hurry. Do ye understand, Richard?" Edna squeezed Maggie's hand, encouraging her to continue with the incantation. "Hurry, Richard," she called through the flames. She watched as he did as she had requested, touching each man in turn and lastly laying his hand on the woman's shoulder.

"Come, we must leave quickly. Follow me," Richard grasped Angelina's hand and led the way to the front entrance of the castle.

"Richard, Angelina, I brought yer weapons." Nick tossed their swords and dirks towards them while the others grabbed their own swords from the table and ran after Richard, Nick and Angelina.

Edna and Maggie were tiring swiftly, and could only hold the others in place for a few moments longer, but Edna hoped it was long enough to give Richard and the others a good head start. The fire began to die out in both the inn's fireplace, and the one in Malcolm's great hall and Edna turned to Maggie and hugged her. "My things are by the door, your Uncle Angus is waiting for me on the other side of the bridge. I must be there when Richard arrives, and then I hope to see my daughter and her family. I love ye Maggie, dear. Take good care of the inn and the bridge while I'm away."

"I will," Maggie promised. "You can count on me."

* * *

Richard and the others ran like the devil himself was chasing them, and in some ways he was. They all kept pace, turning occasionally to see if they were being followed. The night was warm for November. There was a dampness in the air from the fog that was settling over the city and as they hit the Marina Green, they kept running. The sounds of shouting and running men behind them floated across the marina and had them pushing themselves to breakneck speeds. Angelina had been keeping up, but she was beginning to falter. Richard pulled her up next to him and placed an arm around her waist to keep her going. If he had to, he'd throw her over his shoulder and run with her that way. They couldn't allow themselves to be caught, not now. Not when he had the chance to go home with the woman he loved.

As they approached the spot Edna had chosen, Richard yelled to the others. "If you don't want to travel back in time with us, you would be wise to go your own way."

"Zeke, you know what to do with the school. I have faith that you can make a good business out of it," Nick said, his breathing heavy.

"Thank you, Nick. I won't let you down," Zeke answered, gasping for breath.

"Nick, give him the key to the house," Angelina suggested.

"I'm a step ahead of ye, lass. I already did." Nick grinned and clapped Zeke on the back. The others waved goodbye and called out their good wishes as they veered away to head back into the heart of the city. "Shall we?" Nick said.

Angelina, Nick and Richard continued to run. They could see the whirling blanket of fog in front of them, but before they got there, Richard stopped and faced Angelina. "You said you thought you were born in the wrong century, are you sure you want to discover if you are right?"

Angelina's eyes were alight with excitement. "Yes. Let's go."

Richard smiled at her response. He was happy to know she wanted to go with him, because there was no way he intended on leaving her behind with Malcolm Granger. He began to run once again, Angelina and Nick by his side. Richard saw the familiar and colorful sparks in the mist and began to experience a little bit of relief. A few more steps and they'd be there. He ran even faster, pulling Angelina along with him as they ducked under tree branches and around bushes. Nick had gotten ahead of them and gleefully leaped into the fog when he reached it. Richard risked one last backward glance, only to see Malcolm and his men heading their way at breakneck speed. He could only hope the fog would dissipate before they reached it.

* * *

Edna stood at the bridge waiting impatiently for the fog to come and take her to her husband. Angus had decided to stay when he'd returned to Breaghacraig with their niece Maggie a few months back; he'd gone to help Maggie protect the MacKenzie clan from the evil witch Brielle. When the danger was over, he'd chosen to stay with his and Edna's daughter, Arlena in medieval Scotland and sent a message through Maggie and Dylan, to ask Edna to travel across the bridge so they could all be together for the first time in many years.

Edna had never possessed a great capacity to tolerate delays, and waiting even a few more minutes was something she found trying, but she knew better than anyone that the fog had a mind of its own and while she could control it most of the time, occasionally it would prove stubborn. It seemed as if the fog knew patience was not a virtue Edna Campbell possessed. She only hoped that it had appeared in a timely manner for Richard and his friends. She'd know soon enough, because as she watched, the fog appeared and Edna walked nervously through it for her first time-travelling experience. She'd been the keeper of the bridge for many, many years, but she had never taken advantage of its magic herself - so while she was excited, she was also experiencing a mild anxiety attack. She forced herself to keep walking and was surprised at the sensation of the fog as it wrapped around her like a warm blanket. She felt safe and protected and she let go of any uneasiness she had been suffering. As the fog cleared, it revealed her handsome husband. Absence had indeed made her heart grow fonder and she flew to Angus, throwing herself into his waiting arms. "Oh, Angus, how I've missed ye," she cried. Tears of happiness flooded her cheeks.

"Not nearly as much as I've missed ye, *mo chroi,* my heart." They held on tightly to each other and Angus spoke softly in Edna's ear. "My love, I knew that if I didnae stay, you would always find a reason why you couldnae come to see yer daughter and grand babes, so I'm afraid I forced yer hand. I hope yer nae angry with me."

"Nae, of course I cannae be angry with ye. I should have come a long time ago and now that I'm here, I'm very anxious to see my family."

Angus smiled, apparently relieved that his wife was happy to be with him again. He tipped her chin up and offered her a smoldering kiss, which left Edna unsteady on her feet. He held her tightly to keep her from falling and when they could finally tear their lips away from one another, Edna spoke. "Well now, if I'd known I'd get a kiss like that one, I'd have been here much sooner."

Angus laughed and lifting her off the ground, spun her around. "Angus, please you'll make me dizzy and I have one more thing to do before we go. Did ye bring the extra horses I asked fer?"

"Aye, I did. They're grazing just beyond the trees. Who are they fer?"

"Ye'll soon see."

The fog started forming again and as it swirled in their direction, Angus held on tightly to Edna. "I'll nae let it take ye from me, Edna."

"'Tis nae here to take anyone. 'Tis here to bring someone back."

As the fog thinned, Angelina, Richard and Nick emerged. The men looked overjoyed, while the young woman appeared to be in shock as she took in her surroundings.

"Richard, come quickly. I've horses fer ye just yonder. I cannae be sure that ye have nae been followed, so 'tis best we leave right away."

"They were right behind us," Richard stated, glancing back over his shoulder.

"Come, the fog has nae left yet and that concerns me." Edna led the way to the horses that had been saddled and waiting for them. "We'll have time enough for introductions later." They mounted and cantered off through the trees. Richard stayed close by Angelina's side, not knowing her equestrian skills, but he was pleased to discover she seemed quite comfortable on her mount. As soon as they hit a clearing, they kicked the horses into a gallop, and headed in the direction of Castle Fionn.

* * *

Malcolm couldn't believe his luck. He had watched the fog swallow Nick and his companions, never believing that he'd reach it in time to follow them, but he had, as had his men. He had made it to the year 1514! He knew he was in the right year, because as they emerged from the fog he spied Nick, Angelina and Richard riding away with two others. Their friends had apparently stayed behind in San Francisco, which suited Malcolm just fine.

"We're here! We did it," he said to Pierce, who was looking suitably amazed.

"Where are we?" Gabe asked. "What just happened?"

"We're in sixteenth century Scotland. The year 1514, to be exact. Gentlemen, we have just experienced time travel."

Dane and Nash appeared completely dumbfounded by this announcement, turning in slow circles to study their surroundings.

"We'll need to find the site where I've been told the sword was hidden, and then we'll need to find our *friends*. They're our ticket home." Malcolm glanced around, trying to figure out what time of day it was. The sun was attempting to peek through the clouds to the east, which made him think it was early morning, perhaps around eight a.m. "We'll have plenty of time to locate a campsite for tonight. Perhaps we'll run across a village and we can find some food." Malcolm was exhilarated and it showed in his voice. "Isn't this exciting?" When his men didn't respond, he set off in the direction

Nick and the others had gone. He'd follow their horses' tracks, in hopes of getting his bearings. He had a map tucked away in his pocket and he'd need time to study it before they could set off in earnest on their search for the sword.

"First things first. We need food, water, shelter and…" he glanced down at what he was wearing, "…appropriate clothing." Again, none of the men answered him, apparently still too stunned by what had just happened. Malcolm bristled angrily. Just because they weren't in San Francisco any longer, was no reason for his men to cease doing his bidding. "Come on! Get your asses in gear and let's go." Malcolm started marching through the trees, not bothering to check if they followed. *Naturally, they would follow him,* he thought smugly. What choice did they have?

* * *

Richard and the others rode hard through the whole day, until they were forced to stop for the night when darkness fell. Richard wasn't particularly worried about Malcolm catching up with them, because he knew they had no horses. Setting up camp was easily accomplished with everyone's help and when he had a moment, he stopped to speak with Edna. "Thank you for getting us back safely, I wasn't sure if you'd hear me when I called your name."

"Never fear, laddie. I've been keeping track of ye since I sent ye on yer way, always waiting to hear my name called if ye needed me."

Nick joined them. "Edna, I'm Nick Mackall. I'm pleased to make yer acquaintance."

Edna took his hand in greeting. "And who is this lovely young woman ye've brought back with ye, Richard?"

"Angelina Lawson, this is Edna Campbell."

"Edna, I have so many questions, I don't even know where to begin." Angelina reached out and grasped Edna's hand in hers.

"Well, I'm sure I can answer them all, but first, let's get some food in our bellies, shall we?" Edna kept hold of Angelina's hand and drew her towards the fire.

The fire was blazing and Angus pulled more food from his saddlebags than Richard thought seemed possible. Edna smiled happily while she watched him. Richard had the distinct impression that every time Angus put his hand in the bags, Edna was manifesting another item for him to reveal. If she was capable of transporting him through time to a distant land, he had no doubt she could feed them with little effort. He shook his head at the things he'd once considered unbelievable, which he now accepted without question.

"Are you alright, Angelina?" Richard sat down next to her, concerned about how she was handling this transition. Her eyes were wide with wonder as she observed the goings on of the camp. She clung to Richard's arm tightly, a sensation he was enjoying. As she had told him on more than one occasion, she was perfectly capable of taking care of herself, so the fact that she was leaning on him to get her through this situation warmed his heart.

"I'm fine. Just a little shocked I guess. I'm happy to be here with you, though." She smiled up at him and his heart skipped a beat.

Richard glanced over Angelina's head, to discover Edna appeared quite happy and proud as she observed the two of them. "Where do we go from here?" he asked.

"We'll head to Castle Fionn. After a good night's sleep, Angus will guide us on our way. He tells me it's only a few short hours from here."

"Can you tell if Malcolm followed us here?" Richard asked.

"Let me see." Edna spent a minute or two staring into the flames of the fire and then shook her head in dismay. "It appears that he did indeed come through the mist and he brought four others with him. He is on foot though, so that is in our favor. The fact that he's here for the Twin Sword frightens me. We cannae allow him to get to it."

"We won't," Angelina stated confidently.

"I like you," Edna said, cocking her head and gazing at Angelina. "You're a good strong woman and that will come in verra handy."

Handy for what? Richard wondered. He was hoping to get Angelina back to his home in England without further incident. As far as he was concerned, there was no need for her to be a part of whatever was going to happen with Malcolm. He was more than willing to help, but wanted Angelina safely away from the danger. "I would like to take Angelina back to my home as soon as possible."

"Of course, of course," Edna said. She rose, and went to sit with Angus, but Richard had the uneasy sensation that there was something else Edna wasn't telling them.

* * *

Angelina awoke with a smile on her face, despite the fact that she was shivering with cold. She had spent the entire night snuggled in Richard's warm embrace, but now that he wasn't there beside her, she was a bit cold. She wrapped herself in the blanket she'd been given the night before and sat up. The others were already up and moving about the campsite. She smiled again - this was better than the best Ren Faire she had been to. She rose and moved closer to the fire to get warm.

"Make no mistake, Angelina, this is nae a Renaissance Faire. This is verra, verra real." Edna's voice came from behind her and Angelina turned to discover the older woman carrying a bowl of food towards her. *Had Edna just read her thoughts?* "Ye'll need to eat a good breakfast. We'll be leaving soon." Edna handed her a steaming bowl of stew left over from the night before, along with a thick piece of bread. "Eat. And Angelina, if ye ever decide that ye don't want to be here, just tell me. I'll see to it that ye get safely returned to San Francisco." Edna turned and walked away, leaving Angelina thinking about what she'd said. At this very moment, Angelina couldn't think of one reason why she'd want to leave. She'd imagined a world like this for so long, and now she was actually going to experience it. How could there possibly be any reason she'd want to leave?

Angelina held the bowl between her hands, enjoying the warmth. Gazing around the camp, she located Richard as he returned from the forest with an armload of wood for the fire.

"Good morning," he called cheerily. "You were sleeping so soundly this morning, I hope I didn't disturb you when I rose." He placed some of the wood he had brought on the fire and placed the rest nearby, before he came to sit beside her. "I see Edna got you some food."

She took a spoonful of the stew and nodded in acknowledgement, chewing and swallowing before she spoke. "Did you sleep well?" she asked.

"Very well," came his happy response. "In fact, I don't think I've ever had a better night's sleep." He leaned in and kissed her temple, lingering to brush an errant lock of hair from her face with his fingers and leaving her speechless. Angelina wasn't exactly certain when she had come to love Richard - perhaps it had been right from the very first moment she'd seen him at the Marina. No matter when it had happened, she was over the moon to be here with him and couldn't wait to see his home and meet his family. She didn't know a lot about Richard's life in medieval England, but she knew him to be a kind, gentle and honorable man. She was excited to learn more.

* * *

Riding through the Scottish countryside on MacKenzie lands brought back some memories for Richard that left him ill at ease. He should really have a conversation with Angelina about his past, but the right time had simply not presented itself. What he needed was some time alone with her and then he'd tell her. He felt guilty for not telling her before they found themselves fleeing from Malcolm Granger. If he'd told her the truth, he worried that there was every possibility she would have stayed behind and he would have been the most miserable man on earth. He knew he had to tell her the truth about his past, but at the same time, he very much feared her reaction.

Angelina had spent the morning chatting with Edna about time travel and witchcraft and as one would expect, she was utterly fascinated. Richard rode alongside Nick and Angus, who were deep in conversation, and he quietly contemplated his future and hoped that Angelina would still be a part of it, after she found out what kind of man he had been for most of his life. He was comfortable with his own thoughts, having spent a good deal of time on his own. Even when he was with his men, he rarely took the time to join in on their conversations. The dark cloud that had always hung over him, got in the way of enjoying himself. So, no one, other than Nick, knew him to be anything other than a man who should not be provoked.

They were rapidly approaching Castle Fionn, Ewan and Lena MacKenzie's home. Richard had no idea what his welcome would be, if they welcomed him at all and he suffered a pang of anxiety in his gut. Gazing back at Angelina, he saw her smile and wave to him before turning back to Edna. He worried that this might be the last time she gazed on him with such loving eyes, the last time he'd hear her sweet voice. Worst of all, perhaps this was the last time he'd see her.

Chapter 23

TWO LITTLE REDHEADED WHIRLWINDS RAN their way, as soon as the gates to the castle were opened. They were followed by a troop of barking dogs and then Lena and Ewan MacKenzie, who waved excitedly in their direction.

Angelina had learned from her conversation with Edna that this was the first time she had time travelled as well. And even more importantly, it was the first time she was meeting her own daughter in years, meeting her son-in-law and the first time she'd get to see her grandbabes. Angelina's heart was full at the sight of this whole family heading their way. She peeked in Edna's direction, only to see the older woman shedding tears of joy as she saw her family together for the first time. Lena rushed toward her mother's horse, shedding tears of her own. Angus jumped down from his horse and went to Edna's side, helping her dismount into the waiting arms of her daughter. The two women could do nothing more than stare at each other, crying and hugging. Angelina found her own eyes had dampened at this emotional scene. She was so caught up in what was happening that she hadn't noticed Richard dismount and come over to her. He laid a hand on her thigh and she jumped.

"I'm sorry, love, it was not my intention to frighten you. Come. Let me help you down from there." He handed her reins off to a nearby stableboy and then lifted her down easily. Her feet touched the ground for the first time in hours and it took a minute for her to regain her balance. Richard kept a steadying hand on her back as he guided her towards the others. For a moment, they simply stood and watched the family reunion, taking place in front of their eyes.

"'Tis a beautiful sight," Nick said when he joined them. "I can hardly wait to see my own family. I hope they remember me." And in typical Nick fashion, he chuckled, although Angelina was sure he was just as anxious to see them, as Edna had been to see her family.

The two little boys were adorable. They were wrapped around Edna's legs as she was being introduced to Ewan, and soon enough she bent down to hug them both and to take an extra-long look at their sweet little faces. They each grabbed one of her hands and dragged Edna into the castle.

Feeling like outsiders, Angelina, Richard and Nick weren't sure whether to join them or not, but Angus detached himself from the family and came back to get them. "Dinnae stand there, come inside. Once Edna has calmed herself, I'll introduce ye to the family." They followed Angus through the castle doors and into the great hall.

Ewan left the group and approached them. "Welcome. I be Ewan MacKenzie." He held his hand out to Nick, who shook it.

"Nick Mackall. Pleased to meet you." Nick turned to Angelina. "This is Angelina Lawson." Ewan bowed in her direction. "And this is Sir Richard Jefford. I'm sure ye've heard of him."

Richard cringed at the thought of what might come next.

"Sir Richard, I'm pleased to finally meet ye. We're verra grateful for what ye did, to help rid us of Brielle," Ewan said.

Richard's face heated. "I didn't do all that much. Maggie and Dylan were the ones who ultimately rid the world of the witch."

"The way I hear it, you stood with them, even at the risk of your own demise."

Richard didn't respond, instead he gazed down at Angelina who was watching him with adoration in her eyes. It would be wrong not to tell her everything. She thought him a hero, but if she knew the truth, she'd surely loathe him. It was probably what he deserved.

"I can see I'm embarrassing you, but you are far too modest Sir Richard. Let me introduce you to my lovely wife and my two young sons." Ewan led the way to where Edna and Angus stood with Lena and the boys. Things had calmed down a bit and Lena and Edna were catching up on what had been happening in their lives. "Lena, let me introduce you to our guests. This is Angelina Lawson, Nick Mackall and Sir Richard Jefford."

Lena stopped mid-sentence and turned to them. "Forgive me. I've been so excited to have my mother here, I'm afraid I've been quite rude. I'm pleased to meet you all and I welcome you to Castle Fionn. You are honored guests in our home. These are my two sons, Rowan and Ranald." Turning to the two boys, Lena said, "Behave yerselves. Dinnae bother our guests, do ye ken?"

"Aye, Ma," both boys said in unison.

"They can be wee devils when they put their minds to it, which seems to be all the time." Lena's motherly smile contradicted her words.

The boys marched up to Richard and Nick and held out their little hands.

"Now which is which," Nick teased.

"I be Ranald and he be Rowan." The twins were identical and Richard wasn't certain he'd ever be able to tell them apart, but he couldn't deny the fact that they were quite the handsome little men.

"You all must be exhausted from your ride. Let's get you settled in your rooms so you can rest before we eat." Lena led the way upstairs to the guest quarters, putting Nick and Richard in one and Angelina in another. "You're welcome to join us downstairs, or if you'd like to rest, I'll send someone up for you when 'tis time to eat."

All three opted to stay upstairs. Richard thought it was only right to let Edna spend some uninterrupted time with her family, and on top of that, they had ridden quite a distance today without rest.

"There's a warm bath downstairs, if you're interested. We have a hot spring underground and it makes for a lovely, relaxing bath. If ye've a mind to use it, I can show ye where it is."

"I'd like that," Angelina said. "My muscles are pretty sore from two days of riding. I'll see you two later." She gave the men a small wave and followed Lena downstairs.

* * *

"Would you care to join her?" Nick asked, with a glint of humor in his eyes.

"Not at the moment," Richard said. Despite how well things had gone so far, he was still worrying about what he should tell Angelina and when.

The men entered their quarters and Richard sat in a chair beside the fire. Nick sat across from him. "I'm happy to see there are two beds," Nick chuckled.

Richard didn't respond, he was deep in thought and not paying any attention to his friend.

"Richard are ye with me?" Nick said, hitting Richard on the knee.

Richard jumped and rubbed his hand across his jaw. "I'm sorry, I was just thinking."

"About what? Only something verra good, or verra bad, would keep ye from being fascinated by what I've just said."

"Bad." Richard didn't offer anything else. He didn't think he had to. Nick knew him well enough to know most of Richard's misdeeds. It's why Nick had ridden away from him all those years before. He hadn't liked the person Richard had become.

"Does it have something to do with our Angelina?"

"Yes." Richard sighed heavily, leaning back in the chair. "I'm afraid to tell her about my past. She'll be very disappointed and I think she'll want nothing to do with me. I don't know what to do. It's only a matter of time before she finds out the whole truth." Richard closed his eyes, as if doing so would block out the reality that was now threatening to ruin the one good thing he'd had in his life. "Every time I meet someone who knows about my past, I'll be worried that they'll let something slip and she'll hate me."

"I ken yer fear, but ye must tell her before she hears it from someone else." The fire crackled in the hearth and the two friends sat in silence as Richard mulled this advice over.

"I haven't had a moment alone with her, and I cannot tell her in front of everyone else." His eyes roamed the room, taking in the furnishings, the small wooden swords, and two rocking horses taking up positions beneath the windows. "I believe they've given us the twins' room," he remarked.

"Yer just noticing? Ye must be in a bad way, my friend. If ye wish to be alone with Angelina, now might be the perfect time. Why dinnae ye see if ye can find her? I'm going to take this time for a well-deserved nap." Nick rose and went over to one of the beds, and he flopped down, placing a pillow beneath his head. "Dinnae wake me until the evening meal is being served."

After a few moments, the slow, even sound of Nick's breathing told Richard that he had indeed fallen asleep. Unfortunately for Richard, the war going on inside his head did not cease. Should he go to Angelina? Should he wait? Fear, not an emotion that was familiar to him, lay heavy upon his shoulders. Trying to be a good man and do all the right things, was leaving him both worried and overwhelmed. Eventually, he made the decision to seek out Angelina and bear his soul, no matter what the outcome may be.

* * *

The warm water soothed Angelina's sore muscles from the minute she sank into the large bath, enjoying the sensation of the water all the way up to her chin. This room was unlike anything she'd seen before and certainly, unlike anything she'd expected to see in medieval Scotland. Lena had explained it had been created at her request and to her specifications. To Angelina, it resembled a spa, carved into the rock walls beneath the castle. A large rectangular pool of heated water filled the room with steam, and stone shelves for sitting had been carved into the interior. The atmosphere was serene and meant for relaxing.

A noise alerted her to the fact that she was not alone and she spun to see who was there. "Hello?" Her voice echoed off the stone walls. "Is someone there?" Suddenly, her warm, soothing bath no longer seemed relaxing. She waited, holding her breath, but heard nothing else. Angelina swam across to the other side of the pool, so she could see if anyone was about to enter. The move helped to calm her frazzled nerves and before long, when no one appeared, she was able to get back into her peaceful mindset.

Naturally, her thoughts turned to Richard. A humble hero. It was so like him, to downplay his part in whatever it was that happened when he'd assisted the MacKenzie clan. She'd have to ask him about it. Angelina closed her eyes and imagined his smoldering gaze on her, his lips kissing hers - at first soft and then with passionate ferocity - his hands stroking her skin. Why hadn't she thought to ask him to join her? That kind of thing was probably frowned upon here, which made it seem so much more enticing.

Glancing down at her hands, Angelina realized she was rapidly turning into a prune and should probably get out. She was just pulling herself up out of the water when she heard the distinct sound of a male voice and a female response. Moments later, a serving girl came in with a drying cloth in her hands.

"The gentleman asked me to bring this to ye, m'lady." The girl handed the cloth to Angelina. "Would ye like me to help ye?"

Angelina smiled at the obviously shy girl, whose eyes hadn't left her feet since she entered the bath. "What gentleman?"

The girl, continuing to examine the floor, shrugged her shoulders in response. "I dinnae ken. Not someone I know."

That was certainly believable - if this girl couldn't look Angelina in the eye, she surely wouldn't have looked directly at whoever had asked her to give Angelina the cloth. "Thank you." Angelina began to dry herself, turning her back, embarrassed to be seen nude by the girl who remained standing nearby. "What's your name?"

"Elspeth, ma'am." She dropped into a low curtsy.

"You can go, Elspeth. I can get dressed on my own." Angelina watched as Elspeth backed out of the room and took off down the passageway towards the stairs.

She couldn't help but giggle to herself. There were so many things she was going to have to get used to in the sixteenth century. For instance, the cloth she'd been given to dry herself, which was surprisingly absorbent. She finished drying herself off and was dressed in no time. *Now to find out who was watching me,* she thought.

* * *

Richard bolted for the stairs, as soon as he saw Angelina emerging from the bath. He had come down here with the intentions of speaking to her about his past, but had not thought the idea through particularly well. Once his eyes had locked onto her naked body, his own body reacted in the most natural of ways. He had groaned aloud and startled her, so he had remained hidden just outside the doorway until she relaxed again. Despite knowing it was wrong to do so, he had continued to peek at her from around the doorway until she'd decided to emerge from the bath. Spinning on his heels to leave before she discovered him, he'd practically run down the small servant girl headed toward the bath. "The lady needs a drying cloth," he'd spat out, praying she wouldn't notice the obvious bulge which had formed in his now far-too-tight breeches . He hurried on his way and now that he was upstairs, safe in his room, he paced back and forth, cursing himself for his foolish behavior. He was Sir Richard Jefford - or at least, he used to be, before his trip to San Francisco. Now he was thoughtful, caring, kind and seemingly, without any bad qualities he could name. Unless, of course, he considered spying on a naked woman, which he had done without thought for anything but his own carnal lust. Mayhap he wasn't as noble as he'd thought. What he had really wanted was to join her in the bath. To take her in his arms and make her his, but he couldn't. He wouldn't, not until she knew everything she needed to about him and then *she* definitely wouldn't. This dilemma was tearing him apart. Was there any way he could spirit Angelina from here to his home, without running across anyone who knew him? He shook his head ruefully. What a ridiculous thought. What would he do once he got there? He couldn't keep her locked up in his castle forever. No. He had to tell her, but he feared he couldn't work up the courage.

A knock at the door brought him back to the present. "Yes?" he called. He glanced across at Nick, but his friend didn't move. He had always been a very sound sleeper.

"It's Angelina. Can I come in?"

Richard went to the door and opened it. "Nick is asleep."

She pushed past him and into the room. Glancing Nick's way, she giggled before turning back to him. "Hey, were you just down in the bath area?"

"Me?" He gestured to himself and felt like a complete oaf.

"Yes, you. Is there anyone else here who's awake?" She wandered closer to him and all Richard could see was a very wet, very naked Angelina emerging from the water, like a goddess from the sea. He stumbled backwards as she continued her approach. "You know, if it was you, I don't have a problem with that. I just wish you had joined me."

"Angelina, I…" She was pressing herself up against him. Surely, she would feel the impact she was having on him, and back away.

"What, Richard?" Her hands roamed across his chest and down to his belly and then even lower.

"It was me. I'm so sorry I didn't announce my presence. I wanted to join you, but I cannot compromise your good name. Things are different in this time." He backed away again, but her hand lingered and the throbbing of his shaft was making it difficult to think.

"You two should really have your own room." Nick stretched and yawned as he sat up. "You've disturbed my sleep and what I've seen is enough to keep me awake for days. As they say in Angelina's time, I'll never be able to unsee that, Richard."

Angelina removed her hand and grabbed a pillow, tossing it at Nick's head with pinpoint accuracy. It hit him with a thud. "Ow," he said, feigning injury.

"You could join me in my room, Richard. That way Nick could get back to his nap."

"I'm afraid that would not be appropriate behavior. We are guests here with the MacKenzies and they've given us separate rooms. We must bow to their wishes." *There, that should settle things,* he thought. But there was one thing it wasn't settling. "Why is it that my breeches are suddenly too tight." Richard pulled and tugged at them to relieve his anguish.

Nick and Angelina laughed so hard, they were practically in tears.

"I'd better leave," Angelina hiccoughed her way to the door. "I'm just across the hall, should you be looking for me."

The door closed and Richard breathed a sigh of relief, turning to stare daggers at Nick.

"I heard everything. I take it you haven't told her yet, or this may have ended differently." Nick threw his legs over the side of the bed and stood.

"I couldn't tell her. The opportunity simply did not present itself." He went to his bed and sat down, running his hands through his hair.

"I dinnae believe I've ever seen you so affected by a woman, Richard. In the past, you always saw what you wanted and took it. What's the hold up here?"

"Love." There he'd said it. He was smitten and he had no idea what he could do about it.

"Aye. That does make a difference." Nick was eyeing him with a pitying expression on his face.

"I went down to the bath to tell her about my past, and instead, I hid and peeked at her like a young lad who was seeing his first naked lass. Is love always like this, Nick?"

"I wouldnae ken it." Nick sat down next to him. "I dinnae believe I've ever truly been in love meself. And from the looks of it, I'm nae so sure I want to be. It seems painful."

"It is. I thought I loved Irene, but now that I've experienced these feelings I have for Angelina, I know it was not love at all that drew me to Irene. But what I did because of it, could ruin the only true love I've ever known."

Chapter 24

MALCOLM GRANGER AND HIS ARMY of four slogged through the damp forest, heading where, they didn't know. They'd long ago stopped avoiding the rain dripping from the trees and the puddles they found themselves plodding through almost constantly. The fallen leaves in the path made their trek treacherous. More than once a man had slipped and landed on the ground, cursing the rain that had poured down nonstop for the last twenty-four hours. They were all cold, wet and extremely irritable.

"Malcolm, is there any chance we could stop soon?" Pierce Holmes questioned. His voice was filled with resentment.

Malcolm glared at him. "And just where would you like to stop? I don't see any place that would shelter us from the rain and cold, do you? Or perhaps you'd like to sit down right here with no fire and no shelter. Is that what you want?"

"That's not what I meant, Malcolm. I'm just wondering if we could start searching for some shelter? Maybe a cave, or a rocky overhang." Pierce must have realized his mistake, because he changed his tone to one more conciliatory.

Malcolm knew Pierce was at the end of his rope, otherwise he'd never have spoken to him in such a manner. One thing he didn't need was a mutiny on his hands. "Fine. Keep your eyes open - all of you."

They walked on in silence, but it wasn't long before Nash called out. "Over there! Looks like a cave."

Malcolm spotted it. "Let's go." He led the way, barely able to lift his legs because he was so tired. Fallen tree branches and a slick forest floor didn't help their situation, but determination carried them towards their goal. Pierce had been right to question him, but he'd never tell him that. They all needed to rest and get their strength back. He had no idea how much further they needed to go. As soon as they got a fire started, he planned to take a better look at the map Joel had made for him.

* * *

Angelina leaned on the castle doorframe, watching the rain as it fell in the courtyard. It had been coming down nonstop for hours, but she'd always loved the rain, so it could continue indefinitely as far as she was concerned.

"Angelina!" Edna called. "Come join us."

She closed the door and went inside where the others were all seated around the fire. Some were drinking whiskey, some had tea and some had whiskey in their tea. She took a seat near Richard, who'd been acting oddly ever since they'd arrived. Maybe he'd changed his mind about her, although that didn't seem likely, but she could see that her presence was making him uncomfortable and she suffered a pang of anxiety. Maybe when they'd settled this issue with Malcolm, she'd have to ask Edna to send her home. Not that she wanted to go, but she wasn't about to stay somewhere she wasn't wanted.

Elspeth poured her some tea and at Edna's urging, added a tot of whiskey.

"It'll warm you up from the inside out, my dear." Edna was smiling in that motherly way she had.

"Thanks," Angelina replied, sipping the tea and enjoying the warmth of the whiskey wending its way down to her belly.

"Now that we're all here and relatively comfortable," Edna started, "I'd like to talk about Malcolm." She gazed around at the others, and Angelina noted that everyone was paying very close attention. "He's on his way here. Dinnae worry. He won't make it for a few more days. His men are tired and wet, and their progress has been slowed by the rain."

"You say they're on the way here?" The concern on Ewan's face was completely understandable. He had a family to protect.

"Aye, but there's nothing to worry about. When they arrive, Angus and I will have escorted the three of ye away from Castle Fionn." She waved a hand in the direction of Angelina, Richard and Nick. "Ewan, ye will entertain them as guests. They will only stay for a day and then they'll be on their way. Give them whatever they need to complete their journey. If they want horses, see to it that they get them. We dinnae wish to be waiting for them forever to come for the sword. I'd like this over with as quickly as possible, so I can come back and spend more time with all of ye. Just as I'm sure you, Nick, would like to go home and Richard would like to take Angelina back to England to meet his family."

"That sounds reasonable. We'll be gracious hosts." Lena glanced at Ewan and he nodded in approval.

As for the rest of us, we'll leave in the morning. Our journey will take us to Campbell land. Angus will see to it that we are welcomed there." She glanced at Angus and furrowed her brow in concern. "They havenae seen you for quite a long time. I hope they'll recognize ye."

"Dinnae fear, I'm sure they will. We'll need their help in finding the location of the sword. Hopefully, someone there will be able to guide us." Angus sipped his whiskey. "Ewan tells me my Uncle Tavish is the Campbell laird now. I always had a good relationship with him, although I'm sure he believes me to be dead. 'Twill come as quite a shock to him, when I ride into their stronghold."

Angelina listened intently as the plans were made. She wasn't sure what her part would be, but she wanted to help in any way possible. "I have my sword, and I'm prepared to use it," she announced. Ewan and Angus sent a skeptical look her way. "I'm quite good with a weapon," she added, "Richard and Nick can attest to that."

"She is very good with a sword. I would hope she wouldn't need to be involved in the fray, but if she is, it would be invaluable protection for her and for Edna." Richard glanced Angelina's way and she smiled stiffly at him. He was trying to protect her, when he knew good and well there was no need. Hadn't he been there when she took down Nash Roydon at the Faire? She knew this and was aware of the fact that any *fray* they entered would be a real one.

"I won't need a sword, dear. I've my magic." Edna proudly sat up a little straighter.

"So you'll use your magic to fight Malcolm," Richard stated.

"I don't foresee any trouble, but one never knows. Malcolm cannot fight my powers, but if he gets his hands on that sword, well then, we'll have a problem. It's best we stop him before he ever gets to it."

Murmurs of agreement came from the group. Angelina glanced Richard's way and as she suspected, his eyes were focused on her. They were going to have to get a few things straightened out, but all that would have to wait until after the Twin Sword was safely secured.

* * *

Luck was on their side as the sun broke through the clouds and blessed them with sunshine for their journey. They said their good-byes to Lena, Ewan and the boys, with the intention that they would see them again soon and rode off towards the Campbell lands.

"The two of ye have hardly spoken," Nick observed as he rode up beside Angelina. "Would ye care to tell me about it?"

"There's not much to tell. In the last day or so, Richard has distanced himself from me. I don't know why, but I've seen this before with other men I've spent time with and it's not something I will tolerate. If he doesn't want me around anymore, then he should just say so."

"Richard is a complicated man, Angelina. I'm nae sure even he kens what goes on in his head at times. Don't give up so quickly. I feel the two of ye were meant to be together."

"He's hiding something, I know the signs. I just don't know what it is."

"There are some things… things that he wishes were long forgotten, but they cannae be. He wishes to speak with ye about them, but fears yer reaction. 'Tis why he's been acting so strangely."

"If we're to even stand a chance at a life together, then he's going to have to trust me. Do you know what he's hiding?"

"Aye. But 'tis not my place to tell ye. He's the one you need to ask."

"How much further do we have to go?"

"We're still traversing MacKenzie land. Once we cross the hills you see off in the distance, we'll be on Campbell land. Then 'twill be up to Angus to find the location of the sword."

"Angus hasn't been back here in decades, from what I heard. How does he know that anyone from his past is still alive?"

"Well, ye heard him say that Ewan informed him about his uncle, Tavish. Ewan is familiar with his clan and while some are no longer with us, there are others who are and Angus will surely be glad to see them."

Angelina adjusted her position in the saddle and Nick smiled warmly at her. He'd known from the instant he'd seen her with Richard that they were meant to be together. He wished he could help, but it was up to the two of them to sort this mess out. He'd be there if either one of them needed him.

* * *

The clip clopping of the horses hooves sounded at a steady pace as they travelled along a road framed on either side by the greenest of pastures. Wagon ruts along their route were filled with water from the previous day's rain. The horses cautiously stepped around them. Richard, coward that he was, rode alongside Angus and adeptly avoided Angelina. It wasn't that he didn't want to be with her, on the contrary, that was the only place he wished to be, but he was working out a way to tell her about his past mistakes - one that wouldn't end up with her walking away from him. This was something he needed to settle soon, before his avoidance did more damage than his actual misdeeds. She was losing patience with him, of that there was no doubt.

Richard noted Nick riding alongside her and hoped that he would put in a good word or two for him. He'd find out soon enough, because Nick was moving forward away from Angelina, leaving her in the capable hands of Edna. As Nick approached, he nodded his greeting.

"How is m'lady?" Richard asked, worry etching his features.

"She willnae be yer lady fer much longer, if ye dinnae speak with her. Her patience is wearing thin." Nick cast a glance back in Angelina's direction and turned to Richard, shaking his head. "Dinnae let this one slip away from ye."

Richard knew Nick was right and he nodded. "Yer right. I'll speak with her and whatever she decides, it's out of my hands. I love her, Nick, and I don't want to lose her, but the decision is ultimately hers to make."

Richard was preparing to turn back to Angelina when a line of riders appeared in the road up ahead of them. "Damn. The MacKenzies," Richard muttered. "I don't believe this will end well for me."

"They're no longer angry with ye, Richard. Ewan said as much."

"They may not be, but they do hold the key to my secret." His heart sank as he watched their approach - his future would surely end before it even had a chance to begin.

Angus held up his hand for them all to stop and wait as the MacKenzie's approached. There appeared to be six of them as far as Richard could tell. He couldn't see who was in their group, but he had a bad feeling in the pit of his belly. Nothing good could come of this unexpected meeting.

The riders drew closer and Richard could see Robert, Cailin and Cormac along with three others riding behind. They greeted Angus as they approached and gave a cursory glance at the others. Robert spotted him and rode his way. Richard wasn't sure whether he should prepare himself for an attack or a welcome.

"Sir Richard. The last time we met was not under such friendly circumstances." Robert reached out to clasp Richard's arm.

Richard didn't know what to say in response, but knew he must say something. "I extend my deepest apologies to you and the MacKenzie clan. I hope that you and your family can find it in your hearts to forgive me. I am a changed man."

Robert nodded his head and Richard breathed a little easier. "We hear that ye were on yer way to visit us with yer regrets, but became embroiled in battle with the witch, Brielle. We thank ye fer yer help in that matter."

"You are most welcome, Sir, but Maggie did the bulk of the work."

"Aye. And ye were dragged off and lost to us for a time. Where did Edna send ye?" Robert's expression told Richard that he was more interested in his time travel adventures, than jealousy.

"San Francisco, in the year 2014," Richard answered.

"Where our Ashley and Jenna are from! I'd love to see it with my own two eyes, but I dinnae believe I'll ever be able to do so."

Angelina had ridden up to join them. "Did I hear you say Ashley and Jenna? Are they the same Ashley and Jenna that I know?"

"They may well be, lass. Ashley and Jenna are time travelers from San Francisco. Are ye as well?"

"Yes. Are they here? And is that Cormac I see?" Angelina was obviously very excited.

"Aye. 'Tis indeed." Cormac greeted her with a warm smile. "You're a long way from home, lass."

"I know. I can hardly believe it myself. Where are Jenna and Ashley?" she asked again.

"Back at Breaghacraig, of course. Ye must come and stay with us." Robert turned in his saddle and called Angus over. "Angus where are ye off to?"

"We're on our way to Campbell lands. There's a man come from the future, in search of the Twin Sword. We must keep it from him, at all costs."

"Ye must stop for the night. Ye'll stay at Breaghacraig and ye can be on yer way tomorrow. Jenna and Ashley would nae forgive any of us if we didnae bring ye back."

"Edna?" Angus asked, "What do ye think?"

"I think 'tis a grand idea. We cannae go much further as it is, so we may as well join our friends for the night. I'd love to see the castle I've been sending the ladies to."

Cailin and Cormac joined them. Both men leaned across in their saddles and greeted Edna with a warm hug. Richard couldn't help noticing that Cailin was eyeing him with some mistrust. He couldn't blame him for his reaction. "You all go on ahead," he suggested. "I think I'll make camp out here. That way I can keep watch for Malcolm and his men."

"Nonsense," Edna responded. "Ye'll do nae such thing. Malcolm will be staying the night at Castle Fionn. I know this, because Lena has spoken with me and told me they just arrived. So, there's no need for ye to sacrifice yerself." Edna gave Richard a knowing glance.

Richard sighed heavily. "All right. I defer to your wisdom, madam."

The MacKenzie's turned their horses and headed back in the direction from which they had come. Richard and his group followed. Angelina rode between Cailin and Cormac, who dwarfed her with their size. The soft, sweet sound of her laughter drifted back to Richard as she reacted to whatever they were telling her. So far, no one mentioned Ashley, but he knew that would come. It was inevitable.

Chapter 25

EVERYONE BUT RICHARD SEEMED HAPPY to arrive at Breaghacraig. In stark contrast, Richard looked as if he was being led to the gallows. Angelina watched him carefully. This was not the man she had met and come to love in San Francisco. This was a man about to have his secret revealed. How could she know that? She didn't, but he had some sort of secret, she was certain of it and ever since their arrival in Scotland, he had begun to avoid being alone with her. As each day passed, he became more withdrawn and now as he sat atop his horse, he seemed the most uncomfortable she'd seen him yet.

Robert turned to speak to him. "We have your horse here. We've taken verra good care of him. I've ridden him myself on occasion. He is a fine warhorse. I'm sure you'd be happy to see him straight away."

"I would. I appreciate your kindness in caring for him. I have missed him greatly. Arion was a gift to me from my father before his death." He dismounted, handing the reins of his current mount to one of the stable boys. "If you don't mind, I'll go and see him now. I'll join you inside later." Richard followed the stable boy as he walked the horse away from the group gathered in the courtyard.

Angelina leaned over and whispered to Nick, "He sure was in a hurry to get away from us."

"You dinnae understand what Arion means to him. Before coming to San Francisco, he spent every day riding and training him into a fine warhorse. I understand his need to see his horse." Nick dismounted and came to her side. She waved him off and lithely slipped down from her own mount. More stable boys arrived to take the other horses. "Shall we?" Nick asked, extending his arm for her to take.

Angelina giggled at this show of formality on Nick's part. "We're not in San Francisco anymore."

"I believe I always behaved the gentleman, even there, where others are not always on their best behavior."

Again, she couldn't help but laugh. "You're absolutely right. You have always treated me like a lady." She took his arm and walked with him into the great hall of Breaghacraig. "This is beautiful." Angelina's mouth dropped open at the magnificence of the hall. She noticed Edna being greeted by three women. Angelina assumed they were the ladies of the house and as she and Nick approached, they turned to her and she was both shocked and surprised to discover Ashley and Jenna standing near the third, dark-haired woman. She hadn't recognized them, dressed as they were in their medieval clothing. All three women shrieked in delight, and the men turned to stare in amusement as they jumped up and down and hugged one another.

"I can't believe I'm seeing you both!" Angelina said. "So *this* is where you went to on your Scottish vacations!"

"You can't be that shocked to see us. You've seen Cormac." Jenna's smile couldn't have been brighter and Ashley's was a close second.

"We'll be populating this little section of Scotland with all the women we know from San Francisco," Ashley laughed.

"Where's Dylan?" Angelina glanced around, expecting to see him.

"He's in Glendaloch, with Maggie." Jenna said, as if Angelina should know exactly what that meant. When Angelina looked at her blankly, Jenna continued. "Glendaloch is where Edna's from. The Thistle & Hive Inn."

Angelina shook her head. "But I thought he was here. I'm confused."

"He was, but he met Maggie and fell in love. It was so romantic," Jenna gushed. "Maggie needed to go back to Glendaloch, so naturally, Dylan went with her."

Angelina smiled and nodded. "I'm so happy to see you both and to know that you're safe and happy."

"And who's this handsome man?" Jenna asked, nodding in Nick's direction.

"That's Nick Mackall. He's originally from this time, but for the past few years, he's been living in San Francisco. I'm not sure how he got there, but he's pleased to have returned here now."

Ashley and Jenna both said, "Edna," simultaneously. They were giggling like two excited schoolgirls.

"Did I hear you young ladies call my name?" Edna asked with a bright smile. She'd been speaking to the dark haired woman nearby. "Angelina, let me introduce you to Irene. She's the lady of the castle. Robert's wife."

"I'm pleased to meet ye. Welcome to our home." Irene smiled warmly and Angelina immediately felt at ease with her.

"Thank you so much for taking such good care of my niece and her friend."

"'Tis their husbands, my brothers, who take good care of them. I'm blessed to have them in my household. They've made my life much easier with their helpful ways, so ye could say 'tis they who take care of me. I'll go see to some tea. It seems the men already have their whiskey. Would ye care for a little something to eat? Ye must be hungry." Without waiting for an answer, Irene hurried off. "I'll be right back," she called as she left the hall."

Everyone was standing around, chatting happily together. Nick and Angus were filling the MacKenzie men in on their mission to protect the Twin Sword from Malcolm Granger's clutches. Angelina kept checking the doorway, expecting Richard to join them at any moment, but he still hadn't returned.

"Is something wrong?" Jenna asked.

"No. I'm just waiting for Richard. He's in the stable visiting with his horse. I thought he'd be back by now."

"Who's this Richard?" Jenna tipped her head in a knowing manner.

"A friend of mine. He's from this time, too. He was in San Francisco and I met him, I guess, when he first arrived. We never really talked about it, but now that I think of it, I'll bet I met him the minute he dropped out of the fog."

"So, you're not *with* Nick?" Ashley asked, placing emphasis on the 'with'.

"No! We're just good friends. We're more like brother and sister than anything else."

Angelina had her back to the door, but she knew someone had entered because Ashley's face turned ghostly white and she ran across to Cailin, taking refuge behind him. Turning, she was surprised to discover Richard had evoked such a visceral response from Ashley. But why? Did this have something to do with his odd behavior? She'd bet money on it.

Nick hurried over to her side. "Don't jump to conclusions," he warned.

"What's going on? Ashley is obviously terrified of Richard - look at her! She's hiding behind her husband!"

"No matter what you hear, you must give Richard a chance to explain himself."

Angelina shook her head, suddenly angry. "He's had plenty of time to do that. He had time in San Francisco and he's had time since we've been here, but instead he's been avoiding me and while I might not know the particulars, apparently I now know why."

She watched Richard, who had come to a standstill just inside the doorway. He'd seen Ashley run for Cailin and his gaze darted back and forth between Ashley and herself. Richard visibly shook himself and entered the hall, striding across to Cailin and Ashley. He dropped to his knees on the floor in front of them. "My Lady Ashley. I must apologize to you for the terrible treatment you received, not only from me, but also from my men. As you know, Thomas and Roger are no longer a threat to you, but I want you to know that I too, am no longer a threat. I have become a new man, I hope, a much better man. I wish nothing more than to return to my home, where I will leave behind my jealousy and hatred and live my life in the company of my own family. I was on my way here to apologize to you all, when I came across Maggie and Dylan. They accepted me into their camp and treated me as a friend. I believe they saw the man I wanted to become and they were willing to give me that chance. Unfortunately, before I could come here to Breaghacraig to apologize to you, I found myself saved from certain death by Edna, and sent to San Francisco to learn a lesson or two about life and love. I believe I have learned those lessons. I will no longer pose a threat to the MacKenzie Clan. I hope that you'll accept my apology in the spirit in which it has been given. I understand that you may never forgive me and I will have to accept that." He continued to kneel, waiting for what, Angelina didn't know. Ashley slowly came out from behind Cailin.

"I accept your apology and while I will forgive you, I can never forget what you've done," she said, clutching Cailin's hand.

"Cailin, I am at your mercy. I will accept whatever punishment you may wish to mete out," Richard said in a low voice.

By now, Irene was returning to the hall. She had brought a blonde haired woman with her, who carried a tray containing tea and some food. "Richard, get up from your knees. No one is going to mete out punishment, no matter how much you may deserve it."

He stood up and glanced in Angelina's direction. She knew he could see the anger and confusion in her expression. He started to walk in her direction, but she held up a hand to stop him. "I have to know what you did. I cannot and will not go anywhere with you, until I know." Everyone stood in silence and Angelina suspected they were all holding their breath. She turned to her friend. "Ashley. What did he do to you?"

Ashley looked at her feet and took a deep breath before she spoke. "I'd rather tell you in privacy, if you don't mind."

"Gentlemen, let us take our whiskey and go out into the courtyard. There may still be some sun which we may stand in to keep warm," Robert announced. The men turned and left the great hall in silence. Richard was the last to go, his eyes pleading with Angelina, but she turned away from him.

"Would ye like us to go as well, Ashley?" Irene asked quietly.

"No, you know the story. I couldn't bear retelling it in front of the men, that's all. Please, sit down." Ashley walked across to the chairs gathered around the fire and sat down. "Thank you, Helene," she said, addressing the blonde woman, who was handing her a cup of tea. The other women took a seat and each accepted a cup from the tray Helene was carrying. The young woman set the tray on a small table by the fire and excused herself.

"Did he do something to hurt you?" Angelina demanded.

Ashley seemed to be collecting her thoughts. When she finally spoke, she seemed to have regained control of her nerves. "He did. I thought I had gotten past it, but seeing him today without any prior warning, it brought everything back in a rush." Ashley twirled her hair around her fingers and lapsed into silence for a minute. "Are you in love with Richard?" she asked when she spoke again.

"I thought I was, but now I'm not so sure." Angelina glanced at Edna, who seemed somewhat embarrassed by the entire situation.

Ashley sipped her tea before she continued. "Well, the condensed version of the story is that Richard was in love with

Irene." Angelina's head whipped around to catch Irene nodding her head sadly. So *she* was the Irene Nick had spoken about. "He had been in love with her for many years, but she had married Robert, her true love and Richard spent years obsessing about finding a way to get her back. Eventually, he saw his opportunity, and he kidnapped both Irene and me. Richard's man, Thomas…" when Ashley said his name, she cringed, "…he tried to rape me and his other man, Roger, choked me before Thomas stopped him. " She paused, obviously replaying these events in her mind and Angelina felt terrible that she was the cause of Ashley having to relive the memories. "Richard may or may not have known what was going on, as he wasn't there when we were kidnapped, but he was so focused on Irene, he really didn't care what happened to me."

"I'm so sorry, Ashley, but I have to know. Did *he* hurt you?" She hoped the answer would be a negative, but up until this point, she'd heard nothing that would make her want to pursue a relationship with Richard.

"Yes." Hesitating, Ashley turned to Jenna, who nodded. "He hit me."

"Oh my God. He hit you?"

Ashley nodded focusing her gaze on Angelina.

Edna cleared her throat. "I'd like to say something, if ye dinnae mind."

"Of course not. Please, go ahead." Angelina said, turning her attention to Edna. She wasn't certain how much more she could deal with, as she was already feeling queasy after hearing Ashley's tale.

"Ashley, thank ye for sharing yer story with us. I ken it was painful fer ye to relive it." Edna inhaled sharply before she continued. "There is no excuse for Richard's behavior, but I believe that everyone deserves a second chance in life. I gave him a nudge in the right direction and since that time, he has maintained a spotless record. Angelina, ye ken what he did with Maggie and Dylan. He wants to be a good man and he can be. When I sent him to San Francisco, I wanted him to learn what it was like to be in love. Truly in love. Not the type of love he imagined he had with you, Irene. He fell in love with ye, Angelina, and he never once thought about possessing you. He was happy just to be in yer presence. He was willing to let you go if ye didnae wish to return to Scotland with him. It would have hurt him terribly, but he learned that he cannae possess you, he wants you to be in his life because that was what ye want. Ye ken?"

"I do, but I can't possibly be with him now. I can't tolerate a man hitting a woman. As you said, there is no excuse for his behavior," Angelina said sadly.

"Well, I'm sorry to hear it, but I cannae force ye to do something ye dinnae feel right about."

The men were heard entering the hall again. Cailin hurried to Ashley's side and searched her face. "Are ye well, Ashley?"

She nodded and buried her face in his chest, as he wrapped his strong arms around her and held her tightly.

"Where's Richard?" Jenna asked Cormac.

"He's outside, saddling up Arion." Cormac poured himself another whiskey before settling next to his wife by the fire.

"He's leaving, Angelina." Nick had come to Angelina's side and spoke softly, so only she would hear. "Go to him. He's miserably unhappy."

"I can't. I know what he did and I don't want to see him again. It's better that he leaves."

Without a word, Nick turned away from her and strode back out through the door.

Angelina suspected her heart was broken. She had thought she'd found her man, but he had turned out to be no different from all the others. It was time to pick up the pieces of her shattered dreams and put her heart on lock down, once again.

* * *

Richard was slumped against the castle wall. Arion was snuffling his hair and face with his nose, but while he was obviously happy to have Richard back, he couldn't seem to understand what was wrong with him.

"Richard," Nick called to him as he approached.

Richard stood and adjusted his saddle. "It's done, isn't it?"

"I think she just needs some time to digest it all," Nick said, rubbing his hand across Arion's shoulders. "It's been a shock for her. Stay. Give her some time. She'll come around, you'll see."

"Thank you for trying to help, Nick, but I think it's best if I leave. I cannot bear to be around her when she looks at me with such disdain. To know I've disappointed her so." Richard vaulted up onto Arion's back and turned him towards the gate.

"At least stay for the night, Richard!" Nick grabbed the reins, in an effort to get him to stay.

"I cannot. Take care of Angelina and keep her out of harm's way. It has been good to see you again, my friend, but perhaps you were right to have ridden away from me those many years ago. Perhaps one day, I'll see you again."

"Where are you going?" Nick demanded.

"I don't really know." With that, Richard urged Arion into a gallop and took off like a shot through the gates and out of sight of the castle.

Chapter 26

RICHARD WAS DOING AN EXCELLENT job of pitying himself. So good, in fact, he hadn't noticed the five riders heading his way until they were almost upon him. Looking up, Richard realized there was no escape; he was being surrounded on all sides by Malcolm Granger and his men. It was too late to save himself, there was nothing he could do now, except hope that his death would come quickly. He suspected that was all he had to look forward to, given that he did not intend to assist Granger in any way.

"Richard, fancy meeting you here!" Malcolm laughed, as if he'd said something amusing. "Where are you headed to, without your friends?" Malcolm's mount was prancing in place, filled with energy and ready to run.

"I'm heading back to England. So, if you'll excuse me, I've a long ride ahead of me." Richard made to move his horse through Malcolm's men, but they didn't budge.

"You'll be coming with us, Richard. I'll need your help," Malcolm said.

"I cannot help you. I don't know where the sword is, nor do I care."

"I know where the sword is, but I'll need you to return us to San Francisco."

Richard huffed out an impatient breath. "What you still don't seem to understand, is that I have *no* control over the fog. I can't call upon it to take you anywhere."

"I disagree. It seems you were able to call it to you, just before we left San Francisco." When Richard didn't respond, Malcolm shook his head before he continued. "Richard, Richard. I can make you a very wealthy man, if only you'll help me."

"I am a very wealthy man, here in my own time. I have no wish to go back to San Francisco with you."

Malcolm glanced around. "Why are you alone? Where's the lovely Angelina?"

"Being the intelligent woman she is, Angelina realized I was all wrong for her. She is safely ensconced with a friend.

"Mackall?"

"He is there, also."

"Well then, will you come with us willingly, or must we force the issue? You are a good swordsman, perhaps one of the best I've seen, but you are no match for five of us."

Richard knew the truth of Malcolm's statement. He could see no way of getting out of this alive, other than accompanying them on their quest. He'd go, but he'd bide his time until he could escape them. "I see I have no other choice but to join you." He reluctantly relinquished his weapons to Gabe.

"I like that. A reasonable man. I'm warning you though, don't try anything or you'll regret it immediately."

Richard turned his horse back the way he had come and Malcolm's men surrounded him once again. They rode off to the east, towards what Richard knew to be Campbell land.

* * *

Why couldn't she stop thinking about him? She'd tried everything to block Richard from her thoughts, but nothing was working. Angelina had watched from the doorway, hidden from his sight, when he left. She could still envision him, sitting against the castle wall, legs drawn up and his arms folded across his knees. He had looked so sad, so terribly dejected.

She shouldn't feel sorry for him. He'd lied to her. Well, he hadn't actually lied. He just hadn't told her some very important information about himself. Information that would, if she'd had it, have prevented her from getting involved with him in the first place. Angelina wanted to be angry. She wanted to hate him for what he'd done, but somehow, she couldn't see him as that awful man, the one who'd done such horrible things to Ashley. She knew him only as kind, caring, protective, honorable Richard Jefford. Maybe he really had changed for the better. Didn't everyone deserve a second chance? Didn't he?

Nick came out of the stable with his horse saddled and ready to depart. "Good morn, to ye."

"Hi. Where are you going? I thought we were waiting for Edna and Angus, and then we were going to head off to find Malcolm."

"There's been a change of plans. Edna and Angus are going to see Tavish Campbell and I'm going to see if I can find Richard."

"And what am I supposed to do?"

"You can stay and visit with Jenna and Ashley."

It only took a split second for Angelina to make her decision. "I'm going with you."

Nick smiled knowingly. "Are ye sure? I'm nae sure where he was headed, although I think I might have a good idea."

Angelina nodded determinedly. "Yes. I have to see him. I should have given him a chance to explain himself."

"All right then," Nick said, leaning forward in his saddle and inclining his head towards the stable. "Ye'd best hurry, m'lady."

Angelina ran toward the stable, just as one of the boys exited with her horse, already saddled and prepared to leave. She turned to Nick and narrowed her eyes. "You…"

Nick's smile was smug. "Yes."

"Never mind." The stable boy gave her a leg up and she joined Nick.

"Thank you, for knowing me better than I know myself."

"Ye may not know this about me, but I'm a romantic at heart, Angelina. Ye and Richard are my friends. I cannae bear to see either of ye so unhappy."

They nudged their horses into a canter and hurried through the gates of Breaghacraig, heading south.

"So where are we going?" Angelina questioned.

"To England. To Richard's home."

A small thrill of excitement ran through Angelina's heart at the thought of seeing Richard again. She wasn't sure what would happen when she did, but she needed to confirm he was all right.

They rode hard and fast for two straight days, stopping only long enough to obtain fresh horses, grab a bite to eat and get some much-needed sleep. On the morning of the third day, they came upon a river and a beautiful castle nestled on the opposite bank. The gates stood open and Angelina could see people moving about in the courtyard. A tall young man on horseback exited the gates and Nick called out to him. "Edward!" He sat up tall in his saddle and waved at the other man.

"Nick?" the young man said. "Is that you?"

"Aye. 'Tis me, Nick Mackall."

"Follow me down the bank. There's a shallow spot where you can cross," the other man suggested.

They made their way about a quarter of a mile down the bank, and just as Edward said, there was a safe spot to cross in a sparsely wooded area, which led into dense forest behind them. Nick went first, letting his horse pick his way across safely. Angelina followed, taking the same route and they both reached the opposite bank safely.

"Edward, 'tis good to see ye." Nick said, reaching out to grasp Edward's hand.

"It's good to see you, as well. Where are you coming from? And who is this lovely lady you've brought with you?"

"This is Angelina Lawson. Angelina, this is Edward Jefford, Richard's brother. We've travelled from MacKenzie lands to the north."

"I am very pleased to meet you, m'lady." Edward reached out to Angelina and when she took his hand, he brought hers to his lips for a brief kiss, all the while examining her with his soft green eyes.

Angelina smiled, although she thought Edward looked nothing like Richard. He was blonde, fair and had a lightness to his personality, where Richard was dark and brooding. The thought that she might see Richard soon set a rush of butterflies free in her belly and a blush spread across her cheeks.

"We're here to see Richard," Nick said.

Edward reined in his horse and they headed through the castle gates together. Once in the courtyard they dismounted, leaving their horses in the hands of a young stable boy.

"Richard isn't here, but I know Mother will be happy to see you, Nick. You were always one of her favorites."

Angelina was in awe. Unlike Breaghacraig and Castle Fionn, this castle seemed much more like a home. As they entered the castle, she noticed beautifully woven rugs strewn across the floors and brilliantly colored tapestries covering the walls. Light poured in through large windows on the lower portion of the walls and smaller, circular windows higher up. Cathedral ceilings gave the room a sense of grandness, but everything else about it was cozy and warm. The large hearth was set into an interior wall, and the fire blazed, warming the room to a comfortable temperature. "This is beautiful," Angelina whispered.

"I'm sorry. What was that? I didn't quite hear you." Edward came closer and took Angelina's arm, guiding her further into the room.

"I said that this room is beautiful."

"Mother has a talent for decorating. She has made this cold, utilitarian castle into a home. Speaking of Mother, I'll go and see if I can find her. Please, make yourselves at home." Edward exited the room and Angelina turned to Nick, who was observing her with a huge grin plastered across his handsome face.

"What?" she asked.

"I can read ye like a book, lass. Ye love it, dinnae ye?"

Angelina shrugged. "What's not to love? It's just like every fairytale castle I ever dreamt of as a little girl." Angelina would never tell anyone, but this really was her dream come true, right down to every little detail she had envisioned as a ten-year-old. "I can't believe it." She wandered the room, imagining Richard growing up here. What must it have been like for him? She couldn't imagine it being anything but wonderful.

The sound of a woman's voice approaching caught their attention. Both Nick and Angelina turned towards the sound as a tall, blonde haired woman entered.

"Nicholas! I am so pleased to see you again!" The woman glided across the room and placed her hand in his. Nick offered her a short, formal bow.

"Lady Catherine, it's been many years since I've seen you and you haven't changed a bit."

"You can't fool me with your charm, Sir, but I thank you." Lady Catherine turned to Angelina, lifting one delicately arched eyebrow. "Who have you brought with you, Nicholas?" she asked, smiling warmly at Angelina.

"This is Angelina Lawson, Lady Catherine. A friend of Richard's."

"Quite a lovely friend, I would say. Where have you both been?" She examined their clothing, and Angelina suddenly felt extremely underdressed, as she was still wearing her competition clothing. The people at Breaghacraig hadn't mentioned the way she was dressed and Angelina assumed it was because they knew she wasn't from their time, but here she stood in front of Richard's mother, in a pair of dusty, dirty leather breeches, knee high boots, and a once-clean white tunic and leather belt. While she'd bathed at Irene's castle, she had yet to find an opportunity to locate some new clothes. What must Lady Catherine think? "Are you good with a sword, Angelina?"

"I am." Angelina had forgotten she had her sword sheathed and strapped across her back. "Please excuse the way I'm dressed, Lady Catherine. We've ridden for the past two days to get here."

Lady Catherine looked from Angelina, to Nick and back again. "Have you? But why?"

"We're searching for Richard," Nick interjected.

"He's not here. He left several weeks ago to head to the Mac-Kenzies and we've not seen him since. Is everything alright?" Lady Catherine sounded distressed.

"He was with us, up until a couple of days ago. He was well, but he left Breaghacraig and I thought he would be returning home."

"Perhaps he has stopped somewhere along the way and is en-route now. You must stay and wait for him."

Nick exchanged a worried frown with Angelina.

"Please, at least join me for the evening meal and stay the night. I would enjoy the company."

Nick inclined his head in agreement. "Very well. We'd be happy to, m'lady."

"Good. I will have baths drawn for you both, and Angelina, I will find a suitable gown for you to wear." Lady Catherine exited the room in a gentle glide, much the way she had entered. Angelina was fascinated by the way she managed to walk across the room without appearing to take a step, almost as if she were being drawn on a hidden track. Angelina decided it must have taken her years of practice to perfect such a regal air.

Once Lady Catherine was safely out of earshot, Angelina turned to Nick. "Where do you think Richard could be?"

"I'm nae sure. I would've bet my life he was on his way back here. I hope he hasn't run into any trouble."

"We have to find him," Angelina was suffering a rising sense of panic.

"We will, but some fine food and a good night's sleep will do us both good."

"Richard's mother must think I'm odd, with the way I'm dressed."

"Ye'd have no way of knowing this, but she is quite good with a sword herself. She felt if she were to be left here in the castle when her children were young, she wanted to be able to protect herself and her family. Richard's father saw to it that she had the best instructor he could find. So I doubt she thinks yer too odd."

A servant entered the room and bowed deeply before speaking. "Lady Catherine has asked me to show you to your baths. If you'll follow me, my Lord and m'lady."

As they made their way down the passageway leading to their rooms, Angelina couldn't help but wonder once again where Richard was - and if he was all right.

Chapter 27

LADY CATHERINE, ANGELINA, Nick and Edward sat around the fireplace, sipping wine after enjoying a delicious dinner and lively conversation.

"Everything was delicious," Angelina said, her gaze focused on the fire. The crackling and popping of the wood created nostalgic images of times when she was younger. She had loved to sit by the fireplace, staring into the flames as her mother sat nearby and read. Because of those precious memories, she'd always preferred an open fire.

"I'm glad you enjoyed it. Tell me, Angelina, how is it that you know my son and why hasn't he mentioned you to me before now?"

"We haven't known each other for very long. We met rather unexpectedly and found we had a lot in common." Angelina didn't want to lie to Lady Catherine, but wasn't sure she'd understand the whole time traveling thing.

"Edward, would ye care to join me outside for a wee walk?" Nick gave Angelina a meaningful nod and rose to his feet.

"I would be happy to join you." Edward stood up and the two men departed the room, leaving Catherine and Angelina alone.

"I'm glad they've gone," Lady Catherine said. She moved to sit beside Angelina. "I sense there's something you're not sharing with me."

Angelina's cheeks heated. "I don't know what you mean."

"You and Nick rode here with some urgency, based on the state of your clothing upon your arrival. Would you care to tell me about it?"

"Richard and I had a disagreement. I came here to talk to him." Angelina lifted her eyes to meet Lady Catherine's appraising gaze. "Richard asked me to come here with him, but I've found out some things about him that I found very disturbing. I told him I couldn't be in a… uh… relationship with him because of what I'd learned and he left Breaghacraig the same day. After I'd had a little time to think, I decided I wanted to be sure he was alright."

"What did you find out that has upset you?" Lady Catherine's face expressed a keen interest in what Angelina had to say.

"I don't know if I should say."

"There's nothing that I do not know, dear. Please continue."

Angelina inhaled sharply before she spoke again. "We were at the MacKenzies and Richard had been acting very strangely. You see, he was so happy to have me with him and all of a sudden that changed and he started avoiding me. None of it made sense until I saw him apologizing to my friend Ashley for some unspeakable things that were done to her."

"Ah, yes. I know all about those most unfortunate events. He was quite distraught the last time I saw him, and it was his intention to go to Breaghacraig to express his sincere sorrow for what he had done. He did not expect forgiveness, but rather sought to be able to live with himself and perhaps start his life anew here with us. He must have met you fairly recently, then."

"Only a few weeks ago." Angelina sighed heavily, turning her attention back to the flickering fire. "I've mistrusted men for most of my life and I had intended to remain a single woman, rather than get involved with an untrustworthy man. And most of the men I've met have been exactly that. Richard was so different. I didn't intend to fall in love with him, but I did. I thought I'd surely be meeting you under very different circumstances. I just don't know if I can pursue a relationship with him now."

"Angelina, let me tell you some things you most probably don't know about Richard. Perhaps they will help you to understand him better." Lady Catherine took Angelina's hand and gazed into her face. Her honesty and sincerity was evident to Angelina, who prepared herself for the worst. "Richard is my oldest son, Edward the youngest. I have two other sons and two daughters, none of whom lives here any longer. The boys left by choice and my daughters are now married and have homes of their own." She squeezed Angelina's fingers, her soft green eyes moist with unshed tears. "Richard's father was a stern man and despite that, Richard admired and loved him so much. He wanted nothing more than to please his father no matter the cost. Matthew was not the easiest man to live with and I didn't always agree with the way he handled our children, but I did my best to be a good wife and to stand by him. Because Richard was the oldest, it was he who would inherit everything that his father had worked so hard to gain. Richard was soft in his father's eyes, so Matthew was very hard on him, always finding ways to make Richard prove he was worthy to be his heir. When Richard was about fifteen, he met a girl named Irene MacBayne. He fell instantly in love. She was a beauty and he was so young he didn't realize what he was experiencing was merely infatuation. At any rate, Irene was already in love with Robert MacKenzie and while she was kind to Richard, she wanted nothing more than friendship from him. When he returned home and told Matthew of his disappointment, he was berated for losing this girl to another, for shaming the family name by letting a Scotsman have her. His father beat him soundly and Richard, ashamed of disappointing his father, spent the next few days sleeping in the stable. Matthew told him it was his duty to take what rightly belonged to him and that he should not rest until Irene was his. Richard, of course, wanting nothing more than to please his father, became an angry, jealous man whose only purpose in life was to retrieve Irene. The fact that she was married and had children never came into play. Nothing would stand in his way. He was determined to have her, no matter the cost. He was determined to show his father he was worthy of his approval and love. His father, even on his deathbed, reminded Richard of his continual disappointment in him. It was a cruel thing to do and unfortunately, there was little I could do to stop Matthew. I tried talking to Richard about it, but he left home shortly afterwards and… well, he was so young and impressionable and he loved his father and wanted his approval so much. It took years of abusive treatment, both mental and physical to create the angry, vindictive Richard you are so afraid of discovering. I'm sure you can understand that this treatment greatly changed my son from the warm, caring boy he had been to a man who was almost an exact replica of his father. I cannot excuse or condone his behavior and I cannot tell you what to do. I can only say that I fervently believe Richard is worth saving from a lonely life, filled with regret."

With that, Lady Catherine left the room, leaving Angelina to stare into the fireplace and wonder what she should do. She knew what her heart was telling her, but the very last thing she wanted to do was put herself into a bad situation. If Lady Catherine had stayed, maybe Angelina could have explained why she was afraid. That she didn't want to suffer through what she had seen her mother experience with her father. Her mother hadn't been very wise when it came to choosing men, and Angelina's father had been the worst. He had been an alcoholic, a chronic cheater, and any time her mother challenged him regarding those two issues, he would beat her. Angelina had seen enough of it to know she couldn't tolerate that behavior in her own life and so, rather than get involved in a meaningful relationship, she had kept all her relationships casual and had never once let her heart fall into the hands of any man.

Because how would she know which one, if any, she could trust?

* * *

Angelina slept fitfully that night, her dreams haunted by images of Richard trapped in an unfamiliar place. He called to her, but she couldn't seem to reach him. He was searching for a way to escape, but there didn't seem to be any. When she woke, Angelina was utterly exhausted. In her dreams, she had spent the entire night trying to get to Richard. She'd ridden down paths, through forests, down more paths, up hills, across rivers and still she couldn't find him. She'd searched everywhere, calling his name, but he'd never answered. She experienced a heightened sense of urgency when her feet hit the floor. Throwing on her dirty tournament clothes, Angelina knew she had to convince Nick that there was something very wrong. She opened the door to her chamber and headed across the passageway to Nick's. The door opened just as she was about to knock.

"Angelina, we must leave. Something is wrong." The usually upbeat Nick, who took nothing seriously, appeared more disturbed than she had ever seen him before. He took her by the arms and practically shouted at her. "Richard is in trouble. He needs us." Letting go of her, he brushed past her and hurried down the stairs.

Lady Catherine was waiting for them as they descended the last few steps. "Did we all have the same dream?" She searched their faces, as if searching for some sign to ease her worry. "Something is very wrong. You must save him from whatever danger has befallen him."

Angelina took a deep breath and tried to collect her thoughts and calm herself for Lady Catherine's sake. "I believe we did have the same dream. Nick?"

"Aye. Richard is in trouble. I dinnae ken his whereabouts, but we must find him. We'll leave immediately."

"I have the stable boys preparing your horses and the kitchen staff are preparing food for your journey. Please don't let anything happen to Richard. Please." Lady Catherine, who had seemed so poised and calm the night before, was practically in a panic this morning.

"We'll find him," Angelina said, trying to reassure Richard's mother, almost as much as she was trying to reassure herself.

Edward rushed down the stairs. "I'm going with you."

"Edward, please stay here with me. I wish no harm to come to you." Lady Catherine grabbed hold of her youngest son's sleeve.

"I must go, Mother. I will take care and return to you unharmed. I promise." Lady Catherine had latched onto his hands now and Angelina could see she wasn't willing to let go.

"Don't worry," Angelina said. "We'll take very good care of him. Something tells me we're going to need his help."

"Aye. The lad will be fine with us. We'll see to it. When the situation Richard finds himself in is resolved, we'll all return." Nick gently kissed Lady Catherine on the cheek and squeezed her hands reassuringly.

Angelina did the same and then Edward crushed his mother to him in a fierce hug. "Don't worry, Mother. We'll find him and bring him home."

* * *

The horses awaited them in the courtyard, and they mounted and prepared to leave. Edward had assembled his men, leaving some behind to safe guard the castle. Lady Catherine watched from the doorway, clutching a handkerchief to her lips. Angelina could see how worried Lady Catherine was and wished more than anything to ease her of that burden. The only way to accomplish that would be to ensure Richard was safely returned to her and his home.

"We'll make this trip, much the same way we came here, Angelina," Nick said. He seemed worried about whether Angelina could make it, and she had to admit - her thighs and back were aching from all the riding - but she shook her head resolutely.

"Don't worry about me. I can handle anything if it means Richard will be saved." She kicked her horse into a gallop and the men followed swiftly on her heels.

They soon left the bucolic English countryside behind and headed for the Scottish Highlands. Angelina couldn't fathom how, but they seemed to instinctively know where they were going without question or thought. And for now, she was willing to go with her gut instincts, especially considering Nick seemed to be thinking exactly the same thing.

* * *

Sullen and irritable, Richard rode beside Malcolm Granger, who was chatting happily about finding the Twin Sword and how it would give him the power he had always deserved. "We're getting closer. According to my map, we've crossed onto Campbell land and should be at the mouth of the rock vault holding the sword before sundown." He sounded gleeful and Richard wanted to wipe that smile from his face more than anything.

"Finding the vault will do you no good, if you have no way to gain entry," Richard observed with some satisfaction.

"Don't you worry, Jefford, I brought a little something along that will guarantee my entrance." Malcolm was humming cheerfully as he rode further ahead and Pierce took up his vacated position next to Richard.

"What is he talking about? Is he out of his mind?" Richard didn't expect an answer, but Pierce gave him one anyway.

"Not at all. We brought some explosives from the twenty first century. Malcolm had everything ready and waiting when we ran after you that night. He shouldn't have any trouble at all getting that sword. And then, you, of course, will see to it that we return home."

"I keep telling you, returning you to San Francisco isn't up to me. That eventuality won't be an issue, however, as the people here will never allow you to get your hands on the Twin Sword."

"They will. We've got you as a hostage, which means they'll do whatever we tell them to do," Pierce smirked.

Laughter bubbled up from Richard's chest. "You fools. I'm the worst hostage you could possibly have taken! They don't care what happens to me. I am a hated man in this time, but of course, you had no way of knowing that fact." The surprised expression on Pierce's face gave him some small satisfaction and he was delighted when the other man lapsed into a sullen silence.

* * *

The following morning saw Nick, Angelina, Edward and his men camouflaged by an abundant number of trees. They had gathered around a large rock outcropping, at the foot of a craggy hill. They remained as still as possible while they watched Malcolm Granger, arms flapping about, as he paced back and forth in front of what appeared to be a cave opening, which had been sealed by a rock fall. His men could be seen, scurrying back and forth between their horses and the rocks. They couldn't see Richard, which terrified Angelina, but Arion was clearly visible.

Leaving their horses hidden amongst the trees, Nick signaled the others to follow as they carefully made their way closer to Malcolm's position. Angelina searched the area frantically for Richard and was relieved when Nick pointed him out to her. He was sitting with his back against the rocks, with Nash Roydon, Angelina's opponent in the tournament, standing guard over him. She suddenly felt a little better, knowing that Nash was hardly any competition with a sword.

"What are they doing?" she whispered, crawling on her belly to Nick's position.

"I'm nae sure. Malcolm is ranting about something and the others seem to be following his orders."

At the sound of brush breaking behind them, they turned to see the MacKenzies joining them.

"What are ye doing here?" Nick asked, a relieved smile spreading across his lips.

"Ye didnae think to ask us to join ye? Surely ye ken we enjoy a good fight as much as the next man," Cormac replied in a low voice.

Robert chuckled. "Dinnae listen to him. We told Edna we'd meet her here, to help in any way we can. She'll be arriving shortly with the Campbell's, if all went well."

"In the meantime, I believe we should attempt to get a wee bit closer, so we can hear what they're discussing," Nick suggested.

"What is Richard doing with them?" Cailin asked.

"He's not helping them, if that's what you think," Angelina said, sounding a bit defensive even to her own ears.

"I can see that he's nae helping them, lass. He has nae sword and there's a big oaf standing over him. I'm surprised to see him, 'tis all." Cailin exchanged a concerned look with Nick.

Nick raised himself onto his knees, to speak to the group. "Cailin, Cormac... come with me. The rest of ye stay here. We'll discover what they're doing and we'll be right back."

"I'm coming with you," Angelina insisted.

"Nae. Yer staying here and I won't hear another word about it." Nick and the others stayed low to the ground as they made their way to a closer position, remaining out of Malcolm's sight.

Angelina intended to follow them, but Robert had obviously read her body language and lowered himself to the ground next to her. "There is strength to be found in waiting, lass. Ye'll get yer chance, but first let them get the information we need to plan our next move." He placed one large hand on her shoulder and Angelina relaxed under its warmth.

"Okay. I'm just afraid for Richard."

"We're going to do our best to get him out of there safely," Robert said.

"But why? Surely you don't really care about him? Especially after all the terrible things he did to you and your family. Why would you even *want* to save him?" She really was confounded by the situation. Why was she the one who was the angriest with Richard? Shouldn't they have all wanted him dead?

"When ye've lived in this time long enough, lass, ye'll see that friends and adversaries change like the weather. Richard was our enemy, but he has made amends and done something he didnae have to do to help us, so he is our friend. He made some poor choices early on, but he is a man grown now. He finally sees the difference between right and wrong. We are ever changing, lass. From birth to death, our families, where we live and the circumstances we find ourselves in often dictate how we behave. To be able to rise above that, as Richard seems to have done, is an impressive feat. He has earned our respect and will carry it with him, until such time as he proves himself unworthy, though I dinnae believe that will happen." He smiled warmly at her. "Now, let's keep our eyes on our true enemies, shall we?"

Robert's words made a lot of sense and left Angelina with much to think about. Her own family and circumstances had definitely played a part in how she lived her life. Until she had met Richard, she would have been happy to live her life without love - or at least, that's what she told herself. All a result of having a terrible father and a mother who made poor choices. Richard had suffered a terrible father too. It had almost ruined his life, but Edna had helped him rediscover his conscience. If everyone else had forgiven him, including Ashley, why was she holding back? Could she let go of her own past to accept a future here in this time and place with Richard? She was beginning to believe she could. The only thing standing in her way was Malcolm Granger.

Chapter 28

WATCHING AND WAITING, RICHARD realized the chances of getting out of this situation alive were not good, but at the very least, he would see to it that Malcolm Granger didn't get his hands on that sword. He'd bide his time until Malcolm appeared ready to use his explosives and then he'd act. He wasn't completely sure what he intended to do, but somehow, he had to stop him, at least until the Campbell's and Edna made an appearance.

He had already taken note of Nick and the MacKenzie's arrival. They had hidden in the brush off to his right. They were a stealthy bunch and not easily detected by those who didn't have knowledge of their tactics. He kept an eye on them, without giving them away. Richard prayed that Angelina wasn't with them. There was no reason to put herself in harm's way and he hoped that Nick had seen to it that she stayed far away.

Malcolm and his men stopped dead in their tracks a minute later, shielding their eyes from the sun and staring off toward the nearby hills. Coming up over the rise was an army of Campbell men. Richard couldn't see them clearly yet, but he was certain Edna and Angus would be leading the group. Relief flooded his chest - there was hope yet that they'd be able to stop Malcolm from retrieving the sword.

"Hurry!" Malcolm shouted. His men picked up their pace and worked to get the explosives in place quickly. They had been using extreme care in dealing with the explosives until now. With the imminent arrival of the Campbell men, care had gone out the window in exchange for speed. If Richard was going to do anything, it would have to be done now.

* * *

The sight of the Campbell's coming up over the rise sent relief flooding through Angelina's body. What could Malcolm possibly do, against such a large number of men and a very wily witch? Between the MacKenzie's, Edward and his men, and the Campbell's, Malcolm would surely have no choice but to surrender. She glanced around at the others, who all seemed to be taking this very seriously. There were no smiles anywhere among their group, despite the arrival of rein-forcements.

Angelina decided to take the opportunity to get closer to Rich-ard's position. Everyone seemed focused on the Campbell's and no one noticed as she slithered through the brush, moving close enough to see and hear what was happening. She avoided Nick, positioning herself out to his side, far enough away to avoid him discovering she was there.

Malcolm's men scurried back and forth, with something that looked a lot like dynamite. In fact, it *was* dynamite. They were setting fuses and placing them in any crevices they could find in the rocks. Her heart started beating wildly in her chest. Richard needed to escape before the dynamite exploded, or he would be caught in the blast. With single-minded focus and a stubborn streak a mile wide, Angelina was certain she was the only person who could save him.

When it became apparent that they were ready to light the fuses, Richard leapt to his feet and took a swing at the man guarding him. Knocking him out with a single blow, Richard grabbed the man's sword and turned on the others, taking up an offensive stance.

Malcolm yelled at Richard, before he pulled a pistol from his waistband. Malcolm - *Mr. Medieval* - had bought a gun with him. Angelina's heart leapt into her throat. She had to stop Malcolm, but what could she do? Without conscious thought, she bolted upright and ran straight at Malcolm, intent on knocking him off his feet before he could pull the trigger. She heard Nick curse and events seemed to move in slow motion. Just as she reached Malcolm, he turned in her direction, pointing the weapon at her. Before he could fire a shot, Angelina hit the ground and rolled to safety behind a large boulder. Richard was charging at Malcolm now, but Malcolm still held the gun. "Stop!" he ordered, but Richard paid no attention. He continued barreling directly towards Malcolm, who cocked the pistol and fired. The shot hit Richard, and he fell backwards and slumped to the ground.

"No!" Angelina heard herself screaming as she got to her feet and ran toward Richard. Before she could reach him, she was seized around the waist in an iron grip, thwarting her attempts to get away. Tears coursed down her cheeks. "No!" she cried repeatedly.

"Everyone, clear the area. Light the fuse!" Malcolm snapped. Angelina found herself dragged further away from Richard, who still lay motionless on the ground.

The Campbell clan was running towards the scene with Edna leading the way, but it was apparent they were too far away to stop Malcolm. The dynamite exploded, raining pieces of rock and dirt over the surrounding area. Angelina couldn't see Richard through the smoke and debris, and she prayed he was still alive and had survived the explosion.

Before the dust had a chance to settle, Malcolm bolted toward the mouth of the cave. Fortunately, Edna had arrived and she chanted a spell, casting it in his direction. Malcolm was frozen mid-stride, resembling a marble statue.

"Would anyone else care to join him?" Edna challenged with a determined gleam in her eye. Malcolm's men turned to run, but Edna stopped them with a firm warning. "Dinnae move or ye'll find yerselves in a similar position to yer boss." They all immediately stopped. Angelina pried herself loose and ran to where she'd seen Richard fall. Miraculously, he'd been unharmed by the rocks that had exploded all around them. Malcolm's man Nash hadn't been so lucky. He was buried under the debris, his arm the only visible evidence of where he lay.

"Richard!" Angelina cried, dropping to her knees. "Richard! Please, wake up!"

Edna joined her, kneeling at Richard's side. "Richard, 'tis Edna. I'm going to do my best to help ye, lad, but ye must want to come back to us." She tore open Richard's shirt to locate the bullet wound and found it in his right shoulder. "Angus, bring my saddlebag, dear."

Angus did as she asked and placed it by her side. "Robert, Cailin, I'll need yer help. Angus yer in charge of the saddlebag. Cailin, I need ye to hold Richard down in case he wakes while we work. Robert, I believe ye've more experience in treating battlefield wounds than I, so 'tis you who'll remove the bullet. Do ye ken?"

"Aye." Robert removed his dirk from his boot and joined Edna at Richard's side.

Edna instructed Angus to retrieve a bottle of rubbing alcohol from the saddlebag. He reached in and pulled it out, along with gauze and other bandaging supplies. "Robert, let's disinfect that blade, if ye dinnae mind." Robert placed the dirk in her hand and she poured rubbing alcohol over the blade. She also poured some on Richard's wound, for good measure.

Robert retrieved his knife and inserting it into the wound, carefully probed the wound to locate the bullet. When he found it, he asked Edna to pour more alcohol over his hands, before he used his fingers to grasp the bullet and remove it. "I believe it hit the bone, Edna." Robert showed them a piece of bone fragment, which had come away along with the bullet.

"Never fear, Robert. Whilst a broken bone in these times can be a death sentence, especially if infection sets in, I assure ye I can make sure that doesnae happen." She passed her hand over Richard's wound, chanting a spell as she did so. She repeated this incantation a number of times and everyone watched in amazement as the wound began to close up, before their eyes.

"He's going to be alright, dear," Edna said, resting a comforting hand on Angelina's shoulder. "He's going to be alright. Your tears, mixed with my spell are what did it. You see, my spell alone would nae have worked, but your love for him seeped into that wound, along with your tears - and that's what saved him." Edna got to her feet with a little help from Angus. "He'll need some time to heal. Although the wound is no longer visible, he will still suffer the pain of it."

"Why isn't he waking up?" Angelina demanded.

"He needs to sleep, to recover. Now, I must reset these stones. We cannae take the chance of anyone else getting their hands on the Twin Sword. Believe me, it would be a terrible disaster. The longer the cave entrance remains open, the more likely it is that someone will answer the call of the sword as it seeks its entrance back into the world." She hurried away leaving Angelina crouched over Richard's prone body.

"Are ye alright, lass?" Nick asked when he joined her. Edward joined them and knelt beside his brother. Both men gazed on Richard with brotherly love and eyes filled with unshed tears.

Edward brushed the loose dirt away from Richard's face. "He's a good man."

"That he is, lad." Nick placed a comforting hand on Edward's shoulder and his other on Angelina's. The three stayed at Richard's side, determined to be there when he awoke.

* * *

Edna was preparing to reseal the vault.

"What do ye plan to do with that one?" Angus asked, pointing at Malcolm's motionless figure.

"There's nae I can do fer him now. He chose his own fate. He wanted the sword, and now he will share its resting place for all of eternity." Edna began chanting and waved her arms across the cave entrance. With each new wave, the rocks began to drop back into place at the mouth of the cave. She gathered up the rocks covering Nash's body, returning them to their original positions in the same manner. When the vault was completely sealed, Edna cast a second spell, leaving the cave entrance seamless. No one would ever know the cave had ever been there.

With that accomplished, Edna stood over Nash's lifeless body. "I see nae need that ye should suffer for the misdeeds of yer master." She ran her hands over his broken body, paying special attention to the areas in which he had suffered major injuries. Slowly, Nash came back to life. His eyes opened wide in sheer terror as he recalled what had happened. "Calm yerself," Edna soothed. "Ye'll be well again, lad. I intend to see that ye and yer friends go safely back to where ye came from with no memory of ever having been here. Ye will also spend yer days doing good, and avoiding evil from this point forward. Do ye ken?"

Nash nodded in agreement, as Edna called his friends to his side to assist him. The power of speech seemed to elude them, so Edna repeated what she had told Nash and left them to care for their friend.

"Angus, my love? Once we are finished here, I would like to go back to visit with the Campbell's for a brief time. Yer Uncle Tavish will be relieved to hear that the sword is once again safely hidden away."

"Edna, ye never cease to amaze me." Angus pulled her into his arms and planted a big kiss on her lips. "I love ye, my wife."

She snuggled into his embrace. "After visiting the Campbell's, we'll head back to Castle Fionn for a wee while, before going home to The Thistle & Hive."

"That sounds like a wonderful plan, mo chroi." Angus and Edna stood together and breathed a sigh of relief that it was over.

Chapter 29

ANGELINA, NICK AND EDWARD stood watch over Richard Jefford as he continued to sleep. He hadn't yet awoken from Edna's spell, but he had started to stir, so they had gathered around the bed to wait. The MacKenzie's had kindly offered Breaghacraig as a place for Richard to recuperate and invited Angelina, Nick, Edward and his men to stay indefinitely.

"Do you think he'll awaken soon?" Edward asked, hope tingeing his voice.

"Aye. He will." Nick sounded confident.

The door opened and Ashley entered. "How is he?" she asked, closing the door behind her.

"The same, but he's grown restless. I believe he may wake soon," Nick replied.

"Helene was coming to tell you that the noon meal is being served, but I told her I'd do it as I wanted to check on our patient." Ashley had been spending increasing amounts of time in Richard's room, helping to care for him. Gone was the fear that Angelina had seen that first day they arrived. Ashley seemed to have made peace with her concerns about him. "If you'd like to go down to grab a bite to eat or go outside for some fresh air, I'd be happy to sit with him. I'll send word the minute he wakes."

Angelina's gaze fell on Richard, who seemed to be sleeping deeply again, so she agreed. "Alright, that's a good idea. I think we could all use some nourishment. Nick? Edward?" She motioned toward the door and the two men took one last look at Richard before leaving with her.

* * *

A soft, cool hand brushed across Richard's face, followed by a damp cloth. He struggled to open his eyes and when he managed the feat, he was shocked to see it was Ashley sitting beside him. She had turned her face away as she dipped the cloth into a basin by the bed, and when she turned back, she smiled warmly. "You're awake."

He opened his mouth to speak, not certain if he was dreaming. Ashley was the last person he would have expected to be seated by his bedside. He finally managed to rasp out a word, "Yes," before he struggled to sit up.

Placing a firm hand on his chest, Ashley held him in place. "You shouldn't strain yourself. You've had a bad injury and you need to take it easy while you recover."

He relaxed back onto the pillow, exhausted by the simple act of trying to sit up. "Where is everyone?" His gaze darted around the room, in search of another familiar face. He desperately wanted to know where Angelina was, to ensure she was all right.

"Angelina, Nick and Edward went downstairs for a meal. They'll be back soon, I expect. They haven't left your side for more than a few minutes at a time since you were injured."

"Is she alright? Was she hurt?" Richard questioned anxiously.

"She's fine, but she's very worried about you."

Richard assumed he was at Breaghacraig, because it seemed the only explanation for Ashley being here. "The sword? What happened to the Twin Sword?"

"Edna took care of everything, just as she always does." Ashley proceeded to repeat the stories she'd heard from Cailin.

Richard was relieved to learn Malcolm's attempt to obtain the Twin Sword had been thwarted.

There was a knock at the door and Ashley got up to see who it was. "Yes, Helene?"

"I came to see if you needed anything," Helene said.

"Could you tell everyone Richard is awake?" Ashley requested.

"Aye. 'Twill be a pleasure," Ashley closed the door and Richard could hear the sound of Helene's feet as she hurried down the passageway.

Ashley returned to sit beside him and to his great surprise, she took his hand in her own. "Richard, I've done a lot of thinking and I want you to know that I do believe you have changed for the better. In fact, I'm convinced of it. The Richard Jefford who was abusive to me, was a man possessed by the demons from his past and I believe you have successfully exorcised them."

Richard gazed up at her in wonder. "Thank you, Ashley. I do not deserve your forgiveness, but I am grateful to have it."

The door burst open and three people tried unsuccessfully to push through it simultaneously. Angelina won the battle and ran over to him, tears streaming down her cheeks. "Richard! Thank God!" She put out a hand to touch him, but pulled back at the last instance, as if afraid to do so.

"I will not break, my love." He reached up to grasp her hand, and pulled her down to him. The smell of roses assailed his nostrils with the most wonderful of scents. He hadn't thought he'd see her angelic face ever again, nor be able to run his hands through her silky locks, but here she was and he was overwhelmed with emotion.

"We've been so worried about you," she sniffled, pulling back to look into his eyes.

"Aye, we have. Angelina has barely slept, she's been by yer side almost constantly." Nick leaned over Angelina to place a hand on Richard's arm, as if he weren't convinced he was real.

"Edward. My brother. You're here as well." Richard smiled broadly at the sight of his younger sibling.

"When I heard you were in trouble, I joined Nick and Angelina to search for you. Mother wasn't happy I was going, but I insisted."

Richard smiled warmly. His baby brother was becoming a fine young man and Richard was very proud of him. "I'm happy you're here."

"I wanted to stay until you awoke. Edna told us you'd be all right, but I had to see it with my own eyes so that I could travel home to tell Mother that you are well. She will be very relieved."

"When will you leave?" Richard asked.

"Tomorrow morning. I'd like to get word to her as quickly as possible. You'll need to stay here a while longer, I think." Edward moved around to the other side of the bed, where he leaned in and hugged Richard. "I am happy you'll be coming home Richard. I've missed you greatly." He coughed and cleared his throat, vainly trying to conceal the emotion everyone could hear in his voice.

Angelina flicked her gaze from Nick to Edward. "Would you mind if I had a few minutes alone with Richard?"

"Of course not. We'll see you later, my friend." Nick escorted Ashley from the room and Edward followed them.

When the door closed behind them, Angelina made herself more comfortable, sitting on the edge of the bed. Richard hadn't let go of her hand for a moment and he was watching her warily. "Richard, I want to apologize to you for my behavior."

"You have nothing to apologize for. You did nothing wrong." Richard reached up to cup her cheek against his hand. The love he had for Angelina was beyond anything he'd ever experienced in his life.

"I've spoken with your mother."

Richard was surprised by this announcement. "You've met my mother?"

"Yes. When you left here, Nick and I thought you'd be returning home. He was determined to find you and I went along, because I didn't feel I'd given you a chance to fully explain your actions."

Richard listened quietly, rubbing his thumb tenderly across the back of her hand.

"Anyway, your mother is very sweet. She told me about your father and gave me a far clearer picture of you. I know you wanted to tell me yourself, but the timing has never seemed to be right. I also learned that you were afraid to tell me, because you knew how I'd react and I'm ashamed to say I did exactly what you expected." Vivid blue eyes gazed into his own and he had to remind himself to breathe. "I had to examine my own feelings in order to discover why, if everyone else had forgiven you - even Ashley - why I was still so angry with you."

Richard shook his head. "Angelina, please, this is my shame to bear. None of this was your fault. All I need to know is that you've forgiven me and there's a chance you'll start to love me again." Richard held his breath, awaiting her answer.

Tears began to roll down her cheeks again. "Yes I do forgive you... and I never stopped loving you."

Richard pulled her down to rest her head on his chest and held her close. She loved him. The sweetness of her words went straight to his heart. He'd spend the rest of his days making her happy. It was all he wanted to do. "When can we go home?"

"As soon as you're able." Angelina sat up again. "May I kiss you?"

"That's a question you never need to ask, love." Richard drew her down to him and they shared the sweetest kiss. Sweeter than any they'd experienced thus far. It was a kiss that marked a new and honest beginning, a kiss filled with promise of their future together.

* * *

Edward and his men, along with Nick left the following morning. Nick was returning home to his family, who would undoubtedly be shocked by his return. He had quite the story to tell, whether they believed him or not. He had promised Richard they would meet again soon and Richard warned Nick he was going to hold him to that promise.

Richard was up out of bed and had managed to get himself downstairs and into the courtyard, where he breathed deeply in the cold, fresh air. He was ready to return to his own home, but had promised Angelina they would stay one more day, to be certain he was ready for travel. She had assured him it had nothing to with the fact that she and the MacKenzie women were busily creating a *genuine* medieval gown and cloak for Angelina to wear on their journey. Richard was thankful that everything had worked out and he was more than ready to begin his new life with Angelina.

The MacKenzie men joined him in the courtyard. "'Tis good to see ye up and about, Richard. The weapon Malcolm Granger used to shoot ye was like none we've ever seen. I feared ye wouldnae survive it." Robert put a hand on Richard's shoulder as he spoke.

"I cannot thank you enough for taking me in, and caring for me the way you did. It means more to me than I can ever express." Richard gazed earnestly at each of the men in turn.

"Yer one of us now, Richard," Cormac said. Richard was confused by this pronouncement and it must have shown in his face, because Cormac continued to explain. "Angelina is my Jenna's auntie, ye see and because we are wed, she is my auntie as well. When ye marry me auntie, ye'll be me uncle." Cormac chuckled at this fact.

"I hadn't thought of that. You're right. I will be your uncle." Richard chuckled.

"Welcome to the family," Cailin said, offering him his hand.

"Thank you, Cailin. I'm quite sure you'd rather pummel me than welcome me," Richard smiled.

"Aye. That would've been the case not so long ago, but my wee wife has forgiven ye and as long as she's happy, I am as well. I will say, if ye ever do anything to hurt her again, I willnae be responsible for what happens to ye." Cailin seemed quite serious, which made Richard a little uncomfortable, but then Cailin broke into a wide grin, to reassure Richard all was well.

"We were about to ride out to visit with some of the nearby tenants, if ye'd care to join us. It might be useful to see how ye'll fair tomorrow, when ye leave us."

"That seems like an excellent idea. I'd love to," Richard agreed.

* * *

"When you set your wedding date, you'll let us know, won't you?" Ashley asked, as Angelina tried on her new gown.

"You'll be the first to receive an invitation. Of course, he hasn't officially asked me, but I think it's pretty clear we don't plan on being away from each other, ever again." Angelina slipped the gown over her head and Irene laced up the back.

"The blue is a perfect match fer yer eyes," Irene stated.

The women had taken one of Irene's gowns and modified it to fit Angelina. Their efforts had paid off and it fit like a glove. Angelina admired herself in the mirror. Irene was right, the sapphire blue was perfect. Now they just needed to put the finishing touches on her cape, made of an even deeper blue and lined with fur to keep out the cold. "This is the most luxurious piece of clothing I've ever owned. When I get to my new home, I'll have to find out where I can buy fabric and supplies to make more gowns."

Jenna crossed to the corner of the room and retrieved a beautifully wrapped package, which she handed to Angelina with a warm smile.

"What's this?" Angelina demanded.

"A starter kit," Jenna laughed. "We put this together for you. There's fabric, ribbons, needles and threads. You should have enough there to make two or three more gowns."

Angelina was overcome with affection for these women. She kissed each of them on the cheek and then announced, "Group hug!" They giggled and laughed and held onto each other, enjoying the bonds of sisterhood they all felt. "The only thing that would make this more perfect, would be if I were to live closer."

"We'll make time to come and see you, and if you do the same, I might even see you more often than I did in San Francisco," Jenna said.

"That sounds really good. And Ashley, I don't want to miss seeing your baby when it's born." Angelina grinned happily. "This is so nice! I never thought I'd have a family like this. I had gotten so used to being on my own, I didn't think I needed anyone, but now I know that's not true and there's nothing wrong with needing other people in your life. Right?"

"Right!" they replied in unison.

* * *

Robert and Irene happily hosted a farewell banquet for Richard and Angelina on their final evening at Breaghacraig, and now, everyone stood on the steps of the castle, waving goodbye.

Richard and Angelina were mounted on their horses and ready to ride through the gates, but before they did, they both took one last look at the smiling faces wishing them a safe journey back home.

They both waved and exited the courtyard to start the long journey back to England.

Richard couldn't take his eyes off Angelina. She was a beautiful woman by any standards, but somehow, the sight of her in her new gown and cloak, cheeks rosy from the cold, had completely taken his breath away. As they rode, soft snowflakes began to fall.

"It's snowing!" Angelina cried in delight. She lifted her face to the sky, letting the light flurries land on her face and eyelashes.

Richard couldn't help but laugh and watched adoringly.

"It never snows where I'm from. This is so beautiful! Do you think it will snow any harder?" Her face glowed with happiness.

"I hope not much harder. We will need to stop for the night and I have the perfect place in mind. The snow, no matter how beautiful, will make our journey more difficult, so let's hope it stays like this."

Angelina scooted her horse a little closer to Arion and Richard reached for her hand. They rode that way for many miles, both of them happy and at peace.

Chapter 30

As the sun began to set, they reached the little cottage Richard remembered from his meeting with Maggie and Dylan. He hoped it remained unoccupied. He was sure whoever owned it would welcome them warmly if it wasn't, as was the local custom, but this night he wanted Angelina all to himself. Thoughts of her lying naked beneath him had occupied his mind for many, many miles and relief for his aching manhood was only moments away.

"What do you think?" he asked, pointing in the direction of the small stone cottage.

"It's a sweet little place. Is this where we're spending the night?" Her lashes fluttered as she smiled seductively, suggesting that she too had been having thoughts along the same lines as his.

They approached the cottage, which as Richard had hoped, was empty. He dismounted and hurried to help Angelina. She wasn't used to riding in a gown, and he didn't want to risk her falling. She leaned over and placed her hands on his shoulders and he put his around her waist, lifting her easily and setting her on the ground.

"Oh!" Angelina said. "The snow is so cold!"

Richard lifted her into his arms and carried her into the cottage. "Wait here. I'll be right back. I must see to the horses and then I'll get a fire started." He quickly unsaddled the horses and set them free to roam. He laughed as Arion immediately lay down and rolled in the snow. Angelina's horse apparently thought it an excellent idea, as she followed suit in short order.

Bringing the saddles into the cottage, Richard noted the supply of wood in the fireplace, ready for him to light. He closed the door and made sure the windows were tightly shuttered before setting to work on the fire, which he had burning in moments.

"You're quite the boy scout," Angelina teased.

Richard gave her a quizzical look. "Boy scout?"

"I'll explain it to you some other time. I'm hungry." She grabbed the saddlebags and pulled out some of the food Irene had provided. She daintily sat in front of the fire with Richard at her side.

How can she think about food at a time like this? The expression on his face must have given him away, because Angelina laughed.

"You should eat. You're going to need your strength later," she teased. She offered him a piece of bread.

Richard knew that Angelina knew exactly what she was doing to him and she was enjoying it, so he took the bread and helped himself to some cheese. He uncorked a flask of wine and drank deeply. He offered it to Angelina who took it from him as she gazed seductively into his eyes.

They were cocooned in their own private world. The fire sent a golden glow around the cottage, while the snow continued to fall outside..

"When you said I was going to need my strength, is this what you meant?" He snaked his arm around her waist, hauling her against his chest. His lips were on hers, before she could respond, the need to have her so strong that he had to physically restrain himself from tearing her gown away so he could reach her velvety soft skin.

Angelina, for her part, was right there with him. They were both pulling and tugging at clothing until finally, and thankfully, they were completely naked, free to roam their hands over each other's bodies. Clothes were strewn all over the room as they fell onto the bed, lips and hands seeking and finding. The heated passion of their lovemaking was intense, a smoldering heat that swiftly turned to flame. Richard positioned Angelina beneath him, his hands on her breasts, and he playfully pinched her pebbled nipples. Angelina reacted to his touch in the way he'd dreamed she would. Her response was immediate, a moan of pleasure escaping her lips as she thrust her hips upwards ready for his entry, but he was enjoying this far too much to rush. She wriggled and writhed beneath him, rubbing against his hardened staff in an effort to get what she wanted.

"Not yet," Richard whispered into her ear, nibbling at her ear lobe and then kissing and licking his way down to her beautiful, velvety pink nipples. He took one into his mouth, and Angelina whimpered in ecstasy. His large hands cupped her other breast, squeezing until her back arched towards him in sheer pleasure. She was on the edge, would only need a slight nudge to send her reeling into orgasm, but he wanted to make this last for both of them. He'd been waiting a very long time since that night at her beachside home. He wanted to savor every moment, make it last as long as possible. He continued to twist and tease her nipples, knowing he was driving her wild with desire and loving every minute of it.

Finally, when she could stand it no more, he lowered his mouth to her core, and her orgasm exploded, but still he continued to lap and tease at her. She gripped his hair, grasping and pulling as he brought her to climax repeatedly. When he was done, he smiled in satisfaction, knowing he had pleased his woman greatly. He slithered back up her body and kissed her parted lips.

* * *

Catching her breath, Angelina kissed him back, slipping her tongue into his mouth and forcing him onto his back.

"Your turn," she smiled seductively. She covered his mouth with kisses, preventing him from speaking as her hands sought his shaft and began to massage gently. Richard closed his eyes on a moan and Angelina copied what he had done only minutes before, kissing, licking, and nipping from his ears, to his nipples, and on to his swollen manhood. She skirted around it, knowing that was what he most wanted, but preferring to make him wait. Her hands slithered up his thighs, again coming close to him but not touching. His breath was coming in short gasps when she finally put her mouth over him. He almost came undone, but she saw him take steps to control himself, reaching down to hold her head and play with her hair. She brought him almost to the point of climax and then straddled him, lowering her warm, wet passage over his length, gliding up and down, enjoying the sweet sensations she was creating as much as Richard was. He reached up to cup her breasts and Angelina rode him, her back arched, her hair flowing all around her. She felt powerful knowing she could bring Richard such pleasure, that he wanted her, that he loved her. As Richard got closer to his orgasm, he grabbed Angelina around the waist and placed her beneath him again, this time thrusting into her until they both cried out and reached their release together. They clung to one another, exhausted and sated from their efforts.

* * *

Sometime in the middle of the night, they made love again and when they were done, Richard got up to see to the fire. When he returned, he wrapped Angelina in his warm embrace, confident that he was the luckiest man in the world. She sighed contentedly in his arms and they easily fell back to sleep.

Richard awoke the following morning to the sight of a smiling Angelina, wrapped in his tunic and seated by the fire. She had added some wood and the fire blazed brightly, warming the little cottage and keeping the cold at bay. She set out some food for their breakfast and heated water for tea. Richard joined her on the floor by the fire after pulling on his trewes. She scooted closer and offered him a quick kiss, which Richard swiftly turned into a long, lingering kiss.

"I am so happy to be here with you, Richard. I have to keep pinching myself to make sure I'm not dreaming the most wonderful dream." She tore some bread from the loaf Irene had provided and placed a slice of cheese on top, before putting it into a pan near the fire.

"What's that you're making?" Richard asked curiously.

"It's a grilled cheese, I hope." She removed the pan from the fire, careful not to burn herself. "We should probably let it cool off for a minute."

"I can hardly wait to try it."

After a minute, she tested the bread to ensure it wasn't too hot and lifted it from the pan. "Pretty good for my first attempt without modern cooking tools."

"These *are* modern cooking tools," Richard laughed.

"Oh, yeah. Right." She smiled sweetly at him. "I forgot - from now on I'll be using the latest and greatest in medieval technology."

They ate and Richard thought he'd never tasted anything better, if only because of the fact that Angelina had cooked it for him. He liked her ingenuity and knew she would fit in to his world well. "Will you miss anything about San Francisco?" he asked curiously.

"I'm sure I will. It's a beautiful place, as you've seen, but there's really nothing for me there. Everything I could possibly want is sitting here with me now."

Her words pleased him greatly, as he felt much the same way about her. "We should pack our things and prepare to leave. If we get started now, we'll be to Keswick by nightfall and then it's only a short journey to home."

They cleaned up the little cottage, leaving it exactly as they'd found it. Richard already had fond memories of this place and now he had even more reason to remember it happily, as the place where he began his life anew. He called to the horses, who came running. He gave the horses apples left from their breakfast and some oats mixed with warm water. After the horses were done with their meal, Richard and Angelina saddled them. Angelina was again wearing her new gown and cloak. Her beauty was beyond words and Richard had to give himself a mental shake, so he could continue preparing for the remainder of their journey and not get completely lost in admiring his beautiful woman.

They put out the fire and closed everything up so that the next visitors to the cottage would find a welcoming place to lay their heads. Richard gave Angelina a leg up onto her horse and then mounted Arion. The snow had stopped at some time during the night, leaving a soft powder a few inches deep for them to trek through. The horses had no trouble navigating their way along the road that led to Keswick and then home.

"Richard, does your mother know about time traveling?" Angelina guided her horse around a large icy patch.

"I've told her about it, but I'm not sure whether she believed me or thought I was daft." Richard skirted the same icy patch from the other side of the path.

"I hope she won't mind having me around." He could tell from her tone she was worried and tried to ease her mind.

"She will be more than happy to have you there. My sisters are married and in their own homes now. I think she misses having another woman around to talk with. She's been surrounded by men for years now." He stole a peek to see her reaction and noticed her shoulders relaxing. "She'll love you, because I love you," he added. She'll also love you because like her, you love me."

Angelina offered him another of her brilliant smiles and they urged their horses into a trot, excited to reach the end of their journey.

* * *

"Richard, I see a village up ahead. Is that Keswick?" Angelina craned her neck to see.

"It is. We're almost home."

They cantered the rest of the way into the quaint little village. Angelina found herself fascinated by everything she was seeing. There were small shops dotted here and there, along with an inn for weary travelers. "Will we be able to come back and explore?"

"Mother comes to the village weekly to shop and to visit with the people who reside there. I'm sure she'll be happy to have some-one to take along with her." They had made their way through the village and urged their horses back into a canter. Before she knew it, Angelina saw the beautiful little castle she was going to be calling home. Torches from the courtyard, cast a golden glow, which was visible from the road. As they approached, the gates swung open, granting them entrance.

Richard pulled to a stop in front of the castle doors, and was greeted by a young lad, who took charge of Arion. Richard gently lifted Angelina down from her mare. The young lad gathered her reins as well and headed towards the stable with the horses.

Richard took Angelina's hand and led her through the doors and into the lovely room she recalled from her first visit.

"Richard!" Edward called when they entered. "Mother! Richard is here!"

Lady Catherine must have been close by, because she rushed in-to the room and straight to Richard, whom she captured in her arms. He wrapped his arms around her and hugged her fiercely. Stepping back, she took his face between her hands and gazed lovingly at him. "Richard I'm so happy you're home."

"Mother, I'm so happy to *be* home." Richard held her away from him. "You are as beautiful as always."

"Nonsense. You sound just like your friend, Nick," she blushed.

"He speaks the truth." Richard turned to Angelina and offering her his hand, drew her up to stand beside him. "Mother, I believe you've already met Angelina. I've brought her home with me to be my wife. I hope you'll approve."

"I do more than approve. She will be a good match for you and will serve well as the lady of the castle." Lady Catherine smiled warmly at Angelina, and tipping her head to the side, reached out to touch Angelina's cheek. "She is a beauty to behold. I am so happy for you, my son."

Chapter 31

UNTIL THEY WERE MARRIED, Lady Catherine would not give permission for them to share the same room, but she did place Angelina in a room connected directly to Richard's through a single door. She ignored the fact that they spent every night together and only separated in the morning to return to their own rooms.

A wedding was planned for the New Year and Angelina and Lady Catherine were kept busy making preparations for the event. Invitations had been hand delivered to all their family and friends. Angelina and Lady Catherine had been to the village together on more than one occasion, and Angelina felt certain Lady Catherine told Richard about some of the lovely items they saw, because they always seemed to end up in her possession before another day or two had passed. Richard had bought her a beautiful pendant with matching earrings, and a bolt of the finest silk in a deep purple, along with ribbons and trim to match. He'd purchased a hand carved wooden box for her to keep her trinkets in, and he smiled proudly when he saw how touched she was by his gifts.

Angelina was settling in perfectly to the Jefford household, having learned a lot from Lady Catherine about what was expected of her. Richard and Angelina also sat his mother down one afternoon, and explained how they'd met. Her eyes grew wide at their amazing tale.

"The city of San Francisco sounds like a place that I'd like to see," Lady Catherine announced, after hearing descriptions of the city's beauty and all the wondrous things that could be found there.

"You'd like to time travel?" Angelina asked in surprise.

"Yes. I believe it would be a great adventure." Lady Catherine sat up straighter in her chair, gazing up at the ceiling as if she could spy San Francisco up there. "Anything is possible, as you always say, my dear."

Angelina giggled. The more she'd gotten to know her, the more Angelina appreciated the strength Lady Catherine must have shown to deal with her husband Matthew for all those years. She was as much a free spirit as Angelina, but they both had to keep that secret when they were around anyone who didn't know them well. They had talked long into the night, discussing San Francisco, time travel, the wedding and many other topics. Lady Catherine must have been exhausted, as she began to yawn heavily. "I'm off to bed, my dears. I will see you in the morning."

She left them alone by the fire. Richard placed some cushions on the floor and they abandoned their chairs to wrap themselves in each other's arms on the floor. Angelina rested her head on Richard's shoulder and sighed contentedly.

"Happy?" he asked.

"Very," she replied.

"Angelina, I don't think I have ever properly asked you to marry me. I just assumed we would be together." He lifted her chin so he could see her face.

"I always assumed we'd be together too. It seemed only natural that we would be married."

Richard tucked a finger beneath her chin and turned her face gently to his. His dark eyes were filled with love. "Angelina, will you marry me?"

"There was never a need to ask, but now that you have, my answer is yes." She kissed him soundly, which stretched into another kiss and then another.

"We should go upstairs, my love," Richard said, his voice husky with desire. He took her hand and helped her up from the floor.

"You know, it's a good thing we're getting married soon, Richard." She had started up the stairs and turned to face him.

He gazed up at her expectantly. "And why is that, love?"

"Because there's going to be a little baby Jefford joining the family in about eight months."

Richard stopped on the bottom stair, his mouth agape. "What?"

Angelina smiled happily. "I'm pregnant."

Richard lifted her from the stairs and twirled her around. Angelina had never seen him so animated. "I'm going to be a father!" he shouted.

"Shhh… We can't tell anyone yet. Remember, we're not married. It has to be our little secret for the time being." Angelina touched her finger to his nose and giggled. "I never believed this would happen for me. I always thought I would live my life alone and now I've got you and your family, and our baby to be. I'm a lucky girl."

Richard swept her up into his arms and began to walk up the stairs. "No, my love, 'tis I who am the lucky one."

THE END

About the Author

Jennae was born and raised a New England girl, just outside of Boston, Massachusetts, where her imagination was always bigger than she was. Surrounded by an abundance of nostalgic, historical landmarks her love of history and creative writing was formed. Her large extended Irish and Italian families were not only a great source of support and inspiration, but her home was always filled with laughter, love, lots of good food and amazing story telling.

After years of wearing many different career caps, Jennae was determined to do something she had always loved and her vivid imagination took over once again as she decided to follow her dream of writing stories that tapped into her love of magical people and places.

Jennae now lives in the San Francisco Bay Area with her husband, where they've raised two beautiful and talented children. Along the way they've gathered a menagerie of pets, including dogs, cats, chickens and horses to make their family complete.

www.ingramcontent.com/pod-product-compliance
Lightning Source LLC
Chambersburg PA
CBHW060430180626
46817CB00007B/2742